The Trunchbull
let out a yell. . . .

The Trunchbull lifted the water-jug and poured some water into her glass. And suddenly, with the water, out came the long slimy newt straight into the glass, *plop!*

The Trunchbull let out a yell and leapt off her chair as though a firecracker had gone off underneath her.

She stared at the creature twisting and wriggling in the glass. The fires of fury and hatred were smouldering in the Trunchbull's small black eyes.

"Matilda!" she barked. "Stand up!"

"Who, me?" Matilda said. "What have *I* done?"

"Stand up, you disgusting little cockroach! You filthy little maggot! You are a vile, repellent, malicious little brute!" The Trunchbull was shouting. "You are not fit to be in this school! You ought to be behind bars, that's where you ought to be! I shall have the prefects chase you down the corridor and out of the front-door with hockey-sticks!"

The Trunchbull was in such a rage that her face had taken on a boiled colour and little flecks of froth were gathering at the corners of her mouth. But Matilda was also beginning to see red. She had had absolutely nothing to do with the beastly creature in the glass. By golly, she thought, that rotten Trunchbull isn't going to pin this one on me!

Puffin Books by Roald Dahl

ROALD DAHL

Matilda

ILLUSTRATED BY QUENTIN BLAKE

PUFFIN BOOKS
An Imprint of Penguin Group (USA) Inc.

For Michael and Lucy

PUFFIN BOOKS

Published by the Penguin Group

Penguin Young Readers Group, 345 Hudson Street, New York, New York 10014, U.S.A.

Penguin Group (Canada), 90 Eglinton Avenue East, Suite 700, Toronto, Ontario M4P 2Y3, Canada

(a division of Pearson Penguin Canada Inc.)

Penguin Books Ltd, 80 Strand, London WC2R 0RL, England

Penguin Ireland, 25 St Stephen's Green, Dublin 2, Ireland (a division of Penguin Books Ltd)

Penguin Group (Australia), 707 Collins St., Melbourne, Victoria 3008, Australia

(a division of Pearson Australia Group Pty Ltd)

Penguin Books India Pvt Ltd, 11 Community Centre, Panchsheel Park, New Delhi–110 017, India

Penguin Group (NZ), 67 Apollo Drive, Rosedale, Auckland 0632, New Zealand

(a division of Pearson New Zealand Ltd)

Penguin Books, Rosebank Office Park, 181 Jan Smuts Avenue, Parktown North 2193, South Africa

Penguin China, B7 Jiaming Center, 27 East Third Ring Road North,

Chaoyang District, Beijing 100020, China

Penguin Books Ltd, Registered Offices: 80 Strand, London WC2R 0RL, England

First published in Great Britain by Jonathan Cape Ltd., 1988

First published in the United States of America by Viking Penguin,

a division of Penguin Books USA Inc., 1988

First published in Puffin Books, 1990

Reissued in this edition by Puffin Books, an imprint of

Penguin Young Readers Group, 2007, 2013

29 30 28

Text copyright © Roald Dahl, 1988

Illustrations copyright © Quentin Blake, 1988

All rights reserved

Grateful acknowledgment is made for permission to reprint an excerpt from "In Country Sleep"
from *The Poems of Dylan Thomas*. Copyright 1947, 1952 Dylan Thomas. Reprinted by
permission of New Directions Publishing Corporation.

THE LIBRARY OF CONGRESS HAS CATALOGED THE PREVIOUS PUFFIN BOOKS EDITION AS FOLLOWS:

Dahl, Roald.

Matilda / Roald Dahl; illustrations by Quentin Blake.

p. cm.

Reprint. Originally published: New York, N.Y.: Viking Kestrel, 1988.

Summary: Matilda applies her untapped mental powers to rid the school of the evil, child-hating
headmistress, Miss Trunchbull, and restore her nice teacher, Miss Honey, to financial security.

ISBN: 978-0-14-034294-9

[1. Schools—Fiction. 2. Humorous stories.] I. Blake, Quentin, ill. II. Title.

PZ7.D1515Mat 1990 [Fic]—dc20 89-10604

Puffin Books ISBN 978-0-14-241037-0

Printed in the United States of America

THERE'S MORE TO ROALD DAHL
THAN GREAT STORIES . . .

Did you know that 10% of author royalties* from this book go to help the work of the Roald Dahl charities?

Roald Dahl's Marvellous Children's Charity exists to make life better for seriously ill children because it believes that every child has the right to a marvellous life.

This marvellous charity helps thousands of children each year living with serious conditions of the blood and the brain – causes important to Roald Dahl in his lifetime – whether by providing nurses, equipment or toys for today's children in the UK, or helping tomorrow's children everywhere through pioneering research.

Can you do something marvellous to help others?
Find out how at **www.marvellouschildrenscharity.org**

The Roald Dahl Museum and Story Centre, based in Great Missenden just outside London, is in the Buckinghamshire village where Roald Dahl lived and wrote. At the heart of the Museum, created to inspire a love of reading and writing, is his unique archive of letters and manuscripts. As well as two fun-packed biographical galleries, the Museum boasts an interactive Story Centre. It is a place for the family, teachers and their pupils to explore the exciting world of creativity and literacy.
www.roalddahlmuseum.org

Contents

The Reader of Books

It's a funny thing about mothers and fathers. Even when their own child is the most disgusting little blister you could ever imagine, they still think that he or she is wonderful.

Some parents go further. They become so blinded by adoration they manage to convince themselves their child has qualities of genius.

Well, there is nothing very wrong with all this. It's the way of the world. It is only when the parents begin telling *us* about the brilliance of their own revolting offspring, that we start shouting, "Bring us a basin! We're going to be sick!"

School teachers suffer a good deal from having to listen to this sort of twaddle from proud parents, but they usually get their own back when the time comes to write the end-of-term reports. If I were a teacher I would cook up some real scorchers for the children of doting parents. "Your son Maximilian", I would write, "is a total wash-out. I hope you have a family business you can push him into when he leaves school because he sure as heck won't get a job anywhere else." Or if I were feeling lyrical that day, I might write, "It is a curious truth that grasshoppers have their hearing-organs in the sides of the abdomen. Your daughter Vanessa, judging by what she's learnt this term, has no hearing-organs at all."

I might even delve deeper into natural history and say, "The periodical cicada spends six years as a grub underground, and no more than six *days* as a free creature of sunlight and air. Your son Wilfred has spent six years as a grub in this school and we are still waiting for him to emerge from the chrysalis." A particularly poisonous little girl might sting me into saying, "Fiona has the same glacial beauty as an iceberg, but unlike the iceberg she has absolutely nothing below the surface." I

think I might enjoy writing end-of-term reports for the stinkers in my class. But enough of that. We have to get on.

Occasionally one comes across parents who take the opposite line, who show no interest at all in their children, and these of course are far worse than the doting ones. Mr and Mrs Wormwood were two such parents. They had a son called Michael and a daughter called Matilda, and the parents looked upon Matilda in particular as nothing more than a scab. A scab is something you have to put up with until the time comes when you can pick it off and flick it away. Mr and Mrs Wormwood looked forward enormously to the time when they could pick their little daughter off and flick her away, preferably into the next county or even further than that.

It is bad enough when parents treat *ordinary* children as though they were scabs and bunions, but it becomes somehow a lot worse when the child in question is *extra-*ordinary, and by that I mean sensitive and brilliant. Matilda was both of these things, but above all she was brilliant. Her mind was so nimble and she was so quick to  learn that her ability should have been obvious even to the most half-witted of parents. But Mr and Mrs Wormwood were both so gormless and so wrapped up in their own silly little lives that they failed to notice anything unusual about their daughter. To tell the truth, I doubt they would have noticed had she crawled into the house with a broken leg.

Matilda's brother Michael was a perfectly normal boy, but the sister, as I said, was something to make your eyes pop. By the age of *one and a half* her speech was perfect and she knew as many words as most grown-ups. The parents, instead of applauding her, called her a noisy chatterbox and told her sharply that small girls should be seen and not heard.

By the time she was *three*, Matilda had taught herself to read by studying newspapers and magazines that lay around the house. At the age of *four*, she could read fast and well and she naturally began hankering after books. The only book in the whole of this enlightened household was something called *Easy Cooking* belonging to her mother, and when she had read this from cover to cover and had learnt all the recipes by heart, she decided she wanted something more interesting.

"Daddy," she said, "do you think you could buy me a book?"

"A *book*?" he said. "What d'you want a flaming book for?"

"To read, Daddy."

"What's wrong with the telly, for heaven's sake? We've got a lovely telly with a twelve-inch screen and now you come asking for a book! You're getting spoiled, my girl!"

Nearly every weekday afternoon Matilda was left alone in the house. Her brother (five years older than her) went to school. Her father went to work and her mother went out playing bingo in a town eight miles away. Mrs Wormwood was hooked on bingo and played it five afternoons a week. On the afternoon of the day when her father had refused to buy her a book, Matilda set out all by herself to walk to the public library in the village. When she arrived, she introduced herself to the librarian, Mrs Phelps. She asked if she might sit awhile and read a book. Mrs Phelps, slightly taken aback at the arrival of such a tiny girl unacccompanied by a parent, nevertheless told her she was very welcome.

"Where are the children's books please?" Matilda asked.

"They're over there on those lower shelves," Mrs Phelps told her. "Would you like me to help you find a nice one with lots of pictures in it?"

"No, thank you," Matilda said. "I'm sure I can manage."

From then on, every afternoon, as soon as her mother had left for bingo, Matilda would toddle down to the library. The walk took only ten minutes and this allowed her two glorious hours sitting quietly by herself in a cosy corner devouring one book after another. When she had read every single children's book in the place, she started wandering round in search of something else.

Mrs Phelps, who had been watching her with fascination for the past few weeks, now got up from her desk and went over to her. "Can I help you, Matilda?" she asked.

"I'm wondering what to read next," Matilda said. "I've finished all the children's books."

"You mean you've looked at the pictures?"

"Yes, but I've read the books as well."

Mrs Phelps looked down at Matilda from her great height and Matilda looked right back up at her.

"I thought some were very poor," Matilda said, "but others were lovely. I liked *The Secret Garden* best of all. It was full of mystery. The mystery of

13

the room behind the closed door and the mystery of the garden behind the big wall."

Mrs Phelps was stunned. "Exactly how old are you, Matilda?" she asked.

"Four years and three months," Matilda said.

Mrs Phelps was more stunned than ever, but she had the sense not to show it. "What sort of a book would you like to read next?" she asked.

Matilda said, "I would like a really good one that grown-ups read. A famous one. I don't know any names."

Mrs Phelps looked along the shelves, taking her time. She didn't quite know what to bring out. How, she asked herself, does one choose a famous grown-up book for a four-year-old girl? Her first thought was to pick a young teenager's romance of the kind that is written for fifteen-year-old school-girls, but for some reason she found herself instinctively walking past that particular shelf.

"Try this," she said at last. "It's very famous and very good. If it's too long for you, just let me know and I'll find something shorter and a bit easier."

"*Great Expectations,*" Matilda read, "by Charles Dickens. I'd love to try it."

I must be mad, Mrs Phelps told herself, but to Matilda she said, "Of course you may try it."

Over the next few afternoons Mrs Phelps could hardly take her eyes from the small girl sitting for hour after hour in the big armchair at the far end of the room with the book on her lap. It was necessary to rest it on the lap because it was too heavy for her to hold up, which meant she had to sit leaning forward in order to read. And a strange sight it was, this tiny dark-haired person sitting there with her feet nowhere near touching the floor, totally absorbed in the wonderful adventures of Pip and old Miss Havisham and her cobwebbed house and by the spell of magic that Dickens the great story-teller had woven with his words. The only movement from the reader was the lifting of the hand every now and then to turn over a page, and Mrs Phelps always felt sad when the time came for her to cross the floor and say, "It's ten to five, Matilda."

During the first week of Matilda's visits Mrs Phelps had said to her, "Does your mother walk you down here every day and then take you home?"

"My mother goes to Aylesbury every afternoon to play bingo," Matilda had said. "She doesn't know I come here."

"But that's surely not right," Mrs Phelps said. "I think you'd better ask her."

"I'd rather not," Matilda said. "She doesn't encourage reading books. Nor does my father."

"But what do they expect you to do every afternoon in an empty house?"

"Just mooch around and watch the telly."

"I see."

"She doesn't really care what I do," Matilda said a little sadly.

Mrs Phelps was concerned about the child's safety on the walk through the fairly busy village High Street and the crossing of the road, but she decided not to interfere.

16

Within a week, Matilda had finished *Great Expectations* which in that edition contained four hundred and eleven pages. "I loved it," she said to Mrs Phelps. "Has Mr Dickens written any others?"

"A great number," said the astounded Mrs Phelps. "Shall I choose you another?"

Over the next six months, under Mrs Phelps's

watchful and compassionate eye, Matilda read the following books:

> *Nicholas Nickleby* by Charles Dickens
> *Oliver Twist* by Charles Dickens
> *Jane Eyre* by Charlotte Brontë
> *Pride and Prejudice* by Jane Austen
> *Tess of the D'Urbervilles* by Thomas Hardy
> *Gone to Earth* by Mary Webb
> *Kim* by Rudyard Kipling
> *The Invisible Man* by H. G. Wells
> *The Old Man and the Sea* by Ernest Hemingway
> *The Sound and the Fury* by William Faulkner
> *The Grapes of Wrath* by John Steinbeck
> *The Good Companions* by J. B. Priestley
> *Brighton Rock* by Graham Greene
> *Animal Farm* by George Orwell

It was a formidable list and by now Mrs Phelps was filled with wonder and excitement, but it was probably a good thing that she did not allow herself to be completely carried away by it all. Almost anyone else witnessing the achievements of this small child would have been tempted to make a great fuss and shout the news all over the village and beyond, but not so Mrs Phelps. She was someone who minded her own business and had long since discovered it was seldom worth while to interfere with other people's children.

"Mr Hemingway says a lot of things I don't understand," Matilda said to her. "Especially about men and women. But I loved it all the same. The way he tells it I feel I am right there on the spot watching it all happen."

"A fine writer will always make you feel that," Mrs Phelps said. "And don't worry about the bits you can't understand. Sit back and allow the words to wash around you, like music."

"I will, I will."

"Did you know", Mrs Phelps said, "that public libraries like this allow you to borrow books and take them home?"

"I didn't know that," Matilda said. "Could *I* do it?"

"Of course," Mrs Phelps said. "When you have chosen the book you want, bring it to me so I can make a note of it and it's yours for two weeks. You can take more than one if you wish."

From then on, Matilda would visit the library only once a week in order to take out new books and return the old ones. Her own small bedroom now became her reading-room and there she would sit and read most afternoons, often with a mug of hot chocolate beside her. She was not quite tall enough to reach things around the kitchen, but she kept a small box in the outhouse which she brought in and stood on in order to get whatever she wanted. Mostly it was hot chocolate she made, warming the milk in a saucepan on the stove before mixing it. Occasionally she made Bovril or Ovaltine. It was pleasant to take a hot drink up to her room and have it beside her as she sat in her silent room reading in the empty house in the afternoons. The books transported her into new worlds and introduced her to amazing people who lived exciting lives. She went on olden-day sailing ships with Joseph Conrad. She went to Africa with Ernest Hemingway and to India with Rudyard Kipling. She travelled all over the world while sitting in her little room in an English village.

Mr Wormwood,
the Great Car Dealer

Matilda's parents owned quite a nice house with three bedrooms upstairs, while on the ground floor there was a dining-room and a living-room and a kitchen. Her father was a dealer in second-hand cars and it seemed he did pretty well at it.

"Sawdust", he would say proudly, "is one of the great secrets of my success. And it costs me nothing. I get it free from the sawmill."

"What do you use it for?" Matilda asked him.

"Ha!" the father said. "Wouldn't you like to know."

"I don't see how sawdust can help you to sell second-hand cars, daddy."

"That's because you're an ignorant little twit," the father said. His speech was never very delicate but Matilda was used to it. She also knew that he liked to boast and she would egg him on shamelessly.

"You must be very clever to find a use for something that costs nothing," she said. "I wish I could do it."

"You couldn't," the father said. "You're too stupid. But I don't mind telling young Mike here about it seeing he'll be joining me in the business one day." Ignoring Matilda, he turned to his son and said, "I'm always glad to buy a car when some fool

22

has been crashing the gears so badly they're all worn out and rattle likc mad. I get it cheap. Then all I do is mix a lot of sawdust with the oil in the gear-box and it runs as sweet as a nut."

"How long will it run like that before it starts rattling again?" Matilda asked him.

"Long enough for the buyer to get a good distance away," the father said, grinning. "About a hundred miles."

"But that's dishonest, daddy," Matilda said. "It's cheating."

"No one ever got rich being honest," the father said. "Customers are there to be diddled."

Mr Wormwood was a small ratty-looking man whose front teeth stuck out underneath a thin ratty moustache. He liked to wear jackets with large brightly-coloured checks and he sported ties that were usually yellow or pale green. "Now take mileage for instance," he went on. "Anyone who's buying a second-hand car, the first thing he wants to know is how many miles it's done. Right?"

"Right," the son said.

"So I buy an old dump that's got about a hundred and fifty thousand miles on the clock. I get it cheap. But no one's going to buy it with a mileage like that, are they? And these days you can't just take the speedometer out and fiddle the numbers back like you used to ten years ago. They've fixed it so it's impossible to tamper with it unless you're a ruddy watchmaker or something. So what do I do? I use my brains, laddie, that's what I do."

"How?" young Michael asked, fascinated. He

23

seemed to have inherited his father's love of crookery.

"I sit down and say to myself, how can I convert a mileage reading of one hundred and fifty thousand into only ten thousand without taking the speed-ometer to pieces? Well, if I were to run the car backwards for long enough then obviously that would do it. The numbers would click backwards, wouldn't they? But who's going to drive a flaming car in reverse for thousands and thousands of miles? You couldn't do it!"

"Of course you couldn't," young Michael said.

"So I scratch my head," the father said. "I use my brains. When you've been given a fine brain like I have, you've got to use it. And all of a sudden, the answer hits me. I tell you, I felt exactly like that other brilliant fellow must have felt when he discovered penicillin. 'Eureka!' I cried. 'I've got it!'"

"What did you do, dad?" the son asked him.

"The speedometer", Mr Wormwood said, "is run off a cable that is coupled up to one of the front wheels. So first I disconnect the cable where it joins the front wheel. Next, I get one of those high-speed electric drills and I couple that up to the end of the cable in such a way that when the drill turns, it turns the cable *backwards*. You got me so far? You following me?"

"Yes, daddy," young Michael said.

"These drills run at a tremendous speed," the father said, "so when I switch on the drill the mileage numbers on the speedo spin backwards at

24

a fantastic rate. I can knock fifty thousand miles off the clock in a few minutes with my high-speed electric drill. And by the time I've finished, the car's only done ten thousand and it's ready for sale. 'She's almost new,' I say to the customer. 'She's hardly done ten thou. Belonged to an old lady who only used it once a week for shopping.'"

"Can you really turn the mileage back with an electric drill?" young Michael asked.

"I'm telling you trade secrets," the father said. "So don't you go talking about this to anyone else. You don't want me put in jug, do you?"

"I won't tell a soul," the boy said. "Do you do this to many cars, dad?"

"Every single car that comes through my hands gets the treatment," the father said. "They all have their mileage cut to under under ten thou before they're offered for sale. And to think I invented that all by myself," he added proudly. "It's made me a mint."

Matilda, who had been listening closely, said, "But daddy, that's even more dishonest than the sawdust. It's disgusting. You're cheating people who trust you."

"If you don't like it then don't eat the food in this house," the father said. "It's bought with the profits."

"It's dirty money," Matilda said. "I hate it."

Two red spots appears on the father's cheeks. "Who the heck do you think you are," he shouted, "The Archbishop of Canterbury or something, preaching to me about honesty? You're just an ignorant little squirt who hasn't the foggiest idea what you're talking about!"

"Quite right, Harry," the mother said. And to Matilda she said, "You've got a nerve talking to your father like that. Now keep your nasty mouth shut so we can all watch this programme in peace."

They were in the living-room eating their suppers on their knees in front of the telly. The suppers were TV dinners in floppy aluminium containers with separate compartments for the stewed meat,

the boiled potatoes and the peas. Mrs Wormwood sat munching her meal with her eyes glued to the American soap-opera on the screen. She was a large woman whose hair was dyed platinum blonde except where you could see the mousy-brown bits growing out from the roots. She wore heavy make-up and she had one of those unfortunate bulging figures where the flesh appears to be strapped in all around the body to prevent it from falling out.

"Mummy," Matilda said, "would you mind if I ate my supper in the dining-room so I could read my book?"

The father glanced up sharply. "*I* would mind!" he snapped. "Supper is a family gathering and no one leaves the table till it's over!"

"But we're not at the table," Matilda said. "We never are. We're always eating off our knees and watching the telly."

"What's wrong with watching the telly, may I ask?" the father said. His voice had suddenly become soft and dangerous.

Matilda didn't trust herself to answer him, so she kept quiet. She could feel the anger boiling up inside her. She knew it was wrong to hate her parents like this, but she was finding it very hard not to do so. All the reading she had done had given her a view of life that they had never seen. If only they would read a little Dickens or Kipling they would soon discover there was more to life than cheating people and watching television.

Another thing. She resented being told constantly that she was ignorant and stupid when she knew she wasn't. The anger inside her went on boiling and boiling, and as she lay in bed that night she made a decision. She decided that every time her father or her mother was beastly to her, she would get her own back in some way or another. A small victory or two would help her to tolerate their idiocies and would stop her from going crazy. You must remember that she was still hardly five years old and it is not easy for somebody as small as that to score points against an all-powerful grown-up. Even so, she was determined to have a go. Her father, after what had happened in front of the telly that evening, was first on her list.

The Hat
and the Superglue

The following morning, just before the father left for his beastly second-hand car garage, Matilda slipped into the cloakroom and got hold of the hat he wore each day to work. She had to stand on her toes and reach up as high as she could with a walking-stick in order to hook the hat off the peg, and even then she only just made it. The hat itself was one of those flat-topped pork-pie jobs with a jay's feather stuck in the hat-band and Mr Wormwood was very proud of it. He thought it gave him a rakish daring look, especially when he wore it at an angle with his loud checked jacket and green tie.

Matilda, holding the hat in one hand and a thin tube of Superglue in the other, proceeded to squeeze a line of glue very neatly all round the inside rim of the hat. Then she carefully hooked the hat back on to the peg with the walking-stick. She timed this operation very carefully, applying the glue just as her father was getting up from the breakfast table.

Mr Wormwood didn't notice anything when he put the hat on, but when he arrived at the garage he couldn't get it off. Superglue is very powerful stuff, so powerful it will take your skin off if you pull too hard. Mr Wormwood didn't want to be

scalped so he had to keep the hat on his head the whole day long, even when putting sawdust in gear-boxes and fiddling the mileages of cars with his electric drill. In an effort to save face, he adopted a casual attitude hoping that his staff would think that he actually *meant* to keep his hat on all day long just for the heck of it, like gangsters do in the films.

When he got home that evening he still couldn't get the hat off. "Don't be silly," his wife said. "Come here. I'll take it off for you."

She gave the hat a sharp yank. Mr Wormwood let out a yell that rattled the window-panes. "Ow-w-w!" he screamed. "Don't do that! Let go! You'll take half the skin off my forehead!"

Matilda, nestling in her usual chair, was watching this performance over the rim of her book with some interest.

"What's the matter, daddy?" she said. "Has your head suddenly swollen or something?"

The father glared at his daughter with deep suspicion, but said nothing. How could he? Mrs Wormwood said to him, "It *must* be Superglue. It couldn't be anything else. That'll teach you to go playing round with nasty stuff like that. I expect you were trying to stick another feather in your hat."

"I haven't touched the flaming stuff!" Mr Wormwood shouted. He turned and looked again at Matilda who looked back at him with large innocent brown eyes.

Mrs Wormwood said to him, "You should read the label on the tube before you start messing with dangerous products. Always follow the instructions on the label."

"What in heaven's name are you talking about, you stupid witch?" Mr Wormwood shouted, clutching the brim of his hat to stop anyone trying to pull it off again. "D'you think I'm so stupid I'd glue this thing to my head on purpose?"

Matilda said, "There's a boy down the road who got some Superglue on his finger without knowing it and then he put his finger to his nose."

Mr Wormwood jumped. "What happened to him?" he spluttered.

"The finger got stuck inside his nose," Matilda said, "and he had to go around like that for a week. People kept saying to him, 'Stop picking your nose,' and he couldn't do anything about it. He looked an awful fool."

"Serve him right," Mrs Wormwood said. "He shouldn't have put his finger up there in the first place. It's a nasty habit. If all children had Superglue put on their fingers they'd soon stop doing it."

Matilda said, "Grown-ups do it too, mummy. I saw you doing it yesterday in the kitchen."

"That's quite enough from you," Mrs Wormwood said, turning pink.

Mr Wormwood had to keep his hat on all through supper in front of the television. He looked ridiculous and he stayed very silent.

When he went up to bed he tried again to get the thing off, and so did his wife, but it wouldn't budge. "How am I going to have my shower?" he demanded.

"You'll just have to do without it, won't you," his wife told him. And later on, as she watched her skinny little husband skulking around the bedroom in his purple-striped pyjamas with a pork-pie hat on his head, she thought how stupid he looked. Hardly the kind of man a wife dreams about, she told herself.

Mr Wormwood discovered that the worst thing about having a permanent hat on his head was having to sleep in it. It was impossible to lie comfortably on the pillow. "Now do stop fussing around," his wife said to him after he had been tossing and turning for about an hour. "I expect it will be loose by the morning and then it'll slip off easily."

But it wasn't loose by the morning and it wouldn't slip off. So Mrs Wormwood took a pair of scissors and cut the thing off his head, bit by bit, first the top and then the brim. Where the inner band had stuck to the hair all around the sides and back, she had to chop the hair off right to the skin so that he finished up with a bald white ring round his head, like some sort of a monk. And in the front, where the band had stuck directly to the bare skin, there remained a whole lot of small patches of brown leathery stuff that no amount of washing would get off.

At breakfast Matilda said to him, "You *must* try to get those bits off your forehead, daddy. It looks as though you've got little brown insects crawling about all over you. People will think you've got lice."

"Be quiet!" the father snapped. "Just keep your nasty mouth shut, will you!"

All in all it was a most satisfactory exercise. But it was surely too much to hope that it had taught the father a permanent lesson.

The Ghost

There was comparative calm in the Wormwood household for about a week after the Superglue episode. The experience had clearly chastened Mr Wormwood and he seemed temporarily to have lost his taste for boasting and bullying.

Then suddenly he struck again. Perhaps he had had a bad day at the garage and had not sold enough crummy second-hand cars. There are many things that make a man irritable when he arrives home from work in the evening and a sensible wife will usually notice the storm-signals and will leave him alone until he simmers down.

When Mr Wormwood arrived back from the garage that evening his face was as dark as a thundercloud and somebody was clearly for the high-jump pretty soon. His wife recognised the signs immediately and made herself scarce. He then strode into the living-room. Matilda happened to be curled up in an arm-chair in the corner, totally absorbed in a book. Mr Wormwood switched on the television. The screen lit up. The programme blared. Mr Wormwood glared at Matilda. She hadn't moved. She had somehow trained herself by now to block her ears to the ghastly sound of the dreaded box. She kept right on reading, and for some reason this infuriated the father. Perhaps his anger was

intensified because he saw her getting pleasure from something that was beyond his reach.

"Don't you *ever* stop reading?" he snapped at her.

"Oh, hello daddy," she said pleasantly. "Did you have a good day?"

"What is this trash?" he said, snatching the book from her hands.

"It isn't trash, daddy, it's lovely. It's called *The Red Pony*. It's by John Steinbeck, an American writer. Why don't you try it? You'll love it."

"Filth," Mr Wormwood said. "If it's by an American it's certain to be filth. That's all they write about."

"No daddy, it's beautiful, honestly it is. It's about . . . "

"I don't want to know what it's about," Mr Wormwood barked. "I'm fed up with your reading anyway. Go and find yourself something useful to

40

do." With frightening suddenness he now began ripping the pages out of the book in handfuls and throwing them in the waste-paper basket.

Matilda froze in horror. The father kept going. There seemed little doubt that the man felt some kind of jealousy. How dare she, he seemed to be saying with each rip of a page, how dare she enjoy reading books when he couldn't? How dare she?

"That's a *library* book!" Matilda cried. "It doesn't belong to me! I have to return it to Mrs Phelps!"

"Then you'll have to buy another one, won't you?" the father said, still tearing out pages. "You'll have to save your pocket-money until there's enough in the kitty to buy a new one for your precious Mrs Phelps, won't you?" With that he dropped the now empty covers of the book into the basket and marched out of the room, leaving the telly blaring.

Most children in Matilda's place would have burst into floods of tears. She didn't do this. She sat there very still and white and thoughtful. She seemed to know that neither crying nor sulking ever got anyone anywhere. The only sensible thing to do when you are attacked is, as Napoleon once said, to counter-attack. Matilda's wonderfully subtle mind was already at work devising yet another suitable punishment for the poisonous parent. The plan that was now beginning to hatch in her mind depended, however, upon whether or not Fred's parrot was really as good a talker as Fred made out.

41

Fred was a friend of Matilda's. He was a small boy of six who lived just around the corner from her, and for days he had been going on about this great talking parrot his father had given him.

So the following afternoon, as soon as Mrs Wormwood had departed in her car for another session of bingo, Matilda set out for Fred's house to investigate. She knocked on his door and asked if he would be kind enough to show her the famous bird. Fred was delighted and led her up to his bedroom where a truly magnificent blue and yellow parrot sat in a tall cage.

"There it is," Fred said. "It's name is Chopper."

"Make it talk," Matilda said.

"You can't *make* it talk," Fred said. "You have to be patient. It'll talk when it feels like it."

They hung around, waiting. Suddenly the parrot said, "Hullo, hullo, hullo." It was exactly like a human voice. Matilda said, "That's amazing! What else can it say?"

"Rattle my bones!" the parrot said, giving a wonderful imitation of a spooky voice. "Rattle my bones!"

"He's always saying that," Fred told her .

"What else can he say?" Matilda asked.

"That's about it," Fred said. "But it is pretty marvellous don't you think?"

"It's fabulous," Matilda said. "Will you lend him to me just for one night?"

"No," Fred said. "Certainly not."

"I'll give you all my next week's pocket-money," Matilda said.

That was different. Fred thought about it for a few seconds. "All right, then," he said, "If you promise to return him tomorrow."

Matilda staggered back to her own empty house carrying the tall cage in both hands. There was a large fireplace in the dining-room and she now set about wedging the cage up the chimney and out of sight. This wasn't so easy, but she managed it in the end.

"Hullo, hullo, hullo!" the bird called down to her. "Hullo, hullo!"

"Shut up, you nut!" Matilda said, and she went out to wash the soot off her hands.

That evening while the mother, the father, the brother and Matilda were having supper as usual in the living-room in front of the television, a voice came loud and clear from the dining-room across the hall. "Hullo, hullo, hullo," it said.

"Harry!" cried the mother, turning white. "There's someone in the house! I heard a voice!"

"So did I!" the brother said. Matilda jumped up and switched off the telly. "Ssshh!" she said. "Listen!"

They all stopped eating and sat there very tense, listening.

"Hullo, hullo, hullo!" came the voice again.

"There it is!" cried the brother.

"It's burglars!" hissed the mother. "They're in the dining-room!"

"I think they are," the father said, sitting tight.

"Then go and catch them, Harry!" hissed the mother. "Go out and collar them red-handed!"

The father didn't move. He seemed in no hurry to dash off and be a hero. His face had turned grey.

"Get on with it!" hissed the mother. "They're probably after the silver!"

The husband wiped his lips nervously with his napkin. "Why don't we all go and look together?" he said.

"Come on, then," the brother said. "Come on, mum."

"They're definitely in the dining-room," Matilda whispered. "I'm sure they are."

The mother grabbed a poker from the fireplace. The father took a golf-club that was standing in the corner. The brother seized a table-lamp, ripping the plug out of its socket. Matilda took the knife she had been eating with, and all four of them crept towards the dining-room door, the father keeping well behind the others.

"Hullo, hullo, hullo," came the voice again.

"Come on!" Matilda cried and she burst into the room, brandishing her knife. "Stick 'em up!" she yelled. "We've caught you!" The others followed

her, waving their weapons. Then they stopped. They stared around the room. There was no one there.

"There's no one here," the father said, greatly relieved.

"I heard him, Harry!" the mother shrieked, still quaking. "I distinctly heard his voice! So did you!"

"I'm certain I heard him!" Matilda cried. "He's in here somewhere!" She began searching behind the sofa and behind the curtains.

Then came the voice once again, soft and spooky this time, "Rattle my bones," it said. "Rattle my bones."

They all jumped, including Matilda who was a pretty good actress. They stared round the room. There was still no one there.

"It's a ghost," Matilda said.

"Heaven help us!" cried the mother, clutching her husband round the neck.

"I know it's a ghost!" Matilda said. "I've heard it here before! This room is haunted! I thought you knew that."

"Save us!" the mother screamed, almost throttling her husband.

"I'm getting out of here," the father said, greyer than ever now. They all fled, slamming the door behind them.

The next afternoon, Matilda managed to get a rather sooty and grumpy parrot down from the chimney and out of the house without being seen. She carried it through the back-door and ran with it all the way to Fred's house.

"Did it behave itself?" Fred asked her.

"We had a lovely time with it," Matilda said. "My parents adored it."

Arithmetic

Matilda longed for her parents to be good and loving and understanding and honourable and intelligent. The fact that they were none of these things was something she had to put up with. It was not easy to do so. But the new game she had invented of punishing one or both of them each time they were beastly to her made her life more or less bearable.

Being very small and very young, the only power Matilda had over anyone in her family was brain-power. For sheer cleverness she could run rings around them all. But the fact remained that any five-year-old girl in any family was always obliged to do as she was told, however asinine the orders might be. Thus she was always forced to eat her evening meals out of TV-dinner-trays in front of the dreaded box. She always had to stay alone on weekday afternoons, and whenever she was told to shut up, she had to shut up.

Her safety-valve, the thing that prevented her from going round the bend, was the fun of devising and dishing out these splendid punishments, and the lovely thing was that they seemed to work, at any rate for short periods. The father in particular became less cocky and unbearable for several days after receiving a dose of Matilda's magic medicine.

The parrot-in-the-chimney affair quite definitely

cooled both parents down a lot and for over a week they were comparatively civil to their small daughter. But alas, this couldn't last. The next flare-up came one evening in the sitting-room. Mr Wormwood had just returned from work. Matilda and her brother were sitting quietly on the sofa waiting for their mother to bring in the TV dinners on a tray. The television had not yet been switched on.

In came Mr Wormwood in a loud check suit and a yellow tie. The appalling broad orange-and-green check of the jacket and trousers almost blinded the onlooker. He looked like a low-grade bookmaker dressed up for his daughter's wedding, and he was clearly very pleased with himself this evening. He sat down in an armchair and rubbed his hands together and addressed his son in a loud voice. "Well, my boy," he said, "your father's had a most successful day. He is a lot richer tonight than he was this morning. He has sold no less than five cars, each one at a tidy profit. Sawdust in the gear-boxes, the electric-drill on the speedometer cables, a splash of paint here and there and a few other clever little tricks and the idiots were all falling over themselves to buy."

He fished a bit of paper from his pocket and studied it. "Listen boy," he said, addressing the son and ignoring Matilda, "seeing as you'll be going into this business with me one day, you've got to know how to add up the profits you make at the end of each day. Go and get yourself a pad and a pencil and let's see how clever you are."

The son obediently left the room and returned with the writing materials.

"Write down these figures," the father said, reading from his bit of paper. "Car number one was bought by me for two hundred and seventy-eight pounds and sold for one thousand four hundred and twenty-five. Got that?"

The ten-year-old boy wrote the two separate amounts down slowly and carefully.

"Car number two", the father went on, "cost me one hundred and eighteen pounds and sold for seven hundred and sixty. Got it?"

"Yes, dad," the son said. "I've got that."

"Car number three cost one hundred and eleven pounds and sold for nine hundred and ninety-nine pounds and fifty pence."

"Say that again," the son said. "How much did it sell for?"

"Nine hundred and ninety-nine pounds and fifty pence," the father said. "And that, by the way, is another of my nifty little tricks to diddle the customer. Never ask for a big round figure. Always go just below it. Never say one thousand pounds. Always say nine hundred and ninety-nine fifty. It sounds much less but it isn't. Clever, isn't it?"

"Very," the son said. "You're brilliant, dad."

"Car number four cost eighty-six pounds – a real wreck that was – and sold for six hundred and ninety-nine pounds fifty."

"Not too fast," the son said, writing the numbers down. "Right. I've got it."

"Car number five cost six hundred and thirty-seven pounds and sold for sixteen hundred and forty-nine fifty. You got all those figures written down, son?"

"Yes, daddy," the boy said, crouching over his pad and carefully writing.

"Very well," the father said. "Now work out the profit I made on each of the five cars and add up the total. Then you'll be able to tell me how much money your rather brilliant father made altogether today."

"That's a lot of sums," the boy said.

"Of course it's a lot of sums," the father answered. "But when you're in big business like I am, you've got to be hot stuff at arithmetic. I've practically got a computer inside my head. It took me less than ten minutes to work the whole thing out."

"You mean you did it in your head, dad?" the son asked, goggling.

"Well, not exactly," the father said. "Nobody could do that. But it didn't take me long. When you're finished, tell me what you think my profit was for the day. I've got the final total written down here and I'll tell you if you're right."

Matilda said quietly, "Dad, you made exactly four thousand three hundred and three pounds and fifty pence altogether."

"Don't butt in," the father said. "Your brother and I are busy with high finance."

"But dad . . ."

"Shut up," the father said. "Stop guessing and trying to be clever."

"Look at your answer, dad," Matilda said gently. "If you've done it right it ought to be four thousand three hundred and three pounds and fifty pence. Is that what you've got, dad?"

The father glanced down at the paper in his hand. He seemed to stiffen. He became very quiet. There was a silence. Then he said, "Say that again."

"Four thousand three hundred and three pounds fifty," Matilda said.

There was another silence. The father's face was beginning to go dark red.

"I'm sure it's right," Matilda said.

"You . . . you little cheat!" the father suddenly shouted, pointing at her with his finger. "You looked at my bit of paper! You read it off from what I've got written here!"

"Daddy, I'm the other side of the room," Matilda said. "How could I possibly see it?"

"Don't give me that rubbish!" the father shouted. "Of course you looked! You must have looked! No one in the world could give the right answer just like that, especially a girl! You're a little cheat, madam, that's what you are! A cheat and a liar!"

At that point, the mother came in carrying a large tray on which were the four suppers. This time it was fish and chips which Mrs Wormwood had picked up in the fish and chip shop on her way home from bingo. It seemed that bingo afternoons left her so exhausted both physically and emotionally that she never had enough energy left to cook an evening meal. So if it wasn't TV dinners it had to be fish and chips. "What are you looking so red in the face about, Harry?" she said as she put the tray down on the coffee-table.

"Your daughter's a cheat and a liar," the father said, taking his plate of fish and placing it on his knees. "Turn the telly on and let's not have any more talk."

The Platinum-Blond Man

There was no doubt in Matilda's mind that this latest display of foulness by her father deserved severe punishment, and as she sat eating her awful fried fish and fried chips and ignoring the television, her brain went to work on various possibilities. By the time she went up to bed her mind was made up.

The next morning she got up early and went into the bathroom and locked the door. As we already know, Mrs Wormwood's hair was dyed a brilliant platinum blonde, very much the same glistening silvery colour as a female tightrope-walker's tights in a circus. The big dyeing job was done twice a year at the hairdresser's, but every month or so in between, Mrs Wormwood used to freshen it up by giving it a rinse in the washbasin with something called PLATINUM BLONDE HAIR-DYE EXTRA STRONG. This also served to dye the nasty brown hairs that kept growing from the roots underneath. The bottle of PLATINUM BLONDE HAIR-DYE EXTRA STRONG was kept in the cupboard in the bathroom, and underneath the title on the label were written the words *Caution, this is peroxide. Keep away from children.* Matilda had read it many times with fascination.

Matilda's father had a fine crop of black hair

which he parted in the middle and of which he was exceedingly proud. "Good strong hair," he was fond of saying, "means there's a good strong brain underneath."

"Like Shakespeare," Matilda had once said to him.

"Like who?"

"Shakespeare, daddy."

"Was he brainy?"

"Very, daddy."

"He had masses of hair, did he?"

"He was bald, daddy."

To which the father had snapped, "If you can't talk sense then shut up."

Anyway, Mr Wormwood kept his hair looking
bright and strong, or so he thought, by rubbing into
it every morning large quantities of a lotion called
OIL OF VIOLETS HAIR TONIC. A bottle of this smelly
purple mixture always stood on the shelf above the
sink in the bathroom alongside all the tooth-
brushes, and a very vigorous scalp massage with
OIL OF VIOLETS took place daily after shaving was
completed. This hair and scalp massage was always
accompanied by loud masculine grunts and heavy

breathing and gasps of "Ahhh, that's better! That's the stuff! Rub it right into the roots!" which could be clearly heard by Matilda in her bedroom across the corridor.

Now, in the early morning privacy of the bathroom, Matilda unscrewed the cap of her father's OIL OF VIOLETS and tipped three-quarters of the contents down the drain. Then she filled the bottle up with her mother's PLATINUM BLONDE HAIR-DYE EXTRA STRONG. She carefully left enough of her father's original hair tonic in the bottle so that when she gave it a good shake the whole thing still looked reasonably purple. She then replaced the bottle on the shelf above the sink, taking care to put her mother's bottle back in the cupboard. So far so good.

At breakfast time Matilda sat quietly at the dining-room table eating her cornflakes. Her brother sat opposite her with his back to the door devouring hunks of bread smothered with a mixture of peanut-butter and strawberry jam. The mother was just out of sight around the corner in the kitchen making Mr Wormwood's breakfast which always had to be two fried eggs on fried bread with three pork sausages and three strips of bacon and some fried tomatoes.

At this point Mr Wormwood came noisily into the room. He was incapable of entering any room quietly, especially at breakfast time. He always had to make his appearance felt immediately by creating a lot of noise and clatter. One could almost hear him saying, "It's me! Here I come, the great man himself, the master of the house, the wage-earner, the one who makes it possible for all the rest of you to live so well! Notice me and pay your respects!"

On this occasion he strode in and slapped his son on the back and shouted, "Well my boy, your father feels he's in for another great money-making day today at the garage! I've got a few little beauties I'm going to flog to the idiots this morning. Where's my breakfast?"

"It's coming, treasure," Mrs Wormwood called from the kitchen.

Matilda kept her face bent low over her corn-flakes. She didn't dare look up. In the first place she wasn't at all sure what she was going to see. And secondly, if she did see what she thought she was going to see, she wouldn't trust herself to keep a straight face. The son was looking directly ahead out of the window stuffing himself with bread and peanut-butter and strawberry jam.

The father was just moving round to sit at the head of the table when the mother came sweeping out from the kitchen carrying a huge plate piled high with eggs and sausages and bacon and tomatoes. She looked up. She caught sight of her husband. She stopped dead. Then she let out a scream that seemed to lift her right up into the air and she dropped the plate with a crash and a splash on to the floor. Everyone jumped, including Mr Wormwood.

"What the heck's the matter with you, woman?" he shouted. "Look at the mess you've made on the carpet!"

"Your *hair*!" the mother was shrieking, pointing a quivering finger at her husband. "Look at your *hair*! What've you done to your *hair*?"

"What's wrong with my hair for heaven's sake?" he said.

"Oh my gawd dad, what've you done to your hair?" the son shouted.

A splendid noisy scene was building up nicely in the breakfast room.

Matilda said nothing. She simply sat there admiring the wonderful effect of her own handiwork. Mr Wormwood's fine crop of black hair was now a dirty silver, the colour this time of a tightrope-walker's tights that had not been washed for the entire circus season.

"You've . . . you've . . . you've *dyed* it!" shrieked the mother. "Why did you do it, you fool! It looks absolutely frightful! It looks horrendous! You look like a freak!"

"What the blazes are you all talking about?" the father yelled, putting both hands to his hair. "I most certainly have not dyed it! What d'you mean I've dyed it? What's happened to it? Or is this some sort of a stupid joke?" His face was turning pale green, the colour of sour apples.

"You *must* have dyed it, dad," the son said. "It's the same colour as mum's only much dirtier looking."

"Of course he's dyed it!" the mother cried. "It can't change colour all by itself! What on earth were you trying to do, make yourself look handsome or something? You look like someone's grandmother gone wrong!"

"Get me a mirror!" the father yelled. "Don't just stand there shrieking at me! Get me a mirror!"

The mother's handbag lay on a chair at the other end of the table. She opened the bag and got out a powder compact that had a small round mirror on the inside of the lid. She opened the compact and handed it to her husband. He grabbed it and held it before his face and in doing so spilled most of

the powder all over the front of his fancy tweed jacket.

"Be *careful*!" shrieked the mother. "Now look what you've done! That's my best Elizabeth Arden face powder!"

"Oh my gawd!" yelled the father, staring into the little mirror. "What's happened to me! I look terrible! I look just like *you* gone wrong! I can't go down to the garage and sell cars like this! How did it happen?" He stared round the room, first at the mother, then at the son, then at Matilda. "How *could* it have happened?" he yelled.

"I imagine, daddy," Matilda said quietly, "that you weren't looking very hard and you simply took mummy's bottle of hair stuff off the shelf instead of your own."

"*Of course* that's what happened!" the mother cried. "Well really Harry, how stupid can you get? Why didn't you read the label before you started splashing the stuff all over you! Mine's *terribly* strong. I'm only meant to use one tablespoon of it in a whole basin of water and you've gone and put it all over your head neat! It'll probably take all your hair off in the end! Is your scalp beginning to burn, dear?"

"You mean I'm going to lose all my hair?" the husband yelled.

"I think you will," the mother said. "Peroxide is a very powerful chemical. It's what they put down the lavatory to disinfect the pan only they give it another name."

"What are you saying!" the husband cried. "I'm not a lavatory pan! I don't want to be disinfected!"

"Even diluted like I use it," the mother told him, "it makes a good deal of *my* hair fall out, so goodness knows what's going to happen to you. I'm surprised it didn't take the whole of the top of your head off!"

"What shall I do?" wailed the father. "Tell me quick what to do before it starts falling out!"

Matilda said, "I'd give it a good wash, dad, if I were you, with soap and water. But you'll have to hurry."

"Will that change the colour back?" the father asked anxiously.

"Of course it won't, you twit," the mother said.

"Then what do I do? I can't go around looking like this for ever?"

"You'll have to have it dyed black," the mother said. "But wash it first or there won't be any there to dye."

"Right!" the father shouted, springing into action. "Get me an appointment with your hairdresser this instant for a hair-dyeing job! Tell them it's an emergency! They've got to boot someone else off their list! I'm going upstairs to wash it now!" With that the man dashed out of the room and Mrs Wormwood, sighing deeply, went to the telephone to call the beauty parlour.

"He does do some pretty silly things now and again, doesn't he, mummy?" Matilda said.

The mother, dialling the number on the phone, said, "I'm afraid men are not always quite as clever as they think they are. You will learn that when you get a bit older, my girl."

Miss Honey

Matilda was a little late in starting school. Most children begin Primary School at five or even just before, but Matilda's parents, who weren't very concerned one way or the other about their daughter's education, had forgotten to make the proper arrangements in advance. She was five and a half when she entered school for the first time.

The village school for younger children was a bleak brick building called Crunchem Hall Primary School. It had about two hundred and fifty pupils aged from five to just under twelve years old. The head teacher, the boss, the supreme commander of this establishment was a formidable middle-aged lady whose name was Miss Trunchbull.

Naturally Matilda was put in the bottom class, where there were eighteen other small boys and girls about the same age as her. Their teacher was called Miss Honey, and she could not have been more than twenty-three or twenty-four. She had a lovely pale oval madonna face with blue eyes and her hair was light-brown. Her body was so slim and fragile one got the feeling that if she fell over she would smash into a thousand pieces, like a porcelain figure.

Miss Jennifer Honey was a mild and quiet person who never raised her voice and was seldom seen to smile, but there is no doubt she possessed that rare gift for being adored by every small child under her care. She seemed to understand totally the bewilderment and fear that so often overwhelms young children who for the first time in their lives are herded into a classroom and told to obey orders. Some curious warmth that was almost tangible shone out of Miss Honey's face when she spoke to a confused and homesick newcomer to the class.

Miss Trunchbull, the Headmistress, was something else altogether. She was a gigantic holy terror, a fierce tyrannical monster who frightened the life out of the pupils and teachers alike. There was an aura of menace about her even at a distance, and when she came up close you could almost feel the dangerous heat radiating from her as from a red-hot rod of metal. When she marched – Miss Trunchbull never walked, she always marched like a storm-trooper with long strides and arms aswinging – when she marched along a corridor you could actually hear her snorting as she went, and if a group of children happened to be in her path, she ploughed right on through them like a tank, with small people bouncing off her to left and right. Thank goodness we don't meet many people like her in this world, although they do exist and all of us are likely to come across at least one of them in a lifetime. If you ever do, you should behave as you would if you met an enraged rhinoceros out in the bush – climb up the nearest tree and stay there until it has gone away. This woman, in all her eccentricities and in her appearance, is almost im-

possible to describe, but I shall make some attempt to do so a little later on. Let us leave her for the moment and go back to Matilda and her first day in Miss Honey's class.

After the usual business of going through all the names of the children, Miss Honey handed out a brand-new exercise-book to each pupil.

"You have all brought your own pencils, I hope," she said.

"Yes, Miss Honey," they chanted.

"Good. Now this is the very first day of school for each one of you. It is the beginning of at least eleven long years of schooling that all of you are going to have to go through. And six of those years will be spent right here at Crunchem Hall where, as you know, your Headmistress is Miss Trunchbull. Let me for your own good tell you something about Miss Trunchbull. She insists upon strict discipline throughout the school, and if you take my advice you will do your very best to behave yourselves in her presence. Never argue with her. Never answer her back. Always do as she says. If you get on the wrong side of Miss Trunchbull she can liquidise you like a carrot in a kitchen blender. It's nothing to laugh about, Lavender. Take that grin off your face. All of you will be wise to remember that Miss Trunchbull deals very very severely with anyone who gets out of line in this school. Have you got the message?"

"Yes, Miss Honey," chirruped eighteen eager little voices.

"I myself", Miss Honey went on, "want to help you to learn as much as possible while you are in this class. That is because I know it will make things easier for you later on. For example, by the end of this week I shall expect every one of you to know the two-times table by heart. And in a year's time I hope you will know all the multiplication tables up to twelve. It will help you enormously if you do. Now then, do any of you happen to have learnt the two-times table already?"

Matilda put up her hand. She was the only one.

Miss Honey looked carefully at the tiny girl with dark hair and a round serious face sitting in the second row. "Wonderful," she said. "Please stand up and recite as much of it as you can."

Matilda stood up and began to say the two-times table. When she got to twice twelve is twenty-four she didn't stop. She went right on with twice thirteen is twenty-six, twice fourteen is twenty-eight, twice fifteen is thirty, twice sixteen is . . ."

"Stop!" Miss Honey said. She had been listening slightly spellbound to this smooth recital, and now she said, "How far can you go?"

"How far?" Matilda said. "Well, I don't really

know, Miss Honey. For quite a long way, I think."

Miss Honey took a few moments to let this curious statement sink in. "You mean", she said, "that you could tell me what two times twenty-eight is?"

"Yes, Miss Honey."

"What is it?"

"Fifty-six, Miss Honey."

"What about something much harder, like two times four hundred and eighty-seven? Could you tell me that?"

"I think so, yes," Matilda said.

"Are you sure?"

"Why yes, Miss Honey, I'm fairly sure."

"What is it then, two times four hundred and eighty-seven?"

"Nine hundred and seventy-four," Matilda said immediately. She spoke quietly and politely and without any sign of showing off.

Miss Honey gazed at Matilda with absolute amazement, but when next she spoke she kept her voice level. "That is really splendid," she said. "But of course multiplying by two is a lot easier than some of the bigger numbers. What about the other multiplication tables? Do you know any of those?"

"I think so, Miss Honey. I think I do."

"Which ones, Matilda? How far have you got?"

"I . . . I don't quite know," Matilda said. "I don't know what you mean."

"What I mean is do you for instance know the three-times table?"

"Yes, Miss Honey."

"And the four-times?"

"Yes, Miss Honey."

"Well, how many *do* you know, Matilda? Do you know all the way up to the twelve-times table?"

"Yes, Miss Honey."

"What are twelve sevens?"

"Eighty-four," Matilda said.

Miss Honey paused and leaned back in her chair behind the plain table that stood in the middle of the floor in front of the class. She was considerably shaken by this exchange but took care not to show it. She had never come across a five-year-old before, or indeed a ten-year-old, who could multiply with such facility.

"I hope the rest of you are listening to this," she said to the class. "Matilda is a very lucky girl. She has wonderful parents who have already taught her to multiply lots of numbers. Was it your mother, Matilda, who taught you?"

"No, Miss Honey, it wasn't."

"You must have a great father then. He must be a brilliant teacher."

"No, Miss Honey," Matilda said quietly. "My father did not teach me."

"You mean you taught yourself?"

"I don't quite know," Matilda said truthfully. "It's just that I don't find it very difficult to multiply one number by another."

Miss Honey took a deep breath and let it out slowly. She looked again at the small girl with bright eyes standing beside her desk so sensible and solemn. "You say you don't find it difficult to multiply one number by another," Miss Honey said. "Could you try to explain that a little bit."

"Oh dear," Matilda said. "I'm not really sure."

Miss Honey waited. The class was silent, all listening.

"For instance," Miss Honey said, "if I asked you to multiply fourteen by nineteen . . . No, that's too difficult . . . "

"It's two hundred and sixty-six," Matilda said softly.

Miss Honey stared at her. Then she picked up a pencil and quickly worked out the sum on a piece of paper. "What did you say it was?" she said, looking up.

"Two hundred and sixty-six," Matilda said.

Miss Honey put down her pencil and removed her spectacles and began to polish the lenses with a piece of tissue. The class remained quiet, watching her and waiting for what was coming next. Matilda was still standing up beside her desk.

"Now tell me, Matilda," Miss Honey said, still polishing, "try to tell me exactly what goes on inside your head when you get a multiplication like that to do. You obviously have to work it out in some way, but you seem able to arrive at the answer almost instantly. Take the one you've just done, fourteen multiplied by nineteen."

"I . . . I . . . I simply put the fourteen down in my head and multiply it by nineteen," Matilda said. "I'm afraid I don't know how else to explain it. I've always said to myself that if a little pocket calculator can do it why shouldn't I?"

"Why not indeed," Miss Honey said. "The human brain is an amazing thing."

74

"I think it's a lot better than a lump of metal," Matilda said. "That's all a calculator is."

"How right you are," Miss Honey said. "Pocket calculators are not allowed in this school anyway." Miss Honey was feeling quite quivery. There was no doubt in her mind that she had met a truly extraordinary mathematical brain, and words like child-genius and prodigy went flitting through her head. She knew that these sort of wonders do pop up in the world from time to time, but only once or twice in a hundred years. After all, Mozart was only five when he started composing for the piano and look what happened to him.

"It's not fair," Lavender said. "How can she do it and we can't?"

"Don't worry, Lavender, you'll soon catch up," Miss Honey said, lying through her teeth.

At this point Miss Honey could not resist the temptation of exploring still further the mind of this astonishing child. She knew that she ought to be paying some attention to the rest of the class but she was altogether too excited to let the matter rest.

"Well," she said, pretending to address the whole class, "let us leave sums for the moment and see if any of you have begun to learn to spell. Hands up anyone who can spell cat."

Three hands went up. They belonged to Lavender, a small boy called Nigel and to Matilda.

"Spell cat, Nigel."

Nigel spelled it.

Miss Honey now decided to ask a question that normally she would not have dreamed of asking the class on its first day. "I wonder", she said, "whether any of you three who know how to spell cat have learned how to read a whole group of words when they are strung together in a sentence?"

"I have," Nigel said.

"So have I," Lavender said.

Miss Honey went to the blackboard and wrote with her white chalk the sentence, *I have already begun to learn how to read long sentences*. She had purposely made it difficult and she knew that there were precious few five-year-olds around who would be able to manage it.

"Can you tell me what that says, Nigel?" she asked.

"That's too hard," Nigel said.

"Lavender?"

"The first word is I," Lavender said.

"Can any of you read the whole sentence?" Miss Honey asked, waiting for the "yes" that she felt certain was going to come from Matilda.

"Yes," Matilda said.

"Go ahead," Miss Honey said.

Matilda read the sentence without any hesitation at all.

"That really is very good indeed," Miss Honey said, making the understatement of her life. "How much *can* you read, Matilda?"

"I think I can read most things, Miss Honey," Matilda said, "although I'm afraid I can't always understand the meanings."

Miss Honey got to her feet and walked smartly out of the room, but was back in thirty seconds carrying a thick book. She opened it at random and placed it on Matilda's desk. "This is a book of humorous poetry," she said. "See if you can read that one aloud."

Smoothly, without a pause and at a nice speed, Matilda began to read:

"An epicure dining at Crewe
Found a rather large mouse in his stew.
Cried the waiter, "Don't shout
And wave it about
Or the rest will be wanting one too."

Several children saw the funny side of the rhyme

77

and laughed. Miss Honey said, "Do you know what an epicure is, Matilda?"

"It is someone who is dainty with his eating," Matilda said.

"That is correct," Miss Honey said. "And do you happen to know what that particular type of poetry is called?"

"It's called a limerick," Matilda said. "That's a lovely one. It's so funny."

"It's a famous one," Miss Honey said, picking up the book and returning to her table in front of the class. "A witty limerick is very hard to write," she added. "They look easy but they most certainly are not."

"I know," Matilda said. "I've tried quite a few times but mine are never any good."

"You have, have you?" Miss Honey said, more startled than ever. "Well Matilda, I would very much like to hear one of these limericks you say you have written. Could you try to remember one for us?"

"Well," Matilda said, hesitating. "I've actually been trying to make up one about you, Miss Honey, while we've been sitting here."

"About *me*!" Miss Honey cried. "Well, we've certainly got to hear that one, haven't we?"

"I don't think I want to say it, Miss Honey."

"Please tell it," Miss Honey said. "I promise I won't mind."

"I think you will, Miss Honey, because I have to use your first name to make things rhyme and that's why I don't want to say it."

"How do you know my first name?" Miss Honey asked.

"I heard another teacher calling you by it just before we came in," Matilda said. "She called you Jenny."

"I insist upon hearing this limerick," Miss Honey said, smiling one of her rare smiles. "Stand up and recite it."

Reluctantly Matilda stood up and very slowly, very nervously, she recited her limerick:

"The thing we all ask about Jenny
Is, 'Surely there cannot be many
Young girls in the place
With so lovely a face?'
The answer to that is, '*Not any!*'"

The whole of Miss Honey's pale and pleasant face blushed a brilliant scarlet. Then once again she smiled. It was a much broader one this time, a smile of pure pleasure.

"Why, thank you, Matilda," she said, still smiling. "Although it is not true, it is really a very good limerick. Oh dear, oh dear, I must try to remember that one."

From the third row of desks, Lavender said, "It's good. I like it."

"It's true as well," a small boy called Rupert said.

"Of course it's true," Nigel said.

Already the whole class had begun to warm towards Miss Honey, although as yet she had hardly taken any notice of any of them except Matilda.

"Who taught you to read, Matilda?" Miss Honey asked.

"I just sort of taught myself, Miss Honey."

"And have you read any books all by yourself, any children's books, I mean?"

"I've read all the ones that are in the public library in the High Street, Miss Honey."

"And did you like them?"

"I liked some of them very much indeed," Matilda said, "but I thought others were fairly dull."

"Tell me one that you liked."

"I liked *The Lion, the Witch and the Wardrobe*," Matilda said. "I think Mr C. S. Lewis is a very good writer. But he has one failing. There are no funny bits in his books."

"You are right there," Miss Honey said.

"There aren't many funny bits in Mr Tolkien either," Matilda said.

"Do you think that all children's books ought to have funny bits in them?" Miss Honey asked.

"I do," Matilda said. "Children are not so serious as grown-ups and they love to laugh."

Miss Honey was astounded by the wisdom of this tiny girl. She said, "And what are you going to do now that you've read all the children's books?"

"I am reading other books," Matilda said. "I borrow them from the library. Mrs Phelps is very kind to me. She helps me to choose them."

Miss Honey was leaning far forward over her work-table and gazing in wonder at the child. She had completely forgotten now about the rest of the class. "What other books?" she murmured.

"I am very fond of Charles Dickens," Matilda said. "He makes me laugh a lot. Especially Mr Pickwick."

At that moment the bell in the corridor sounded for the end of class.

The Trunchbull

In the interval, Miss Honey left the classroom and headed straight for the Headmistress's study. She felt wildly excited. She had just met a small girl who possessed, or so it seemed to her, quite extra-ordinary qualities of brilliance. There had not been time yet to find out exactly how brilliant the child was, but Miss Honey had learned enough to realise that something had to be done about it as soon as possible. It would be ridiculous to leave a child like that stuck in the bottom form.

Normally Miss Honey was terrified of the Head-mistress and kept well away from her, but at this moment she felt ready to take on anybody. She knocked on the door of the dreaded private study. "Enter!" boomed the deep and dangerous voice of Miss Trunchbull. Miss Honey went in.

Now most head teachers are chosen because they possess a number of fine qualities. They under-stand children and they have the children's best interests at heart. They are sympathetic. They are fair and they are deeply interested in education. Miss Trunchbull possessed none of these qualities and how she ever got her present job was a mystery.

She was above all a most formidable female. She had once been a famous athlete, and even now the muscles were still clearly in evidence. You could see them in the bull-neck, in the big shoulders, in the thick arms, in the sinewy wrists and in the powerful legs. Looking at her, you got the feeling that this was someone who could bend iron bars and tear telephone directories in half. Her face, I'm afraid, was neither a thing of beauty nor a joy for ever. She had an obstinate chin, a cruel mouth and small arrogant eyes. And as for her clothes . . . they were, to say the least, extremely odd. She always had on a brown cotton smock which was pinched in around the waist with a wide leather belt. The belt was fastened in front with an enormous silver buckle. The massive thighs which emerged from out of the smock were encased in a pair of extraordinary breeches, bottle-green in colour and made of coarse twill. These breeches reached to just below the knees and from there on down she sported green stockings with turn-up tops, which displayed her calf muscles to perfection. On her feet she wore flat-heeled brown brogues with leather flaps. She looked, in short, more like a rather eccentric and bloodthirsty follower of the stag-hounds than the headmistress of a nice school for children.

When Miss Honey entered the study, Miss Trunchbull was standing beside her huge desk with a look of scowling impatience on her face. "Yes, Miss Honey," she said. "What is it you want? You're looking very flushed and flustered this morning. What's the matter with you? Have those little stinkers been flicking spitballs at you?"

"No, Headmistress. Nothing like that."

"Well, what is it then? Get on with it. I'm a busy

woman." As she spoke, she reached out and poured herself a glass of water from a jug that was always on her desk.

"There is a little girl in my class called Matilda Wormwood . . . " Miss Honey began.

"That's the daughter of the man who owns Wormwood Motors in the village," Miss Trunchbull barked. She hardly ever spoke in a normal voice. She either barked or shouted. "An excellent person, Wormwood," she went on. "I was in there only yesterday. He sold me a car. Almost new. Only done ten thousand miles. Previous owner was an old lady who took it out once a year at the most. A terrific bargain. Yes, I liked Wormwood. A real pillar of our society. He told me the daughter was a bad lot though. He said to watch her. He said if anything bad ever happened in the school, it was certain to be his daughter who did it. I haven't met the little brat yet, but she'll know about it when I do. Her father said she's a real wart."

"Oh no, Headmistress, that can't be right!" Miss Honey cried.

"Oh yes, Miss Honey, it darn well is right! In fact, now I come to think of it, I'll bet it was she who put that stink-bomb under my desk here first thing this morning. The place stank like a sewer! Of course it was her! I shall have her for that, you see if I don't! What's she look like? Nasty little worm, I'll be bound. I have discovered, Miss Honey, during my long career as a teacher that a bad girl is a far more dangerous creature than a bad boy. What's more, they're much harder to squash.

85

Squashing a bad girl is like trying to squash a bluebottle. You bang down on it and the darn thing isn't there. Nasty dirty things, little girls are. Glad I never was one."

"Oh, but you must have been a little girl once, Headmistress. Surely you were."

"Not for long anyway," Miss Trunchbull barked, grinning. "I became a woman very quickly."

She's completely off her rocker, Miss Honey told herself. She's barmy as a bedbug. Miss Honey stood resolutely before the Headmistress. For once she was not going to be browbeaten. "I must tell you, Headmistress," she said, "that you are completely mistaken about Matilda putting a stink-bomb under your desk."

"I am never mistaken, Miss Honey!"

"But Headmistress, the child only arrived in school this morning and came straight to the classroom . . . "

"Don't argue with me, for heaven's sake, woman! This little brute Matilda or whatever her name is has stink-bombed my study! There's no doubt about it! Thank you for suggesting it."

"But I didn't suggest it, Headmistress."

"Of course you did! Now what is it you want, Miss Honey? Why are you wasting my time?"

"I came to you to talk about Matilda, Headmistress. I have extraordinary things to report about the child. May I please tell you what happened in class just now?"

"I suppose she set fire to your skirt and scorched your knickers!" Miss Trunchbull snorted.

"No, no!" Miss Honey cried out. "Matilda is a genius."

At the mention of this word, Miss Trunchbull's face turned purple and her whole body seemed to swell up like a bullfrog's. "A *genius*!" she shouted. "What piffle is this you are talking, madam? You must be out of your mind! I have her father's word for it that the child is a gangster!"

"Her father is wrong, Headmistress."

"Don't be a twerp, Miss Honey! You have met the little beast for only half an hour and her father has known her all her life!"

But Miss Honey was determined to have her say and she now began to describe some of the amazing things Matilda had done with arithmetic.

"So she's learnt a few tables by heart, has she?" Miss Trunchbull barked. "My dear woman, that doesn't make her a genius! It makes her a parrot!"

"But Headmistress she can *read*."

"So can I," Miss Trunchbull snapped.

"It is my opinion", Miss Honey said, "that Matilda should be taken out of my form and placed immediately in the top form with the eleven-year-olds."

"Ha!" snorted Miss Trunchbull. "So you want to get rid of her, do you? So you can't handle her? So now you want to unload her on to the wretched Miss Plimsoll in the top form where she will cause even more chaos?"

"No, no!" cried Miss Honey. "That is not my reason at all!"

"Oh, yes it is!" shouted Miss Trunchbull. "I can see right through your little plot, madam! And my answer is no! Matilda stays where she is and it is up to you to see that she behaves herself."

"But Headmistress, please . . ."

"Not another word!" shouted Miss Trunchbull. "And in any case, I have a rule in this school that all children remain in their own age groups regardless of ability. Great Scott, I'm not having a little five-year-old brigand sitting with the senior girls and boys in the top form. Whoever heard of such a thing!"

Miss Honey stood there helpless before this great red-necked giant. There was a lot more she would like to have said but she knew it was useless. She said softly, "Very well, then. It's up to you, Headmistress."

"You're darn right it's up to me!" Miss Trunchbull bellowed. "And don't forget, madam, that we are dealing here with a little viper who put a stink-bomb under my desk . . . "

"She did *not* do that, Headmistress!"

"Of course she did it," Miss Trunchbull boomed. "And I'll tell you what. I wish to heavens I was still allowed to use the birch and belt as I did in the good old days! I'd have roasted Matilda's bottom for her so she couldn't sit down for a month!"

Miss Honey turned and walked out of the study feeling depressed but by no means defeated. I am going to do something about this child, she told herself. I don't know what it will be, but I shall find a way to help her in the end.

The Parents

When Miss Honey emerged from the Head-mistress's study, most of the children were outside in the playground. Her first move was to go round to the various teachers who taught the senior class and borrow from them a number of text-books, books on algebra, geometry, French, English Literature and the like. Then she sought out Matilda and called her into the classroom.

"There is no point", she said, "in you sitting in class doing nothing while I am teaching the rest of the form the two-times table and how to spell cat and rat and mouse. So during each lesson I shall give you one of these text-books to study. At the end of the lesson you can come up to me with your questions if you have any and I shall try to help you. How does that sound?"

"Thank you, Miss Honey," Matilda said. "That sounds fine."

"I am sure," Miss Honey said, "that we'll be able to get you moved into a much higher form later on, but for the moment the Headmistress wishes you to stay where you are."

"Very well, Miss Honey," Matilda said. "Thank you so much for getting those books for me."

What a nice child she is, Miss Honey thought. I don't care what her father said about her, she seems very quiet and gentle to me. And not a bit stuck up in spite of her brilliance. In fact she hardly seems aware of it.

So when the class reassembled, Matilda went to her desk and began to study a text-book on geometry which Miss Honey had given her. The teacher kept half an eye on her all the time and noticed that the child very soon became deeply absorbed in the book. She never glanced up once during the entire lesson.

Miss Honey, meanwhile, was making another decision. She was deciding that she would go herself and have a secret talk with Matilda's mother and father as soon as possible. She simply refused to let the matter rest where it was. The whole thing was ridiculous. She couldn't believe that the parents were totally unaware of their daughter's remarkable talents. After all, Mr Wormwood was a successful motor-car dealer so she presumed that he was a fairly intelligent man himself. In any event, parents never *underestimated* the abilities of their own children. Quite the reverse. Sometimes it was well nigh impossible for a teacher to convince the proud father or mother that their beloved offspring was a complete nitwit. Miss Honey felt confident that she would have no difficulty in convincing Mr and Mrs Wormwood that Matilda was something very special indeed. The trouble was going to be to stop them from getting over-enthusiastic.

And now Miss Honey's hopes began to expand even further. She started wondering whether per-

91

mission might not be sought from the parents for her to give private tuition to Matilda after school. The prospect of coaching a child as bright as this appealed enormously to her professional instinct as a teacher. And suddenly she decided that she would go and call on Mr and Mrs Wormwood that very evening. She would go fairly late, between nine and ten o'clock, when Matilda was sure to be in bed.

And that is precisely what she did. Having got the address from the school records, Miss Honey set out to walk from her own home to the Wormwood's house shortly after nine. She found the house in a pleasant street where each smallish building was separated from its neighbours by a bit of garden. It was a modern brick house that could not have been cheap to buy and the name on the gate said COSY NOOK. Nosey cook might have been better, Miss Honey thought. She was given to playing with words in that way. She walked up the path and rang the bell, and while she stood waiting she could hear the television blaring inside.

The door was opened by a small ratty-looking man with a thin ratty moustache who was wearing a sports-coat that had an orange and red stripe in the material. "Yes?" he said, peering out at Miss Honey. "If you're selling raffle tickets I don't want any."

"I'm not," Miss Honey said. "And please forgive me for butting in on you like this. I am Matilda's teacher at school and it is important I have a word with you and your wife."

92

"Got into trouble already, has she?" Mr Worm-wood said, blocking the doorway. "Well, she's your responsibility from now on. You'll have to deal with her."

"She is in no trouble at all," Miss Honey said. "I have come with good news about her. Quite startling news, Mr Wormwood. Do you think I might come in for a few minutes and talk to you about Matilda?"

"We are right in the middle of watching one of our favourite programmes," Mr Wormwood said. "This is most inconvenient. Why don't you come back some other time."

Miss Honey began to lose patience. "Mr Wormwood," she said, "if you think some rotten TV programme is more important than your daughter's future, then you ought not to be a parent! Why don't you switch the darn thing off and listen to me!"

That shook Mr Wormwood. He was not used to being spoken to in this way. He peered carefully at the slim frail woman who stood so resolutely out on the porch. "Oh very well then," he snapped. "Come on in and let's get it over with." Miss Honey stepped briskly inside.

"Mrs Wormwood isn't going to thank you for this," the man said as he led her into the sitting-room where a large platinum-blonde woman was gazing rapturously at the TV screen.

"Who is it?" the woman said, not looking round.

"Some school teacher," Mr Wormwood said. "She says she's got to talk to us about Matilda." He crossed to the TV set and turned down the sound but left the picture on the screen.

"Don't do that, Harry!" Mrs Wormwood cried out. "Willard is just about to propose to Angelica!"

"You can still watch it while we're talking," Mr Wormwood said. "This is Matilda's teacher. She says she's got some sort of news to give us."

"My name is Jennifer Honey," Miss Honey said. "How do you do, Mrs Wormwood."

Mrs Wormwood glared at her and said, "What's the trouble then?"

Nobody invited Miss Honey to sit down so she chose a chair and sat down anyway. "This", she said, "was your daughter's first day at school."

"We know that," Mrs Wormwood said, ratty about missing her programme. "Is that all you came to tell us?"

Miss Honey stared hard into the other woman's wet grey eyes, and she allowed the silence to hang in the air until Mrs Wormwood became uncomfortable. "Do you wish me to explain why I came?" she said.

"Get on with it then," Mrs Wormwood said.

"I'm sure you know", Miss Honey said, "that children in the bottom class at school are not expected to be able to read or spell or juggle with numbers when they first arrive. Five-year-olds cannot do that. But Matilda can do it all. And if I am to believe her . . . "

"I wouldn't," Mrs Wormwood said. She was still ratty at losing the sound on the TV.

"Was she lying, then," Miss Honey said, "when she told me that nobody taught her to multiply or to read? Did either of you teach her?"

"Teach her what?" Mr Wormwood said.

"To read. To read books," Miss Honey said. "Perhaps you *did* teach her. Perhaps she *was* lying. Perhaps you have shelves full of books all over the house. I wouldn't know. Perhaps you are both great readers."

"Of course we read," Mr Wormwood said. "Don't be so daft. I read the *Autocar* and the *Motor* from cover to cover every week."

"This child has already read an astonishing number of books," Miss Honey said. "I was simply trying to find out if she came from a family that loved good literature."

"We don't hold with book-reading," Mr Wormwood said. "You can't make a living from sitting

on your fanny and reading story-books. We don't keep them in the house."

"I see," Miss Honey said. "Well, all I came to tell you was that Matilda has a brilliant mind. But I expect you knew that already."

"Of course I knew she could read," the mother said. "She spends her life up in her room buried in some silly book."

"But does it not intrigue you", Miss Honey said, "that a little five-year-old child is reading long adult novels by Dickens and Hemingway? Doesn't that make you jump up and down with excitement?"

"Not particularly," the mother said. "I'm not in favour of blue-stocking girls. A girl should think about making herself look attractive so she can get a good husband later on. Looks is more important than books, Miss Hunky . . . "

"The name is Honey," Miss Honey said.

"Now look at *me*," Mrs Wormwood said. "Then look at *you*. You chose books. I chose looks."

Miss Honey looked at the plain plump person with the smug suet-pudding face who was sitting across the room. "What did you say?" she asked.

"I said you chose books and I chose looks," Mrs Wormwood said. "And who's finished up the better off? Me, of course. I'm sitting pretty in a nice house with a successful businessman and you're left slaving away teaching a lot of nasty little children the ABC."

"Quite right, sugar-plum," Mr Wormwood said, casting a look of such simpering sloppiness at his wife it would have made a cat sick.

Miss Honey decided that if she was going to get anywhere with these people she must not lose her temper. "I haven't told you all of it yet," she said. "Matilda, so far as I can gather at this early stage, is also a kind of mathematical genius. She can multiply complicated figures in her head like lightning."

"What's the point of that when you can buy a calculator?" Mr Wormwood said.

"A girl doesn't get a man by being brainy," Mrs Wormwood said. "Look at that film-star for instance," she added, pointing at the silent TV screen where a bosomy female was being embraced by a craggy actor in the moonlight. "You don't think she got him to do that by multiplying figures at him, do you? Not likely. And now he's going to marry her, you see if he doesn't, and she's going to live in a mansion with a butler and lots of maids."

Miss Honey could hardly believe what she was hearing. She had heard that parents like this existed all over the place and that their children turned out to be delinquents and drop-outs, but it was still a shock to meet a pair of them in the flesh.

"Matilda's trouble", she said, trying once again, "is that she is so far ahead of everyone else around her that it might be worth thinking about some extra kind of private tuition. I seriously believe that she could be brought up to university standard in two or three years with the proper coaching."

"University?" Mr Wormwood shouted, bouncing up in his chair. "Who wants to go to university for heaven's sake! All they learn there is bad habits!"

"That is not true," Miss Honey said. "If you had a heart attack this minute and had to call a doctor, that doctor would be a university graduate. If you got sued for selling someone a rotten second-hand car, you'd have to get a lawyer and he'd be a university graduate, too. Do not despise clever people, Mr Wormwood. But I can see we're not going to agree. I'm sorry I burst in on you like this." Miss Honey rose from her chair and walked out of the room.

Mr Wormwood followed her to the front-door and said, "Good of you to come, Miss Hawkes, or is it Miss Harris?"

"It's neither," Miss Honey said, "but let it go." And away she went.

Throwing the Hammer

The nice thing about Matilda was that if you had met her casually and talked to her you would have thought she was a perfectly normal five-and-a-half-year-old child. She displayed almost no outward signs of her brilliance and she never showed off. "This is a very sensible and quiet little girl," you would have said to yourself. And unless for some reason you had started a discussion with her about literature or mathematics, you would never have known the extent of her brain-power.

It was therefore easy for Matilda to make friends with other children. All those in her class liked her. They knew of course that she was "clever" because they had heard her being questioned by Miss Honey on the first day of term. And they knew also that she was allowed to sit quietly with a book during lessons and not pay attention to the teacher. But children of their age do not search deeply for reasons. They are far too wrapped up in their own small struggles to worry overmuch about what others are doing and why.

Among Matilda's new-found friends was the girl called Lavender. Right from the first day of term the two of them started wandering round together during the morning-break and in the lunch-hour. Lavender was exceptionally small for her age, a skinny little nymph with deep-brown eyes and with dark hair that was cut in a fringe across her forehead. Matilda liked her because she was gutsy and adventurous. She liked Matilda for exactly the same reasons.

Before the first week of term was up, awesome tales about the Headmistress, Miss Trunchbull, began to filter through to the newcomers. Matilda and Lavender, standing in a corner of the playground during morning-break on the third day, were approached by a rugged ten-year-old with a boil on her nose, called Hortensia. "New scum, I suppose," Hortensia said to them, looking down from her great height. She was eating from an extra large bag of potato crisps and digging the stuff out in handfuls. "Welcome to borstal," she added, spraying bits of crisp out of her mouth like snowflakes.

The two tiny ones, confronted by this giant, kept a watchful silence.

"Have you met the Trunchbull yet?" Hortensia asked.

"We've seen her at prayers," Lavender said, "but we haven't met her."

"You've got a treat coming to you," Hortensia said. "She hates very small children. She therefore loathes the bottom class and everyone in it. She thinks five-year-olds are grubs that haven't yet hatched out." In went another fistful of crisps and when she spoke again, out sprayed the crumbs. "If you survive your first year you may just manage to live through the rest of your time here. But many

102

don't survive. They get carried out on stretchers screaming. I've seen it often." Hortensia paused to observe the effect these remarks were having on the two titchy ones. Not very much. They seemed pretty cool. So the large one decided to regale them with further information.

"I suppose you know the Trunchbull has a lock-up cupboard in her private quarters called The Chokey? Have you heard about The Chokey?"

Matilda and Lavender shook their heads and continued to gaze up at the giant. Being very small, they were inclined to mistrust any creature that was larger than they were, especially senior girls.

"The Chokey", Hortensia went on, "is a very tall but very narrow cupboard. The floor is only ten inches square so you can't sit down or squat in it. You have to stand. And three of the walls are made of cement with bits of broken glass sticking out all over, so you can't lean against them. You have to stand more or less at attention all the time when you get locked up in there. It's terrible."

"Can't you lean against the door?" Matilda asked.

"Don't be daft," Hortensia said. "The door's got thousands of sharp spikey nails sticking out of it. They've been hammered through from the outside, probably by the Trunchbull herself."

"Have you ever been in there?" Lavender asked.

"My first term I was in there six times," Hortensia said. "Twice for a whole day and the other times for two hours each. But two hours is quite bad enough. It's pitch dark and you have to stand up dead straight and if you wobble at all you get spiked either by the glass on the walls or the nails on the door.

"Why were you put in?" Matilda asked. "What had you done?"

"The first time", Hortensia said, "I poured half a tin of Golden Syrup on to the seat of the chair the Trunchbull was going to sit on at prayers. It was wonderful. When she lowered herself into the chair, there was a loud squelching noise similar to that made by a hippopotamus when lowering its foot into the mud on the banks of the Limpopo River. But you're too small and stupid to have read the *Just So Stories*, aren't you?"

"I've read them," Matilda said.

"You're a liar," Hortensia said amiably. "You can't even read yet. But no matter. So when the Trunchbull sat down on the Golden Syrup, the squelch was beautiful. And when she jumped up again, the chair sort of stuck to the seat of those awful green breeches she wears and came up with her for a few seconds until the thick syrup slowly came unstuck. Then she clasped her hands to the seat of her breeches and both hands got covered in the muck. You should have heard her bellow."

"But how did she know it was you?" Lavender asked.

"A little squirt called Ollie Bogwhistle sneaked on me," Hortensia said. "I knocked his front teeth out."

"And the Trunchbull put you in The Chokey for a whole day?" Matilda asked, gulping.

"All day long," Hortensia said. "I was off my rocker when she let me out. I was babbling like an idiot."

"What were the other things you did to get put in The Chokey?" Lavender asked.

"Oh I can't remember them all now," Hortensia said. She spoke with the air of an old warrior who has been in so many battles that bravery has become commonplace. "It's all so long ago," she added, stuffing more crisps into her mouth. "Ah yes, I can remember one. Here's what happened. I chose a time when I knew the Trunchbull was out of the way teaching the sixth-formers, and I put up my hand and asked to go to the bogs. But instead of going *there*, I sneaked into the Trunchbull's

room. And after a speedy search I found the drawer where she kept all her gym knickers."

"Go on," Matilda said, spellbound. "What happened next?"

"I had sent away by post, you see, for this very powerful itching-powder," Hortensia said. "It cost 50p a packet and was called The Skin-Scorcher. The label said it was made from the powdered teeth of deadly snakes, and it was guaranteed to raise welts the size of walnuts on your skin. So I sprinkled this stuff inside every pair of knickers in the drawer and then folded them all up again carefully." Hortensia paused to cram more crisps into her mouth.

"Did it work?" Lavender asked.

"Well," Hortensia said, "a few days later, during prayers, the Trunchbull suddenly started scratching herself like mad down below. A-ha, I said to myself. Here we go. She's changed for gym already. It was pretty wonderful to be sitting there watching it all and knowing that I was the only person in the whole school who realised exactly what was going on inside the Trunchbull's pants. And I felt safe, too. I knew I couldn't be caught. Then the scratching got worse. She couldn't stop. She must have thought she had a wasp's nest down there. And then, right in the middle of the Lord's Prayer, she leapt up and grabbed her bottom and rushed out of the room."

Both Matilda and Lavender were enthralled. It was quite clear to them that they were at this moment standing in the presence of a master. Here was somebody who had brought the art of skulduggery to the highest point of perfection, somebody, moreover, who was willing to risk life and limb in pursuit of her calling. They gazed in wonder at this goddess, and suddenly even the boil on her nose was no longer a blemish but a badge of courage.

"But how *did* she catch you that time?" Lavender asked, breathless with wonder.

"She didn't," Hortensia said. "But I got a day in The Chokey just the same."

"Why?" they both asked.

"The Trunchbull", Hortensia said, "has a nasty habit of guessing. When she doesn't know who the culprit is, she makes a guess at it, and the trouble is she's often right. I was the prime suspect this

108

time because of the Golden Syrup job, and although I knew she didn't have any proof, nothing I said made any difference. I kept shouting, 'How could I have done it, Miss Trunchbull? I didn't even know you kept any spare knickers at school! I don't even know what itching-powder is! I've never heard of it!' But the lying didn't help me in spite of the great performance I put on. The Trunchbull simply grabbed me by one ear and rushed me to The Chokey at the double and threw me inside and locked the door. That was my second all-day stretch. It was absolute torture. I was spiked and cut all over when I came out."

"It's like a war," Matilda said, overawed.

"You're darn right it's like a war," Hortensia cried. "And the casualties are terrific. *We* are the crusaders, the gallant army fighting for our lives with hardly any weapons at all and the Trunchbull is the Prince of Darkness, the Foul Serpent, the Fiery Dragon with all the weapons at her command. It's a tough life. We all try to support each other."

"You can rely on us," Lavender said, making her height of three feet two inches stretch as tall as possible.

"No, I can't," Hortensia said. "You're only shrimps. But you never know. We may find a use for you one day in some undercover job."

"Tell us just a little bit more about what she does," Matilda said. "Please do."

"I mustn't frighten you before you've been here a week," Hortensia said.

"You won't," Lavender said. "We may be small but we're quite tough."

"Listen to this then," Hortensia said. "Only yesterday the Trunchbull caught a boy called Julius Rottwinkle eating Liquorice Allsorts during the scripture lesson and she simply picked him up by one arm and flung him clear out of the open classroom window. Our classroom is one floor up and we saw Julius Rottwinkle go sailing out over the garden like a Frisbee and landing with a thump in the middle of the lettuces. Then the Trunchbull turned to us and said, "From now on, anybody caught eating in class goes straight out the window.""

"Did this Julius Rottwinkle break any bones?" Lavender asked.

"Only a few," Hortensia said. "You've got to remember that the Trunchbull once threw the hammer for Britain in the Olympics so she's very proud of her right arm."

"What's throwing the hammer?" Lavender asked.

"The hammer", Hortensia said, "is actually a ruddy great cannon-ball on the end of a long bit of wire, and the thrower whisks it round and round his or her head faster and faster and then lets it go. You have to be terrifically strong. The Trunchbull will throw anything around just to keep her arm in, especially children."

"Good heavens," Lavender said.

"I once heard her say", Hortensia went on, "that a large boy is about the same weight as an Olympic

110

hammer and therefore he's very useful for practising with."

At that point something strange happened. The playground, which up to then had been filled with shrieks and the shouting of children at play, all at once became silent as the grave. "Watch out," Hortensia whispered. Matilda and Lavender glanced round and saw the gigantic figure of Miss Trunchbull advancing through the crowd of boys and girls with menacing strides. The children drew back hastily to let her through and her progress across the asphalt was like that of Moses going through the Red Sea when the waters parted. A formidable figure she was too, in her belted smock and green breeches. Below the knees her calf muscles stood out like grapefruits inside her stockings. "Amanda Thripp!" she was shouting. "You, Amanda Thripp, come here!"

"Hold your hats," Hortensia whispered.

"What's going to happen?" Lavender whispered back.

"That idiot Amanda", Hortensia said, "has let her long hair grow even longer during the hols and her mother has plaited it into pigtails. Silly thing to do."

"Why silly?" Matilda asked.

"If there's one thing the Trunchbull can't stand it's pigtails," Hortensia said.

Matilda and Lavender saw the giant in green breeches advancing upon a girl of about ten who had a pair of plaited golden pigtails hanging over her shoulders. Each pigtail had a blue satin bow at

the end of it and it all looked very pretty. The girl
wearing the pigtails, Amanda Thripp, stood quite
still, watching the advancing giant, and the expression on her face was one that you might find
on the face of a person who is trapped in a small

113

field with an enraged bull which is charging flat-out towards her. The girl was glued to the spot, terror-struck, pop-eyed, quivering, knowing for certain that the Day of Judgment had come for her at last.

Miss Trunchbull had now reached the victim and stood towering over her. "I want those filthy pigtails off before you come back to school tomorrow!" she barked. "Chop 'em off and throw 'em in the dustbin, you understand?"

Amanda, paralysed with fright, managed to stutter, "My m-m-mummy likes them. She p-p-plaits them for me every morning."

"Your mummy's a twit!" the Trunchbull bellowed. She pointed a finger the size of a salami at the child's head and shouted, "You look like a rat with a tail coming out of its head!"

"My m-m-mummy thinks I look lovely, Miss T-T-Trunchbull," Amanda stuttered, shaking like a blancmange.

"I don't give a tinker's toot what your mummy thinks!" the Trunchbull yelled, and with that she lunged forward and grabbed hold of Amanda's pig-tails in her right fist and lifted the girl clear off the ground. Then she started swinging her round and round her head, faster and faster and Amanda was screaming blue murder and the Trunchbull was yelling, "I'll give you pigtails, you little rat!"

"Shades of the Olympics," Hortensia murmured. "She's getting up speed now just like she does with the hammer. Ten to one she's going to throw her."

And now the Trunchbull was leaning back against the weight of the whirling girl and

114

pivoting expertly on her toes, spinning round and round, and soon Amanda Thripp was travelling so fast she became a blur, and suddenly, with a mighty grunt, the Trunchbull let go of the pigtails and Amanda went sailing like a rocket right over the wire fence of the playground and high up into the sky.

"Well thrown, sir!" someone shouted from across the playground, and Matilda, who was mesmerised by the whole crazy affair, saw Amanda Thripp descending in a long graceful parabola on to the playing-field beyond. She landed on the grass and bounced three times and finally came to rest. Then, amazingly, she sat up. She looked a trifle dazed and who could blame her, but after a minute or so she was on her feet again and tottering back towards the playground.

The Trunchbull stood in the playground dusting off her hands. "Not bad," she said, "considering I'm not in strict training. Not bad at all." Then she strode away.

"She's mad," Hortensia said.

"But don't the parents complain?" Matilda asked.

"Would yours?" Hortensia asked. "I know mine wouldn't. She treats the mothers and fathers just the same as the children and they're all scared to death of her. I'll be seeing you some time, you two." And with that she sauntered away.

Bruce Bogtrotter
and the Cake

"How can she get *away* with it?" Lavender said to Matilda. "Surely the children go home and tell their mothers and fathers. I know my father would raise a terrific stink if I told him the Headmistress had grabbed me by the hair and slung me over the playground fence."

"No, he wouldn't," Matilda said, "and I'll tell you why. He simply wouldn't believe you."

"Of course he would."

"He wouldn't," Matilda said. "And the reason is obvious. Your story would sound too ridiculous to be believed. And that is the Trunchbull's great secret."

"What is?" Lavender asked.

Matilda said, "Never do anything by halves if you want to get away with it. Be outrageous. Go the whole hog. Make sure everything you do is so completely crazy it's unbelievable. No parent is going to believe this pigtail story, not in a million years. Mine wouldn't. They'd call me a liar."

"In that case", Lavender said, "Amanda's mother isn't going to cut her pigtails off."

"No, she isn't," Matilda said. "Amanda will do it herself. You see if she doesn't."

"Do you think she's mad?" Lavender asked.

"Who?"

"The Trunchbull."

"No, I don't think she's mad," Matilda said. "But she's very dangerous. Being in this school is like being in a cage with a cobra. You have to be very fast on your feet."

They got another example of how dangerous the Headmistress could be on the very next day. During lunch an announcement was made that the whole school should go into the Assembly Hall and be seated as soon as the meal was over.

When all the two hundred and fifty or so boys and girls were settled down in Assembly, the Trunchbull marched on to the platform. None of the other teachers came in with her. She was carrying a riding-crop in her right hand. She stood up there on centre stage in her green breeches with legs apart and riding-crop in hand, glaring at the sea of upturned faces before her.

"What's going to happen?" Lavender whispered.

"I don't know," Matilda whispered back.

The whole school waited for what was coming next.

"Bruce Bogtrotter!" the Trunchbull barked suddenly. "Where is Bruce Bogtrotter?"

A hand shot up among the seated children.

"Come up here!" the Trunchbull shouted. "And look smart about it!"

An eleven-year-old boy who was decidedly large and round stood up and waddled briskly forward. He climbed up on to the platform.

"Stand over there!" the Trunchbull ordered, pointing. The boy stood to one side. He looked

nervous. He knew very well he wasn't up there to be presented with a prize. He was watching the Headmistress with an exceedingly wary eye and he kept edging farther and farther away from her with little shuffles of his feet, rather as a rat might edge away from a terrier that is watching it from across the room. His plump flabby face had turned grey with fearful apprehension. His stockings hung about his ankles.

"This *clot*," boomed the Headmistress, pointing the riding-crop at him like a rapier, "this *blackhead*, this *foul carbuncle*, this *poisonous pustule* that you see before you is none other than a disgusting criminal, a denizen of the underworld, a member of the Mafia!"

"Who, me?" Bruce Bogtrotter said, looking genuinely puzzled.

"A thief!" the Trunchbull screamed. "A crook! A pirate! A brigand! A rustler!"

"Steady on," the boy said. "I mean, dash it all, Headmistress."

"Do you deny it, you miserable little gumboil? Do you plead not guilty?"

"I don't know what you're talking about," the boy said, more puzzled than ever.

"I'll tell you what I'm talking about, you suppurating little blister!" the Trunchbull shouted. "Yesterday morning, during break, you sneaked like a serpent into the kitchen and stole a slice of my private chocolate cake from my tea-tray! That tray had just been prepared for me personally by the cook! It was my morning snack! And as for the cake, it was my own private stock! That was not boy's cake! You don't think for one minute I'm going to eat the filth I give to you? That cake was made from real butter and real cream! And he, that

robber-bandit, that safe-cracker, that highwayman standing over there with his socks around his ankles stole it and ate it!"

"I never did," the boy exclaimed, turning from grey to white.

"Don't lie to me, Bogtrotter!" barked the Trunchbull. "The cook saw you! What's more, she saw you eating it!"

Thc Trunchbull paused to wipe a fleck of froth from her lips.

When she spoke again her voice was suddenly softer, quieter, more friendly, and she leaned towards the boy, smiling. "You like my special chocolate cake, don't you, Bogtrotter? It's rich and delicious, isn't it, Bogtrotter?"

"Very good," the boy mumbled. The words were out before he could stop himself.

"You're right," the Trunchbull said. "It *is* very

good. Therefore I think you should congratulate the cook. When a gentleman has had a particularly good meal, Bogtrotter, he always sends his compliments to the chef. You didn't know that, did you, Bogtrotter? But those who inhabit the criminal underworld are not noted for their good manners."

The boy remained silent.

"Cook!" the Trunchbull shouted, turning her head towards the door. "Come here, cook! Bogtrotter wishes to tell you how good your chocolate cake is!"

The cook, a tall shrivelled female who looked as though all of her body-juices had been dried out of her long ago in a hot oven, walked on to the platform wearing a dirty white apron. Her entrance had clearly been arranged beforehand by the Headmistress.

"Now then, Bogtrotter," the Trunchbull boomed. "Tell cook what you think of her chocolate cake."

"Very good," the boy mumbled. You could see he was now beginning to wonder what all this was leading up to. The only thing he knew for certain was that the law forbade the Trunchbull to hit him with the riding-crop that she kept smacking against her thigh. That was some comfort, but not much because the Trunchbull was totally unpredictable. One never knew what she was going to do next.

"There you are, cook," the Trunchbull cried. "Bogtrotter likes your cake. He adores your cake. Do you have any more of your cake you could give him?"

"I do indeed," the cook said. She seemed to have learnt her lines by heart.

"Then go and get it. And bring a knife to cut it with."

The cook disappeared. Almost at once she was back again staggering under the weight of an enormous round chocolate cake on a china platter. The cake was fully eighteen inches in diameter and it was covered with dark-brown chocolate icing. "Put it on the table," the Trunchbull said.

There was a small table centre stage with a chair behind it. The cook placed the cake carefully on the table. "Sit down, Bogtrotter," the Trunchbull said. "Sit there."

The boy moved cautiously to the table and sat down. He stared at the gigantic cake.

"There you are, Bogtrotter," the Trunchbull said, and once again her voice became soft, persuasive, even gentle. "It's all for you, every bit of it. As you enjoyed that slice you had yesterday so very much, I ordered cook to bake you an extra large one all for yourself."

"Well, thank you," the boy said, totally bemused.

"Thank cook, not me," the Trunchbull said.

"Thank you, cook," the boy said.

The cook stood there like a shrivelled bootlace, tight-lipped, implacable, disapproving. She looked as though her mouth was full of lemon juice.

"Come on then," the Trunchbull said. "Why don't you cut yourself a nice thick slice and try it?"

"What? Now?" the boy said, cautious. He knew

124

there was a catch in this somewhere, but he wasn't sure where. "Can't I take it home instead?" he asked.

"That would be impolite," the Trunchbull said, with a crafty grin. "You must show cookie here how grateful you are for all the trouble she's taken."

The boy didn't move.

"Go on, get on with it," the Trunchbull said. "Cut a slice and taste it. We haven't got all day."

The boy picked up the knife and was about to cut into the cake when he stopped. He stared at the cake. Then he looked up at the Trunchbull, then at the tall stringy cook with her lemon-juice mouth. All the children in the hall were watching tensely, waiting for something to happen. They felt certain it must. The Trunchbull was not a person who would give someone a whole chocolate cake to eat just out of kindness. Many were guessing that it had been filled with pepper or castor-oil or some other foul-tasting substance that would make the boy violently sick. It might even be arsenic and he would be dead in ten seconds flat. Or perhaps it was a booby-trapped cake and the whole thing would blow up the moment it was cut, taking Bruce Bogtrotter with it. No one in the school put it past the Trunchbull to do any of these things.

"I don't want to eat it," the boy said.

"Taste it, you little brat," the Trunchbull said. "You're insulting the cook."

Very gingerly the boy began to cut a thin slice of the vast cake. Then he levered the slice out. Then he put down the knife and took the sticky thing in his fingers and started very slowly to eat it.

"It's good, isn't it?" the Trunchbull asked.

"Very good," the boy said, chewing and swallowing. He finished the slice.

"Have another," the Trunchbull said.

"That's enough, thank you," the boy murmured.

"I said have another," the Trunchbull said, and now there was an altogether sharper edge to her voice. "Eat another slice! Do as you are told!"

"I don't want another slice," the boy said.

Suddenly the Trunchbull exploded. "Eat!" she shouted, banging her thigh with the riding-crop. "If I tell you to eat, you will eat! You wanted cake! You stole cake! And now you've got cake! What's more, you're going to eat it! You do not leave this platform and nobody leaves this hall until you have eaten the entire cake that is sitting there in front of you! Do I make myself clear, Bogtrotter? Do you get my meaning?"

The boy looked at the Trunchbull. Then he looked down at the enormous cake.

"Eat! Eat! Eat!" the Trunchbull was yelling.

Very slowly the boy cut himself another slice and began to eat it.

Matilda was fascinated. "Do you think he can do it?" she whispered to Lavender.

"No," Lavender whispered back. "It's impossible. He'd be sick before he was halfway through."

The boy kept going. When he had finished the second slice, he looked at the Trunchbull, hesitating.

"Eat!" she shouted. "Greedy little thieves who like to eat cake must have cake! Eat faster boy! Eat faster! We don't want to be here all day! And don't stop like you're doing now! Next time you stop before it's all finished you'll go straight into The Chokey and I shall lock the door and throw the key down the well!"

The boy cut a third slice and started to eat it. He finished this one quicker than the other two and when that was done he immediately picked up the knife and cut the next slice. In some peculiar way he seemed to be getting into his stride.

Matilda, watching closely, saw no signs of distress in the boy yet. If anything, he seemed to be gathering confidence as he went along. "He's doing well," she whispered to Lavender.

"He'll be sick soon," Lavender whispered back. "It's going to be horrid."

When Bruce Bogtrotter had eaten his way through half of the entire enormous cake, he paused for just a couple of seconds and took several deep breaths.

The Trunchbull stood with hands on hips, glaring at him. "Get on with it!" she shouted. "Eat it up!"

Suddenly the boy let out a gigantic belch which rolled around the Assembly Hall like thunder. Many of the audience began to giggle.

"Silence!" shouted the Trunchbull.

The boy cut himself another thick slice and started eating it fast. There were still no signs of flagging or giving up. He certainly did not look as though he was about to stop and cry out, "I can't, I can't eat any more! I'm going to be sick!" He was still in there running.

And now a subtle change was coming over the two hundred and fifty watching children in the audience. Earlier on, they had sensed impending disaster. They had prepared themselves for an unpleasant scene in which the wretched boy, stuffed to the gills with chocolate cake, would have to surrender and beg for mercy and then they would have watched the triumphant Trunchbull forcing more and still more cake into the mouth of the gasping boy.

Not a bit of it. Bruce Bogtrotter was three-quarters of the way through and still going strong. One sensed that he was almost beginning to enjoy himself. He had a mountain to climb and he was jolly well going to reach the top or die in the attempt. What is more, he had now become very conscious of his audience and of how they were all silently rooting for him. This was nothing less than a battle between him and the mighty Trunchbull.

Suddenly someone shouted, "Come on Brucie! You can make it!"

The Trunchbull wheeled round and yelled, "Silence!" The audience watched intently. They were thoroughly caught up in the contest. They were longing to start cheering but they didn't dare.

"I think he's going to make it," Matilda whispered.

"I think so too," Lavender whispered back. "I wouldn't have believed anyone in the world could eat the whole of a cake that size."

"The Trunchbull doesn't believe it either," Matilda whispered. "Look at her. She's turning redder and redder. She's going to kill him if he wins."

The boy was slowing down now. There was no

doubt about that. But he kept pushing the stuff into his mouth with the dogged perseverance of a long-distance runner who has sighted the finishing-line and knows he must keep going. As the very last mouthful disappeared, a tremendous cheer rose up from the audience and children were leaping on to their chairs and yelling and clapping and shouting, "Well done, Brucie! Good for you, Brucie! You've won a gold medal, Brucie!"

The Trunchbull stood motionless on the platform. Her great horsy face had turned the colour of molten lava and her eyes were glittering with fury. She glared at Bruce Bogtrotter who was sitting on his chair like some huge overstuffed grub, replete, comatose, unable to move or to speak. A fine sweat was beading his forehead but there was a grin of triumph on his face.

Suddenly the Trunchbull lunged forward and grabbed the large empty china platter on which the cake had rested. She raised it high in the air and brought it down with a crash right on the top of the wretched Bruce Bogtrotter's head and pieces flew all over the platform.

The boy was by now so full of cake he was like a sackful of wet cement and you couldn't have hurt him with a sledge-hammer. He simply shook his head a few times and went on grinning.

"Go to blazes!" screamed the Trunchbull and she marched off the platform followed closely by the cook.

Lavender

In the middle of the first week of Matilda's first term, Miss Honey said to the class, "I have some important news for you, so listen carefully. You too, Matilda. Put that book down for a moment and pay attention."

Small eager faces looked up and listened.

"It is the Headmistress's custom", Miss Honey went on, "to take over the class for one period each week. She does this with every class in the school and each class has a fixed day and a fixed time. Ours is always two o'clock on Thursday afternoons, immediately after lunch. So tomorrow at two o'clock Miss Trunchbull will be taking over from me for one lesson. I shall be here as well, of course, but only as a silent witness. Is that understood?"

"Yes, Miss Honey," they chirruped.

"A word of warning to you all," Miss Honey said. "The Headmistress is very strict about everything. Make sure your clothes are clean, your faces are clean and your hands are clean. Speak only when spoken to. When she asks you a question, stand up at once before you answer it. Never argue with her. Never answer back. Never try to be funny. If you do, you will make her angry, and when the Headmistress gets angry you had better watch out."

"You can say that again," Lavender murmured.

"I am quite sure", Miss Honey said, "that she will be testing you on what you are meant to have learnt this week, which is your two-times table. So I strongly advise you to swot it up when you get home tonight. Get your mother or father to hear you on it."

"What else will she test us on?" someone asked.

"Spelling," Miss Honey said. "Try to remember everything you have learned these last few days. And one more thing. A jug of water and a glass must always be on the table here when the Headmistress comes in. She never takes a lesson without that. Now who will be responsible for seeing that it's there?"

"I will," Lavender said at once.

"Very well, Lavender," Miss Honey said. "It will be your job to go to the kitchen and get the jug and fill it with water and put it on the table here with a clean empty glass just before the lesson starts."

"What if the jug's not in the kitchen?" Lavender asked.

"There are a dozen Headmistress's jugs and glasses in the kitchen," Miss Honey said. "They are used all over the school."

"I won't forget," Lavender said. "I promise I won't."

Already Lavender's scheming mind was going over the possibilities that this water-jug job had opened up for her. She longed to do something truly heroic. She admired the older girl Hortensia to distraction for the daring deeds she had performed in the school. She also admired Matilda who had sworn her to secrecy about the parrot job she had brought off at home, and also the great hair-oil switch which had bleached her father's hair. It was *her* turn now to become a heroine if only she could come up with a brilliant plot.

On the way home from school that afternoon

136

she began to mull over the various possibilities, and when at last the germ of a brilliant idea hit her, she began to expand on it and lay her plans with the same kind of care the Duke of Wellington had done before the Battle of Waterloo. Admittedly the enemy on this occasion was not Napoleon. But you would never have got anyone at Crunchem Hall to admit that the Headmistress was a less formidable foe than the famous Frenchman. Great skill would have to be exercised, Lavender told herself, and great secrecy observed if she was to come out of this exploit alive.

There was a muddy pond at the bottom of Lavender's garden and this was the home of a colony of newts. The newt, although fairly common in English ponds, is not often seen by ordinary people because it is a shy and murky creature. It is an incredibly ugly gruesome-looking animal, rather like a baby crocodile but with a shorter head. It is quite harmless but doesn't look it. It is about six inches long and very slimy, with a greenish-grey skin on top and an orange-coloured belly underneath. It is, in fact, an amphibian, which can live in or out of water.

That evening Lavender went to the bottom of the garden determined to catch a newt. They are swiftly-moving animals and not easy to get hold of. She lay on the bank for a long time waiting patiently until she spotted a whopper. Then, using her school hat as a net, she swooped and caught it. She had lined her pencil-box with pond-weed ready to receive the creature, but she discovered that it

was not easy to get the newt out of the hat and into the pencil-box. It wriggled and squirmed like quicksilver and, apart from that, the box was only just long enough to take it. When she did get it in at last, she had to be careful not to trap its tail in the lid when she slid it closed. A boy next door called Rupert Entwistle had told her that if you chopped off a newt's tail, the tail stayed alive and grew into another newt ten times bigger than the first one. It could be the size of an alligator. Lavender didn't quite believe that, but she was not prepared to risk it happening.

Eventually she managed to slide the lid of the pencil-box right home and the newt was hers. Then, on second thoughts, she opened the lid just the tiniest fraction so that the creature could breathe.

The next day she carried her secret weapon to school in her satchel. She was tingling with excitement. She was longing to tell Matilda about her plan of battle. In fact, she wanted to tell the whole class. But she finally decided to tell nobody. It was better that way because then no one, even when put under the most severe torture, would be able to name her as the culprit.

Lunchtime came. Today it was sausages and baked beans, Lavender's favourite, but she couldn't eat it.

"Are you feeling all right, Lavender?" Miss Honey asked from the head of the table.

"I had such a huge breakfast", Lavender said, "I really couldn't eat a thing."

Immediately after lunch, she dashed off to the kitchen and found one of the Trunchbull's famous jugs. It was a large bulging thing made of blue-glazed pottery. Lavender filled it half-full of water and carried it, together with a glass, into the class-room and set it on the teacher's table. The class-room was still empty. Quick as a flash, Lavender got her pencil-box from her satchel and slid open the lid just a tiny bit. The newt was lying quite still. With great care, she held the box over the neck of the jug and pulled the lid fully open and tipped the newt in. There was a plop as it landed in the water, then it thrashed around wildly for a few seconds before settling down. And now, to make the newt feel more at home, Lavender de-cided to give it all the pond-weed from the pencil-box as well.

The deed was done. All was ready. Lavender put her pencils back into the rather damp pencil-box and returned it to its correct place on her own desk. Then she went out and joined the others in the playground until it was time for the lesson to begin.

The Weekly Test

At two o'clock sharp the class assembled, including Miss Honey who noted that the jug of water and the glass were in the proper place. Then she took up a position standing right at the back. Everyone waited. Suddenly in marched the gigantic figure of the Headmistress in her belted smock and green breeches.

"Good afternoon, children," she barked.

"Good afternoon, Miss Trunchbull," they chirruped.

The Headmistress stood before the class, legs apart, hands on hips, glaring at the small boys and girls who sat nervously at their desks in front of her.

"*Not* a very pretty sight," she said. Her expression was one of utter distaste, as though she were looking at something a dog had done in the middle of the floor. "What a bunch of nauseating little warts you are."

Everyone had the sense to stay silent.

"It makes me vomit", she went on, "to think that I am going to have to put up with a load of garbage like you in my school for the next six years. I can see that I'm going to have to expel as many of you as possible as soon as possible to save myself from going round the bend." She paused and

141

snorted several times. It was a curious noise. You can hear the same sort of thing if you walk through a riding-stable when the horses are being fed. "I suppose", she went on, "your mothers and fathers tell you you're wonderful. Well, I am here to tell you the opposite, and you'd better believe me. Stand up everybody!"

They all got quickly to their feet.

"Now put your hands out in front of you. And as I walk past I want you to turn them over so I can see if they are clean on both sides."

The Trunchbull began a slow march along the rows of desks inspecting the hands. All went well until she came to a small boy in the second row. "What's your name?" she barked.

"Nigel," the boy said.

"Nigel what?"

"Nigel Hicks," the boy said.

"Nigel Hicks what?" the Trunchbull bellowed. She bellowed so loud she nearly blew the little chap out of the window.

"That's it," Nigel said. "Unless you want my middle names as well." He was a brave little fellow and one could see that he was trying not to be scared by the Gorgon who towered above him.

"I do *not* want your middle names, you blister!" the Gorgon bellowed. "What is *my* name?"

"Miss Trunchbull," Nigel said.

"Then use it when you address me! Now then, let's try again. What is your name?"

"Nigel Hicks, Miss Trunchbull," Nigel said.

"That's better," the Trunchbull said. "Your

hands are filthy, Nigel! When did you last wash them?"

"Well, let me think," Nigel said. "That's rather difficult to remember exactly. It could have been yesterday or it could have been the day before."

The Trunchbull's whole body and face seemed to swell up as though she were being inflated by a bicycle-pump.

"I knew it!" she bellowed. "I knew as soon as I saw you that you were nothing but a piece of filth! What is your father's job, a sewage-worker?"

"He's a doctor," Nigel said. "And a jolly good one. He says we're all so covered with bugs anyway that a bit of extra dirt never hurts anyone."

"I'm glad he's not *my* doctor," the Trunchbull said. "And why, might I ask, is there a baked bean on the front of your shirt?"

"We had them for lunch, Miss Trunchbull."

"And do you usually put your lunch on the front of your shirt, Nigel? Is that what this famous doctor father of yours has taught you to do?"

"Baked beans are hard to eat, Miss Trunchbull. They keep falling off my fork."

"You are disgusting!" the Trunchbull bellowed. "You are a walking germ-factory! I don't wish to see any more of you today! Go and stand in the corner on one leg with your face to the wall!"

"But Miss Trunchbull . . . "

"Don't argue with me, boy, or I'll make you stand on your head! Now do as you're told!"

Nigel went.

"Now stay where you are, boy, while I test you on your spelling to see if you've learnt anything at all this past week. And don't turn round when you talk to me. Keep your nasty little face to the wall. Now then, spell 'write'."

"Which one?" Nigel asked. "The thing you do

with a pen or the one that means the opposite of wrong?" He happened to be an unusually bright child and his mother had worked hard with him at home on spelling and reading.

"The one with the pen, you little fool."

Nigel spelled it correctly which surprised the Trunchbull. She thought she had given him a very tricky word, one that he wouldn't yet have learned, and she was peeved that he had succeeded.

Then Nigel said, still balancing on one leg and facing the wall, "Miss Honey taught us how to spell a new very long word yesterday."

"And what word was that?" the Trunchbull asked softly. The softer her voice became, the greater the danger, but Nigel wasn't to know this.

"'Difficulty'," Nigel said. "Everyone in the class can spell 'difficulty' now."

"What nonsense," the Trunchbull said. "You are not supposed to learn long words like that until you are at least eight or nine. And don't try to tell me *everybody* in the class can spell that word. You are lying to me, Nigel."

"Test someone," Nigel said, taking an awful chance. "Test anyone you like."

The Trunchbull's dangerous glittering eyes roved around the class-room. "You," she said, pointing at a tiny and rather daft little girl called Prudence, "Spell 'difficulty'."

Amazingly, Prudence spelled it correctly and without a moment's hesitation.

The Trunchbull was properly taken aback. "Humph!" she snorted. "And I suppose Miss Honey wasted the whole of one lesson teaching you to spell that one single word?"

"Oh no, she didn't," piped Nigel. "Miss Honey taught it to us in three minutes so we'll never

146

forget it. She teaches us lots of words in three minutes."

"And what exactly is this magic method, Miss Honey?" asked the Headmistress.

"I'll show you," piped up the brave Nigel again, coming to Miss Honey's rescue. "Can I put my other foot down and turn round, please, while I show you?"

"You may do neither!" snapped the Trunchbull. "Stay as you are and show me just the same!"

"All right," said Nigel, wobbling crazily on his one leg. "Miss Honey gives us a little song about each word and we all sing it together and we learn to spell it in no time. Would you like to hear the song about 'difficulty'?"

"I should be fascinated," the Trunchbull said in a voice dripping with sarcasm.

"Here it is," Nigel said.

> "Mrs D, Mrs I, Mrs FFI
> Mrs C, Mrs U, Mrs LTY.

That spells difficulty."

"How perfectly ridiculous!" snorted the Trunchbull. "Why are all these women married? And anyway you're not meant to teach poetry when you're teaching spelling. Cut it out in future, Miss Honey."

"But it does teach them some of the harder words wonderfully well," Miss Honey murmured.

"Don't argue with me, Miss Honey!" the Headmistress thundered. "Just do as you're told! I shall now test the class on the multiplication tables to see if Miss Honey has taught you anything at all in that direction." The Trunchbull had returned to her place in front of the class, and her diabolical gaze was moving slowly along the rows of tiny pupils. "You!" she barked, pointing at a small boy called Rupert in the front row. "What is two sevens?"

"Sixteen," Rupert answered with foolish abandon.

The Trunchbull started advancing slow and soft-footed upon Rupert in the manner of a tigress stalking a small deer. Rupert suddenly became aware of the danger signals and quickly tried again. "It's eighteen!" he cried. "Two sevens are eighteen, not sixteen!"

"You ignorant little slug!" the Trunchbull bellowed. "You witless weed! You empty-headed hamster! You stupid glob of glue!" She had now stationed herself directly behind Rupert, and suddenly she extended a hand the size of a tennis racquet and grabbed all the hair on Rupert's head in her fist. Rupert had a lot of golden-coloured hair. His mother thought it was beautiful to behold and took a delight in allowing it to grow extra long. The Trunchbull had as great a dislike for long hair on boys as she had for plaits and pigtails on girls and she was about to show it. She took a firm grip on Rupert's long golden tresses with her giant hand and then, by raising her muscular right arm, she lifted the helpless boy clean out of his chair and held him aloft.

Rupert yelled. He twisted and squirmed and kicked the air and went on yelling like a stuck pig, and Miss Trunchbull bellowed, "Two sevens are fourteen! Two sevens are fourteen! I am not letting you go till you say it!"

From the back of the class, Miss Honey cried out, "Miss Trunchbull! Please let him down! You're hurting him! All his hair might come out!"

"And well it might if he doesn't stop wriggling!" snorted the Trunchbull. "Keep still, you squirming worm!"

It really was a quite extraordinary sight to see this giant Headmistress dangling the small boy high in the air and the boy spinning and twisting like something on the end of a string and shrieking his head off.

"Say it!" bellowed the Trunchbull. "Say two sevens are fourteen! Hurry up or I'll start jerking you up and down and then your hair really will come out and we'll have enough of it to stuff a sofa! Get on with it boy! Say two sevens are fourteen and I'll let you go!"

"T-t-two s-sevens are f-f-fourteen," gasped Rupert, whereupon the Trunchbull, true to her word, opened her hand and quite literally let him go. He was a long way off the ground when she released him and he plummeted to earth and hit the floor and bounced like a football.

"Get up and stop whimpering," the Trunchbull barked.

Rupert got up and went back to his desk massaging his scalp with both hands. The Trunchbull returned to the front of the class. The children sat there hypnotised. None of them had seen anything quite like this before. It was splendid entertainment. It was better than a pantomime, but with one big difference. In this room there was an enormous human bomb in front of them which was liable to explode and blow someone to bits any moment. The children's eyes were riveted on the Headmistress. "I don't like small people," she was saying. "Small people should never be seen by anybody. They should be kept out of sight in boxes like hairpins and buttons. I cannot for the life of me see why children have to take so long to grow up. I think they do it on purpose."

Another extremely brave little boy in the front row spoke up and said, "But surely *you* were a small person once, Miss Trunchbull, weren't you?"

"I was *never* a small person," she snapped. "I have been large all my life and I don't see why others can't be the same way."

"But you must have started out as a baby," the boy said.

"*Me!* A baby!" shouted the Trunchbull. "How dare you suggest such a thing! What cheek! What infernal insolence! What's your name, boy? And stand up when you speak to me!"

The boy stood up. "My name is Eric Ink, Miss Trunchbull," he said.

"Eric *what*?" the Trunchbull shouted.

"Ink," the boy said.

"Don't be an ass, boy! There's no such name!"

"Look in the phone book," Eric said. "You'll see my father there under Ink."

"Very well, then," the Trunchbull said, "You may be Ink, young man, but let me tell you something. You're not indelible. I'll very soon rub you out if you try getting clever with me. Spell what."

"I don't understand," Eric said. "What do you want me to spell?"

"Spell what, you idiot! Spell the word 'what'!"

"W ... O ... T," Eric said, answering too quickly.

There was a nasty silence.

"I'll give you one more chance," the Trunchbull said, not moving.

"Ah yes, I know," Eric said. "It's got an H in it. W ... H ... O ... T. It's easy."

In two large strides the Trunchbull was behind Eric's desk, and there she stood, a pillar of doom towering over the helpless boy. Eric glanced fearfully back over his shoulder at the monster. "I *was* right, wasn't I?" he murmured nervously.

"You were *wrong*!" the Trunchbull barked. "In fact you strike me as the sort of poisonous little pockmark that will *always* be wrong! You sit wrong! You look wrong! You speak wrong! You are wrong all round! I will give you one more chance to be right! Spell 'what'!"

Eric hesitated. Then he said very slowly, "It's not W ... O ... T, and it's not W ... H ... O ... T. Ah, I know. It must be W ... H ... O ... T ... T."

Standing behind Eric, the Trunchbull reached out and took hold of the boy's two ears, one with each hand, pinching them between forefinger and thumb.

"Ow!" Eric cried. "Ow! You're hurting me!"

"I haven't started yet," the Trunchbull said briskly. And now, taking a firm grip on his two ears, she lifted him bodily out of his seat and held him aloft.

Like Rupert before him, Eric squealed the house down.

From the back of the class-room Miss Honey cried out, "Miss Trunchbull! Don't! Please let him go! His ears might come off!"

"They'll never come off," the Trunchbull

153

shouted back. "I have discovered through long experience, Miss Honey, that the ears of small boys are stuck very firmly to their heads."

"Let him go, Miss Trunchbull, please," begged Miss Honey. "You could damage him, you really could! You could wrench them right off!"

"Ears never come off!" the Trunchbull shouted. "They stretch most marvellously, like these are doing now, but I can assure you they never come off!"

Eric was squealing louder than ever and pedalling the air with his legs.

Matilda had never before seen a boy, or anyone else for that matter, held aloft by his ears alone. Like Miss Honey, she felt sure both ears were going to come off at any moment with all the weight that was on them.

The Trunchbull was shouting, "The word 'what' is spelled W . . . H . . . A . . . T. Now spell it, you little wart!"

Eric didn't hesitate. He had learned from watching Rupert a few minutes before that the quicker you answered the quicker you were released. "W . . . H . . . A . . . T", he squealed, "spells what!"

Still holding him by the ears, the Trunchbull lowered him back into his chair behind his desk. Then she marched back to the front of the class, dusting off her hands one against the other like someone who has been handling something rather grimy.

"That's the way to make them learn, Miss Honey," she said. "You take it from me, it's no good just *telling* them. You've got to *hammer* it into them. There's nothing like a little twisting and twiddling to encourage them to remember things. It concentrates their minds wonderfully."

"You could do them permanent damage, Miss Trunchbull," Miss Honey cried out.

"Oh, I have, I'm quite sure I have," the Trunchbull answered, grinning. "Eric's ears will have stretched quite considerably in the last couple of minutes! They'll be much longer now than they were before. There's nothing wrong with that, Miss Honey. It'll give him an interesting pixie look for the rest of his life."

"But Miss Trunchbull . . . "

"Oh, do shut up, Miss Honey! You're as wet as any of them. If you can't cope in here then you can go and find a job in some cotton-wool private school for rich brats. When you have been teaching for as long as I have you'll realise that it's no good at all being kind to children. Read *Nicholas Nickleby*, Miss Honey, by Mr Dickens. Read about Mr Wackford Squeers, the admirable headmaster of Dotheboys Hall. *He* knew how to handle the little brutes, didn't he! He knew how to use the birch, didn't he! He kept their backsides so warm you could have fried eggs and bacon on them! A fine book, that. But I don't suppose this bunch of morons we've got here will ever read it because by the look of them they are never going to learn to read any thing!"

"I've read it," Matilda said quietly.

The Trunchbull flicked her head round and looked carefully at the small girl with dark hair and deep brown eyes sitting in the second row. "What did you say?" she asked sharply.

"I said I've read it, Miss Trunchbull."

"Read what?"

"*Nicholas Nickleby*, Miss Trunchbull."

"You are lying to me, madam!" the Trunchbull shouted, glaring at Matilda. "I doubt there is a single child in the entire school who has read that book, and here you are, an unhatched shrimp sitting in the lowest form there is, trying to tell me a whopping great lie like that! Why do you do it? You must take me for a fool! Do you take me for a fool, child?"

"Well . . . " Matilda said, then she hesitated. She would like to have said, "Yes, I jolly well do," but that would have been suicide. "Well . . . " she said

156

again, still hesitating, still refusing to say "No".

The Trunchbull sensed what the child was thinking and she didn't like it. "Stand up when you speak to me!" she snapped. "What is your name?"

Matilda stood up and said, "My name is Matilda Wormwood, Miss Trunchbull."

"Wormwood, is it?" the Trunchbull said. "In

that case you must be the daughter of that man who owns Wormwood Motors?"

"Yes, Miss Trunchbull."

"He's a crook!" the Trunchbull shouted. "A week ago he sold me a second-hand car that he said was almost new. I thought he was a splendid fellow then. But this morning, while I was driving that car through the village, the entire engine fell out on to the road! The whole thing was filled with sawdust! The man's a thief and a robber! I'll have his skin for sausages, you see if I don't!"

"He's clever at his business," Matilda said.

"Clever my foot!" the Trunchbull shouted. "Miss Honey tells me that *you* are meant to be clever, too! Well madam, I don't like clever people! They are all crooked! *You* are most certainly crooked! Before I fell out with your father, he told me some very nasty stories about the way you behaved at home! But you'd better not try anything in this school, young lady. I shall be keeping a very careful eye on you from now on. Sit down and keep quiet."

The First Miracle

Matilda sat down again at her desk. The Trunchbull seated herself behind the teacher's table. It was the first time she had sat down during the lesson. Then she reached out a hand and took hold of her water-jug. Still holding the jug by the handle but not lifting it yet, she said, "I have never been able to understand why small children are so disgusting. They are the bane of my life. They are like insects. They should be got rid of as early as possible. We get rid of flies with fly-spray and by hanging up fly-paper. I have often thought of inventing a spray for getting rid of small children. How splendid it would be to walk into this classroom with a gigantic spray-gun in my hands and start pumping it. Or better still, some huge strips of sticky paper. I would hang them all round the school and you'd all get stuck to them and that would be the end of it. Wouldn't that be a good idea, Miss Honey?"

"If it's meant to be a joke, Headmistress, I don't think it's a very funny one," Miss Honey said from the back of the class.

"You wouldn't, would you, Miss Honey," the Trunchbull said. "And it's *not* meant to be a joke. My idea of a perfect school, Miss Honey, is one that has no children in it at all. One of these days

159

I shall start up a school like that. I think it will be very successful."

The woman's mad, Miss Honey was telling herself. She's round the twist. She's the one who ought to be got rid of.

The Trunchbull now lifted the large blue porcelain water-jug and poured some water into her glass. And suddenly, with the water, out came the long slimy newt straight into the glass, *plop*!

The Trunchbull let out a yell and leapt off her chair as though a firecracker had gone off underneath her. And now the children also saw the long thin slimy yellow-bellied lizard-like creature twisting and turning in the glass, and they squirmed and jumped about as well, shouting, "What is it? Oh, it's disgusting! It's a snake! It's a baby crocodile! It's an alligator!"

"Look out, Miss Trunchbull!" cried Lavender. "I'll bet it bites!"

The Trunchbull, this mighty female giant, stood there in her green breeches, quivering like a blancmange. She was especially furious that someone had succeeded in making her jump and yell like that because she prided herself on her toughness. She stared at the creature twisting and wriggling in the glass. Curiously enough, she had never seen a newt before. Natural history was not her strong point. She hadn't the faintest idea what this thing was. It certainly looked extremely unpleasant. Slowly she sat down again in her chair. She looked at this moment more terrifying than ever before. The fires of fury and hatred were smouldering in her small black eyes.

"Matilda!" she barked. "Stand up!"

"Who, me?" Matilda said. "What have I done?"

"Stand up, you disgusting little cockroach!"

"I haven't done anything, Miss Trunchbull, honestly I haven't. I've never seen that slimy thing before!"

"Stand up at once, you filthy little maggot!"

Reluctantly, Matilda got to her feet. She was in

161

the second row. Lavender was in the row behind her, feeling a bit guilty. She hadn't intended to get her friend into trouble. On the other hand, she was certainly not about to own up.

"You are a vile, repulsive, repellent, malicious little brute!" the Trunchbull was shouting. "You are not fit to be in this school! You ought to be behind bars, that's where you ought to be! I shall have you drummed out of this establishment in utter disgrace! I shall have the prefects chase you down the corridor and out of the front-door with hockey-sticks! I shall have the staff escort you home under armed guard! And then I shall make absolutely sure you are sent to a reformatory for delinquent girls for the minimum of forty years!"

The Trunchbull was in such a rage that her face had taken on a boiled colour and little flecks of froth were gathering at the corners of her mouth. But she was not the only one who was losing her cool. Matilda was also beginning to see red. She didn't in the least mind being accused of having done something she had actually done. She could see the justice of that. It was, however, a totally new experience for her to be accused of a crime that she definitely had not committed. She had had absolutely nothing to do with that beastly creature in the glass. By golly, she thought, that rotten Trunchbull isn't going to pin this one on me!

"*I did not do it!*" she screamed.

"Oh yes, you did!" the Trunchbull roared back. "Nobody else could have thought up a trick like that! Your father was right to warn me about you!" The woman seemed to have lost control of herself completely. She was ranting like a maniac. "You are finished in this school, young lady!" she shouted. "You are finished everywhere. I shall personally see to it that you are put away in a place where not even the crows can land their droppings on you! You will probably never see the light of day again!"

"*I'm telling you I did not do it!*" Matilda screamed. "I've never even seen a creature like that in my life!"

"You have put a . . . a . . . a crocodile in my drinking water!" the Trunchbull yelled back. "There is no worse crime in the world against a Headmistress! Now sit down and don't say a word! Go on, sit down at once!"

"*But I'm telling you . . .* " Matilda shouted, refusing to sit down.

"I am telling you to shut up!" the Trunchbull roared. "If you don't shut up at once and sit down I shall remove my belt and let you have it with the end that has the buckle!"

Slowly Matilda sat down. Oh, the rottenness of it all! The unfairness! How dare they expel her for something she hadn't done!

Matilda felt herself getting angrier . . . and angrier . . . and angrier . . . so unbearably angry that something was bound to explode inside her very soon.

The newt was still squirming in the tall glass of water. It looked horribly uncomfortable. The glass was not big enough for it. Matilda glared at the Trunchbull. How she hated her. She glared at the glass with the newt in it. She longed to march up and grab the glass and tip the contents, newt and all, over the Trunchbull's head. She trembled to think what the Trunchbull would do to her if she did that.

The Trunchbull was sitting behind the teacher's table staring with a mixture of horror and fascination at the newt wriggling in the glass. Matilda's eyes were also riveted on the glass. And now, quite slowly, there began to creep over Matilda a most extraordinary and peculiar feeling. The feeling was mostly in the eyes. A kind of electricity seemed to be gathering inside them. A sense of power was brewing in those eyes of hers, a feeling of great strength was settling itself deep inside her eyes. But there was also another feeling which was something else altogether, and which she could not understand. It was like flashes of lightning. Little waves of lightning seemed to be flashing out of her eyes. Her eyeballs were beginning to get hot, as though vast energy was building up somewhere inside them. It was an amazing sensation. She kept her eyes steadily on the glass, and now the power was concentrating itself in one small part of each eye and growing stronger and stronger and it felt as though millions of tiny little invisible arms with hands on them were shooting out of her eyes towards the glass she was staring at.

"Tip it!" Matilda whispered. *"Tip it over!"*

She saw the glass wobble. It actually tilted backwards a fraction of an inch, then righted itself again. She kept pushing at it with all those millions of invisible little arms and hands that were reaching out from her eyes, feeling the power that was flashing straight from the two little black dots in the very centres of her eyeballs.

"Tip it!" she whispered again. *"Tip it over!"*

Once more the glass wobbled. She pushed harder still, willing her eyes to shoot out more power. And then, very very slowly, so slowly she could hardly see it happening, the glass began to lean backwards, farther and farther and farther backwards until it was balancing on just one edge of its base. And there it teetered for a few seconds before finally toppling over and falling with a sharp tinkle on to the desk-top. The water in it and the squirming newt splashed out all over Miss Trunchbull's enormous bosom. The headmistress let out a yell that must have rattled every window-pane in the building and for the second time in the last five minutes she shot out of her chair like a rocket. The newt clutched desperately at the cotton smock where it covered the great chest and there it clung with its little claw-like feet. The Trunchbull looked down and saw it and she bellowed even louder and with a swipe of her hand she sent the creature flying across the class-room. It landed on the floor beside Lavender's desk and very quickly she ducked down and picked it up and put it into her pencil-box for another time. A newt, she decided, was a useful thing to have around.

The Trunchbull, her face more like a boiled ham than ever, was standing before the class quivering with fury. Her massive bosom was heaving in and out and the splash of water down the front of it

made a dark wet patch that had probably soaked
right through to her skin.

"*Who did it?*" she roared. "*Come on! Own up!
Step forward! You won't escape this time! Who is
responsible for this dirty job? Who pushed over
this glass?*"

Nobody answered. The whole room remained
silent as a tomb.

"Matilda!" she roared. "It was you! I know it was you!"

Matilda, in the second row, sat very still and said nothing. A strange feeling of serenity and confidence was sweeping over her and all of a sudden she found that she was frightened by nobody in the world. With the power of her eyes alone she had compelled a glass of water to tip and spill its contents over the horrible Headmistress, and anybody who could do that could do anything.

"Speak up, you clotted carbuncle!" roared the Trunchbull. "Admit that you did it!"

Matilda looked right back into the flashing eyes of this infuriated female giant and said with total calmness, "I have not moved away from my desk, Miss Trunchbull, since the lesson began. I can say no more."

Suddenly the entire class seemed to rise up against the Headmistress. "She didn't move!" they cried out. "Matilda didn't move! Nobody moved! You must have knocked it over yourself!"

"I most certainly did not knock it over myself!" roared the Trunchbull. "How dare you suggest a thing like that! Speak up, Miss Honey! You must have seen everything! Who knocked over my glass?"

"None of the children did, Miss Trunchbull," Miss Honey answered. "I can vouch for it that nobody has moved from his or her desk all the time you've been here, except for Nigel and he has not moved from his corner."

Miss Trunchbull glared at Miss Honey. Miss Honey met her gaze without flinching. "I am telling you the truth, Headmistress," she said. "You must have knocked it over without knowing it. That sort of thing is easy to do."

"I am fed up with you useless bunch of midgets!" roared the Trunchbull. "I refuse to waste any more of my precious time in here!" And with that she marched out of the class-room, slamming the door behind her.

In the stunned silence that followed, Miss Honey walked up to the front of the class and stood behind her table. "Phew!" she said. "I think we've had enough school for one day, don't you? The class is dismissed. You may all go out into the playground and wait for your parents to come and take you home."

The Second Miracle

Matilda did not join the rush to get out of the classroom. After the other children had all disappeared, she remained at her desk, quiet and thoughtful. She knew she had to tell somebody about what had happened with the glass. She couldn't possibly keep a gigantic secret like that bottled up inside her. What she needed was just one person, one wise and sympathetic grown-up who could help her to understand the meaning of this extraordinary happening.

Neither her mother nor her father would be of any use at all. If they believed her story, and it was doubtful they would, they almost certainly would fail to realise what an astounding event it was that had taken place in the classroom that afternoon. On the spur of the moment, Matilda decided that the one person she would like to confide in was Miss Honey.

Matilda and Miss Honey were now the only two left in the class-room. Miss Honey had seated herself at her table and was riffling through some papers. She looked up and said, "Well, Matilda, aren't you going outside with the others?"

Matilda said, "Please may I talk to you for a moment?"

"Of course you may. What's troubling you?"

"Something very peculiar has happened to me, Miss Honey."

Miss Honey became instantly alert. Ever since the two disastrous meetings she had had recently about Matilda, the first with the Headmistress and the second with the dreadful Mr and Mrs Wormwood, Miss Honey had been thinking a great deal about this child and wondering how she could help her. And now, here was Matilda sitting in the classroom with a curiously exalted look on her face and asking if she could have a private talk. Miss Honey had never seen her looking so wide-eyed and peculiar before.

"Yes, Matilda," she said. "Tell me what has happened to you that is so peculiar."

"Miss Trunchbull isn't going to expel me, is she?" Matilda asked. "Because it wasn't me who put that creature in her jug of water. I promise you it wasn't."

"I know it wasn't," Miss Honey said.

"Am I going to be expelled?"

"I think not," Miss Honey said. "The Headmistress simply got a little over-excited, that's all."

"Good," Matilda said. "But that isn't what I want to talk to you about."

"What do you want to talk to me about, Matilda?"

"I want to talk to you about the glass of water with the creature in it," Matilda said. "You saw it spilling all over Miss Trunchbull, didn't you?"

"I did indeed."

"Well, Miss Honey, I didn't touch it. I never went near it."

"I know you didn't," Miss Honey said. "You heard me telling the Headmistress that it couldn't possibly have been you."

"Ah, but it *was* me, Miss Honey," Matilda said. "That's exactly what I want to talk to you about."

Miss Honey paused and looked carefully at the child. "I don't think I quite follow you," she said.

"I got so angry at being accused of something I hadn't done that I made it happen."

"You made what happen, Matilda?"

"I made the glass tip over."

"I still don't quite understand what you mean," Miss Honey said gently.

"I did it with my eyes," Matilda said. "I was staring at it and wishing it to tip and then my eyes went all hot and funny and some sort of power came out of them and the glass just toppled over."

Miss Honey continued to look steadily at Matilda through her steel-rimmed spectacles and Matilda looked back at her just as steadily.

"I am still not following you," Miss Honey said. "Do you mean you actually willed the glass to tip over?"

"Yes," Matilda said. "With my eyes."

Miss Honey was silent for a moment. She did not think Matilda was meaning to tell a lie. It was more likely that she was simply allowing her vivid imagination to run away with her. "You mean you were sitting where you are now and you told the glass to topple over and it did?"

172

"Something like that, Miss Honey, yes."

"If you did that, then it is just about the greatest miracle a person has ever performed since the time of Jesus."

"I did it, Miss Honey."

It is extraordinary, thought Miss Honey, how often small children have flights of fancy like this. She decided to put an end to it as gently as possible. "Could you do it again?" she asked, not unkindly.

"I don't know," Matilda said, "but I think I might be able to."

Miss Honey moved the now empty glass to the middle of the table. "Should I put water in it?" she asked, smiling a little.

"I don't think it matters," Matilda said.

"Very well, then. Go ahead and tip it over."

"It may take some time."

"Take all the time you want," Miss Honey said. "I'm in no hurry."

Matilda, sitting in the second row about ten feet away from Miss Honey, put her elbows on the desk and cupped her face in her hands, and this time she gave the order right at the beginning. *"Tip glass, tip!"* she ordered, but her lips didn't move and she made no sound. She simply shouted the words inside her head. And now she concentrated the whole of her mind and her brain and her will up into her eyes and once again but much more quickly than before she felt the electricity gathering and the power was beginning to surge and the hotness was coming into the eyeballs, and then the millions of tiny invisible arms with hands on them were shooting out towards the glass, and without making any sound at all she kept on shouting inside her head for the glass to go over. She saw it wobble, then it tilted, then it toppled right over and fell with a tinkle on to the table-top not twelve inches from Miss Honey's folded arms.

Miss Honey's mouth dropped open and her eyes stretched so wide you could see the whites all round. She didn't say a word. She couldn't. The shock of seeing the miracle performed had struck her dumb. She gaped at the glass, leaning well away from it now as though it might be a dangerous thing. Then slowly she lifted head and looked at Matilda. She saw the child white in the face, as white as paper, trembling all over, the eyes glazed, staring straight ahead and seeing nothing. The whole face was transfigured, the eyes round and bright and she was sitting there speechless, quite beautiful in a blaze of silence.

Miss Honey waited, trembling a little herself and watching the child as she slowly stirred herself back into consciousness. And then suddenly, *click* went her face into a look of almost seraphic calm. "I'm all right," she said and smiled. "I'm quite all right, Miss Honey, so don't be alarmed."

"You seemed so far away," Miss Honey whispered, awestruck.

"Oh, I was. I was flying past the stars on silver wings," Matilda said. "It was wonderful."

Miss Honey was still gazing at the child in absolute wonderment, as though she were The Creation, The Beginning Of The World, The First Morning.

"It went much quicker this time," Matilda said quietly.

"It's not possible!" Miss Honey was gasping. "I don't believe it! I simply don't believe it!" She closed her eyes and kept them closed for quite a while, and when she opened them again it seemed as though she had gathered herself together. "Would you like to come back and have tea at my cottage?" she asked.

"Oh, I'd love to," Matilda said.

"Good. Gather up your things and I'll meet you outside in a couple of minutes."

"You won't tell anyone about this . . . this thing that I did, will you, Miss Honey?"

"I wouldn't dream of it," Miss Honey said.

Miss Honey's Cottage

Miss Honey joined Matilda outside the school gates and the two of them walked in silence through the village High Street. They passed the greengrocer with his window full of apples and oranges, and the butcher with bloody lumps of meat on display and naked chickens hanging up, and the small bank, and the grocery store and the electrical shop, and then they came out at the other side of the village on to the narrow country road where there were no people any more and very few motor-cars.

And now that they were alone, Matilda all of a sudden became wildly animated. It seemed as though a valve had burst inside her and a great gush of energy was being released. She trotted beside Miss Honey with wild little hops and her fingers flew as if she would scatter them to the four winds and her words went off like fireworks, with terrific speed. It was Miss Honey this and Miss Honey that and Miss Honey I do honestly feel I could move almost anything in the world, not just tipping over glasses and little things like that . . . I feel I could topple tables and chairs, Miss Honey . . . Even when people are sitting in the chairs I think I could push them over, and bigger things too, much bigger things than chairs and tables . . . I only have to take a moment to get my eyes strong and then I can push it out, this strongness, at anything at all so long as I am staring at it hard enough ... I have to stare at it very hard, Miss Honey, very very hard, and then I can feel it all happening behind my eyes, and my eyes get hot just as though they were burning but I don't mind that in the least, and Miss Honey ...

"Calm yourself down, child, calm yourself down," Miss Honey said. "Let us not get ourselves too worked up so early in the proceedings."

"But you do think it is *interesting*, don't you, Miss Honey?"

"Oh, it is *interesting* all right," Miss Honey said. "It is *more* than interesting. But we must tread very carefully from now on, Matilda."

"Why must we tread carefully, Miss Honey?"

"Because we are playing with mysterious forces, my child, that we know nothing about. I do not think they are evil. They may be good. They may even be divine. But whether they are or not, let us handle them carefully."

These were wise words from a wise old bird, but Matilda was too steamed up to see it that way. "I don't see why we have to be so careful?" she said, still hopping about.

"I am trying to explain to you," Miss Honey said patiently, "that we are dealing with the unknown. It is an unexplainable thing. The right word for it is a phenomenon. It is a phenomenon."

"Am I a phenomenon?" Matilda asked.

"It is quite possible that you are," Miss Honey said. "But I'd rather you didn't think about yourself as anything in particular at the moment. What I thought we might do is to explore this phenomenon a little further, just the two of us together, but making sure we take things very carefully all the time."

"You want me to do some more of it then, Miss Honey?"

"That is what I am tempted to suggest," Miss Honey said cautiously.

"Goody-good," Matilda said.

"I myself," Miss Honey said, "am probably far more bowled over by what you did than you are, and I am trying to find some reasonable explanation."

"Such as what?" Matilda asked.

"Such as whether or not it's got something to do with the fact that you are quite exceptionally precocious."

"What exactly does that word mean?" Matilda said.

"A precocious child", Miss Honey said, "is one that shows amazing intelligence early on. You are an unbelievably precocious child."

"Am I really?" Matilda asked.

"Of course you are. You must be aware of that. Look at your reading. Look at your mathematics."

"I suppose you're right," Matilda said.

Miss Honey marvelled at the child's lack of conceit and self-consciousness.

"I can't help wondering", she said, "whether this sudden ability that has come to you, of being able to move an object without touching it, whether it might not have something to do with your brain-power."

"You mean there might not be room in my head for all those brains so something has to push out?"

"That's not quite what I mean," Miss Honey said, smiling. "But whatever happens, and I say it again, we must tread carefully from now on. I have not forgotten that strange and distant glimmer on your face after you tipped over the last glass."

"Do you think doing it could actually hurt me? Is that what you're thinking, Miss Honey?"

"It made you feel pretty peculiar, didn't it?"

"It made me feel lovely," Matilda said. "For a moment or two I was flying past the stars on silver wings. I told you that. And shall I tell you something else, Miss Honey? It was easier the second time, much much easier. I think it's like anything else, the more you practise it, the easier it gets."

Miss Honey was walking slowly so that the small child could keep up with her without trotting too fast, and it was very peaceful out there on the narrow road now that the village was behind them. It was one of those golden autumn afternoons and there were blackberries and splashes of old man's beard in the hedges, and the hawthorn berries were ripening scarlet for the birds when the cold winter came along. There were tall trees here and there on either side, oak and sycamore and ash and occasionally a sweet chestnut. Miss Honey, wishing to change the subject for the moment, gave the names of all these to Matilda and taught her how to recognise them by the shape of their leaves and the pattern of the bark on their trunks. Matilda took all this in and stored the knowledge away carefully in her mind.

They came finally to a gap in the hedge on the left-hand side of the road where there was a five-barred gate. "This way," Miss Honey said, and she opened the gate and led Matilda through and closed it again. They were now walking along a narrow lane that was no more than a rutted cart-track. There was a high hedge of hazel on either side and you could see clusters of ripe brown nuts in their green jackets. The squirrels would be collecting them all very soon, Miss Honey said, and storing them away carefully for the bleak months ahead.

"You mean you *live* down here?" Matilda asked.

"I do," Miss Honey replied, but she said no more.

Matilda had never once stopped to think about where Miss Honey might be living. She had always regarded her purely as a teacher, a person who turned up out of nowhere and taught at school and then went away again. Do any of us children, she wondered, ever stop to ask ourselves where our teachers go when school is over for the day? Do we wonder if they live alone, or if there is a mother at home or a sister or a husband? "Do you

live all by yourself, Miss Honey?" she asked.

"Yes," Miss Honey said. "Very much so."

They were walking over the deep sun-baked mud-tracks of the lane and you had to watch where you put your feet if you didn't want to twist your ankle. There were a few small birds around in the hazel branches but that was all.

"It's just a farm-labourer's cottage," Miss Honey said. "You mustn't expect too much of it. We're nearly there."

They came to a small green gate half-buried in the hedge on the right and almost hidden by the overhanging hazel branches. Miss Honey paused with one hand on the gate and said, "There it is. That's where I live."

Matilda saw a narrow dirt-path leading to a tiny

red-brick cottage. The cottage was so small it looked more like a doll's house than a human dwelling. The bricks it was built of were old and crumbly and very pale red. It had a grey slate roof and one small chimney, and there were two little windows at the front. Each window was no larger than a sheet of tabloid newspaper and there was clearly no upstairs to the place. On either side of the path there was a wilderness of nettles and blackberry thorns and long brown grass. An enormous oak tree stood overshadowing the cottage. Its massive spreading branches seemed to be enfolding and embracing the tiny building, and perhaps hiding it as well from the rest of the world.

Miss Honey, with one hand on the gate which she had not yet opened, turned to Matilda and said, "A poet called Dylan Thomas once wrote some lines that I think of every time I walk up this path."

Matilda waited, and Miss Honey, in a rather wonderful slow voice, began reciting the poem:

"Never and never, my girl riding far and near
 In the land of the hearthstone tales, and spelled
  asleep,
Fear or believe that the wolf in the sheepwhite
  hood
Loping and bleating roughly and blithely shall
  leap, my dear, my dear,
Out of a lair in the flocked leaves in the dew
  dipped year
To eat your heart in the house in the rosy
  wood."

There was a moment of silence, and Matilda, who had never before heard great romantic poetry spoken aloud, was profoundly moved. "It's like music," she whispered.

"It is music," Miss Honey said. And then, as though embarrassed at having revealed such a secret part of herself, she quickly pushed open the gate and walked up the path. Matilda hung back. She was a bit frightened of this place now. It seemed so unreal and remote and fantastic and so totally away from this earth. It was like an illustration in Grimm or Hans Andersen. It was the house where the poor woodcutter lived with Hansel and Gretel and where Red Riding Hood's grandmother lived and it was also the house of The Seven Dwarfs and The Three Bears and all the rest of them. It was straight out of a fairy-tale.

"Come along, my dear," Miss Honey called back, and Matilda followed her up the path.

The front-door was covered with flaky green paint and there was no keyhole. Miss Honey simply lifted the latch and pushed open the door and went in. Although she was not a tall woman, she had to stoop low to get through the doorway. Matilda went after her and found herself in what seemed to be a dark narrow tunnel.

"You can come through to the kitchen and help me make the tea," Miss Honey said, and she led the way along the tunnel into the kitchen – that is if you could call it a kitchen. It was not much bigger than a good-sized clothes cupboard and there was one small window in the back wall with a sink under the window, but there were no taps over the sink. Against another wall there was a shelf, presumably for preparing food, and there was a single cupboard above the shelf. On the shelf itself

there stood a Primus stove, a saucepan and a half-full bottle of milk. A Primus is a little camping-stove that you fill with paraffin and you light it at the top and then you pump it to get pressure for the flame.

"You can get me some water while I light the Primus," Miss Honey said. "The well is out at the back. Take the bucket. Here it is. You'll find a rope in the well. Just hook the bucket on to the end

187

of the rope and lower it down, but don't fall in yourself." Matilda, more bemused than ever now, took the bucket and carried it out into the back garden. The well had a little wooden roof over it and a simple winding device and there was the rope dangling down into a dark bottomless hole. Matilda pulled up the rope and hooked the handle of the bucket on to the end of it. Then she lowered it until she heard a splash and the rope went slack. She pulled it up again and lo and behold, there was water in the bucket.

"Is this enough?" she asked, carrying it in.

"Just about," Miss Honey said. "I don't suppose you've ever done that before?"

"Never," Matilda said. "It's fun. How do you get enough water for your bath?"

"I don't take a bath," Miss Honey said. "I wash standing up. I get a bucketful of water and I heat it on this little stove and I strip and wash myself all over."

"Do you honestly do that?" Matilda asked.

"Of course I do," Miss Honey said. "Every poor person in England used to wash that way until not so very long ago. And *they* didn't have a Primus. They had to heat the water over the fire in the hearth."

"Are *you* poor, Miss Honey?"

"Yes," Miss Honey said. "Very. It's a good little stove, isn't it?" The Primus was roaring away with a powerful blue flame and already the water in the saucepan was beginning to bubble. Miss Honey got a teapot from the cupboard and put some tea leaves into it. She also found half a small loaf of brown bread. She cut two thin slices and then, from a plastic container, she took some margarine and spread it on the bread.

Margarine, Matilda thought. She really must be poor.

Miss Honey found a tray and on it she put two mugs, the teapot, the half bottle of milk and a plate with the two slices of bread. "I'm afraid I don't have any sugar," she said. "I never use it."

"That's all right," Matilda said. In her wisdom she seemed to be aware of the delicacy of the situation and she was taking great care not to say anything to embarrass her companion.

"Let's have it in the sitting-room," Miss Honey said, picking up the tray and leading the way out of the kitchen and down the dark little tunnel into the room at the front. Matilda followed her, but just inside the doorway of the so-called sitting-room she stopped and stared around her in absolute amazement. The room was as small and square and bare as a prison cell. The pale daylight that entered came from a single tiny window in the front wall, but there were no curtains. The only objects in the entire room were two upturned wooden boxes to serve as chairs and a third box between them for a table. That was all. There were no pictures on the walls, no carpet on the floor, only rough unpolished wooden planks, and there were gaps between the planks where dust and bits of grime had gathered. The ceiling was so low that with a jump Matilda could nearly touch it with her finger-tips. The walls were white but the whiteness didn't look like paint. Matilda rubbed her palm against it and a white powder came off on to her skin. It was whitewash, the cheap stuff that is used in cowsheds and stables and hen-houses.

Matilda was appalled. Was this really where her neat and trimly-dressed school teacher lived? Was this all she had to come back to after a day's work? It was unbelievable. And what was the reason for it? There was something very strange going on around here, surely.

Miss Honey put the tray on one of the upturned boxes. "Sit down, my dear, sit down," she said, "and we'll have a nice hot cup of tea. Help yourself

190

to bread. Both slices are for you. I never eat anything when I get home. I have a good old tuck-in at the school lunch and that keeps me going until the next morning."

Matilda perched herself carefully on an upturned box and more out of politeness than anything else she took a slice of bread and margarine and started to eat it. At home she would have been having buttered toast and strawberry jam and probably a piece of sponge-cake to round it off. And yet this was somehow far more fun. There was a mystery here in this house, a great mystery, there was no doubt about that, and Matilda was longing to find out what it was.

Miss Honey poured the tea and added a little milk to both cups. She appeared to be not in the least ill at ease sitting on an upturned box in a bare room and drinking tea out of a mug that she balanced on her knee.

"You know," she said, "I've been thinking very hard about what you did with that glass. It is a great power you have been given, my child, you know that."

"Yes, Miss Honey, I do," Matilda said, chewing her bread and margarine.

"So far as I know," Miss Honey went on, "nobody else in the history of the world has been able to compel an object to move without touching it or blowing on it or using any outside help at all."

Matilda nodded but said nothing.

"The fascinating thing", Miss Honey said, "would be to find out the real limit of this power of yours. Oh, I know you think you can move just about anything there is, but I have my doubts about that."

"I'd love to try something really huge," Matilda said.

"What about distance?" Miss Honey asked. "Would you always have to be close to the thing you were pushing?"

"I simply don't know," Matilda said. "But it would be fun to find out."

Miss Honey's Story

"We mustn't hurry this," Miss Honey said, "so let's have another cup of tea. And do eat that other slice of bread. You must be hungry."

Matilda took the second slice and started eating it slowly. The margarine wasn't at all bad. She doubted whether she could have told the difference if she hadn't known. "Miss Honey," she said suddenly, "do they pay you very badly at our school?"

Miss Honey looked up sharply. "Not too badly," she said. "I get about the same as the others."

"But it must still be very little if you are so dreadfully poor," Matilda said. "Do all the teachers live like this, with no furniture and no kitchen stove and no bathroom?"

"No, they don't," Miss Honey said rather stiffly. "I just happen to be the exception."

"I expect you just happen to like living in a very simple way," Matilda said, probing a little further. "It must make house cleaning an awful lot easier and you don't have furniture to polish or any of those silly little ornaments lying around that have to be dusted every day. And I suppose if you don't have a fridge you don't have to go out and buy all sorts of junky things like eggs and mayonnaise and ice-cream to fill it up with. It must save a terrific lot of shopping."

At this point Matilda noticed that Miss Honey's face had gone all tight and peculiar-looking. Her whole body had become rigid. Her shoulders were hunched up high and her lips were pressed together tight and she sat there gripping her mug of tea in both hands and staring down into it as though searching for a way to answer these not-quite-so-innocent questions.

There followed a rather long and embarrassing silence. In the space of thirty seconds the atmosphere in the tiny room had changed completely and now it was vibrating with awkwardness and secrets. Matilda said, "I am very sorry I asked you

those questions, Miss Honey. It is not any of my business."

At this, Miss Honey seemed to rouse herself. She gave a shake of her shoulders and then very carefully she placed her mug on the tray.

"Why shouldn't you ask?" she said. "You were bound to ask in the end. You are much too bright not to have wondered. Perhaps I even *wanted* you to ask. Maybe that is why I invited you here after all. As a matter of fact you are the first visitor to come to the cottage since I moved in two years ago."

Matilda said nothing. She could feel the tension growing and growing in the room.

"You are so much wiser than your years, my dear," Miss Honey went on, "that it quite staggers me. Although you look like a child, you are not really a child at all because your mind and your powers of reasoning seem to be fully grown-up. So I suppose we might call you a grown-up child, if you see what I mean."

Matilda still did not say anything. She was waiting for what was coming next.

"Up to now", Miss Honey went on, "I have found it impossible to talk to anyone about my problems. I couldn't face the embarrassment, and anyway I lack the courage. Any courage I had was knocked out of me when I was young. But now, all of a sudden I have a sort of desperate wish to tell everything to somebody. I know you are only a tiny little girl, but there is some kind of magic in you somewhere. I've seen it with my own eyes."

Matilda became very alert. The voice she was hearing was surely crying out for help. It must be. It had to be.

Then the voice spoke again. "Have some more tea," it said. "I think there's still a drop left."

Matilda nodded.

Miss Honey poured tea into both mugs and added milk. Again she cupped her own mug in both hands and sat there sipping.

There was quite a long silence before she said, "May I tell you a story?"

"Of course," Matilda said.

"I am twenty-three years old," Miss Honey said, "and when I was born my father was a doctor in this village. We had a nice old house, quite large, red-brick. It's tucked away in the woods behind the hills. I don't think you'd know it."

Matilda kept silent.

"I was born there," Miss Honey said. "And then came the first tragedy. My mother died when I was two. My father, a busy doctor, had to have someone to run the house and to look after me. So he invited my mother's unmarried sister, my aunt, to come and live with us. She agreed and she came."

Matilda was listening intently. "How old was the aunt when she moved in?" she asked.

"Not very old," Miss Honey said. "I should say about thirty. But I hated her right from the start. I missed my mother terribly. And the aunt was not a kind person. My father didn't know that because he was hardly every around but when he did put in an appearance, the aunt behaved differently."

Miss Honey paused and sipped her tea. "I can't think why I am telling you all this," she said, embarrassed.

"Go on," Matilda said. "Please."

"Well," Miss Honey said, "then came the second tragedy. When I was five, my father died very suddenly. One day he was there and the next day he was gone. And so I was left to live alone with my aunt. She became my legal guardian. She had all the powers of a parent over me. And in some way or another, she became the actual owner of the house."

"How did your father die?" Matilda asked.

"It is interesting you should ask that," Miss Honey said. "I myself was much too young to question it at the time, but I found out later that there was a good deal of mystery surrounding his death."

"Didn't they know how he died?" Matilda asked.

"Well, not exactly," Miss Honey said, hesitating, "You see, no one could believe that he would ever have done it. He was such a very sane and sensible man."

"Done what?" Matilda asked.

"*Killed* himself."

Matilda was stunned.
"Did he?" she
gasped.

"That's what it *looked* like," Miss Honey said. "But who knows?" She shrugged and turned away and stared out of the tiny window.

"I know what you're thinking," Matilda said. "You're thinking that the aunt killed him and made it look as though he'd done it himself."

"I am not thinking anything," Miss Honey said. "One must never think things like that without proof."

The little room became quiet. Matilda noticed that the hands clasping the mug were trembling slightly. "What happened after that?" she asked. "What happened when you were left all alone with the aunt? Wasn't she nice to you?"

"Nice?" Miss Honey said. "She was a demon. As soon as my father was out of the way she became a holy terror. My life was a nightmare."

"What did she do to you?" Matilda asked.

"I don't want to talk about it," Miss Honey said. "It's too horrible. But in the end I became so frightened of her I used to start shaking when she came into the room. You must understand I was never a strong character like you. I was always shy and retiring."

"Didn't you have any other relations?" Matilda asked. "Any uncles or aunts or grannies who would come and see you?"

"None that I knew about," Miss Honey said. "They were all either dead or they'd gone to Australia. And that's still the way it is now, I'm afraid."

"So you grew up in that house alone with your

aunt," Matilda said. "But you must have gone to school."

"Of course," Miss Honey said. "I went to the same school you're going to now. But I lived at home." Miss Honey paused and stared down into her empty tea-mug. "I think what I am trying to explain to you," she said, "is that over the years I became so completely cowed and dominated by this monster of an aunt that when she gave me an order, no matter what it was, I obeyed it instantly. That can happen, you know. And by the time I was ten, I had become her slave. I did all the housework. I made her bed. I washed and ironed for her. I did all the cooking. I learned how to do everything."

"But surely you could have complained to *somebody*?" Matilda said.

"To whom?" Miss Honey said. "And anyway, I was far too terrified to complain. I told you, I was her slave."

"Did she beat you?"

"Let's not go into details," Miss Honey said.

"How simply *awful*," Matilda said. "Did you cry nearly all the time?"

"Only when I was alone," Miss Honey said. "I wasn't allowed to cry in front of her. But I lived in fear."

"What happened when you left school?" Matilda asked.

"I was a bright pupil," Miss Honey said. "I could easily have got into university. But there was no question of that."

"Why not, Miss Honey?"

"Because I was needed at home to do the work."

"Then how did you become a teacher?" Matilda asked.

"There is a Teacher's Training College in Reading," Miss Honey said. "That's only forty minutes' bus-ride away from here. I was allowed to go there on condition I came straight home again every afternoon to do the washing and ironing and to clean the house and cook the supper."

"How old were you then?" Matilda asked.

"When I went into Teacher's Training I was eighteen," Miss Honey said.

"You could have just packed up and walked away," Matilda said.

"Not until I got a job," Miss Honey said. "And don't forget, I was by then dominated by my aunt to such an extent that I wouldn't have dared. You can't imagine what it's like to be completely controlled like that by a very strong personality. It turns you to jelly. So that's it. That's the sad story of my life. Now I've talked enough."

"Please don't stop," Matilda said. "You haven't finished yet. How did you manage to get away from her in the end and come and live in this funny little house?"

"Ah, that was something," Miss Honey said. "I was proud of that."

"Tell me," Matilda said.

"Well," Miss Honey said, "when I got my teacher's job, the aunt told me I owed her a lot of money. I asked her why. She said, 'Because I've been feeding you for all these years and buying

your shoes and your clothes!' She told me it added up to thousands and I had to pay her back by giving her my salary for the next ten years. 'I'll give you one pound a week pocket-money,' she said. 'But that's all you're going to get.' She even arranged with the school authorities to have my salary paid directly into her own bank. She made me sign the paper."

"You shouldn't have done that," Matilda said. "Your salary was your chance of freedom."

"I know, I know," Miss Honey said. "But by then I had been her slave nearly all my life and I hadn't the courage or the guts to say no. I was still petrified of her. She could still hurt me badly."

"So how did you manage to escape?" Matilda asked.

"Ah," Miss Honey said, smiling for the first time, "that was two years ago. It was my greatest triumph."

"Please tell me," Matilda said.

"I used to get up very early and go for walks while my aunt was still asleep," Miss Honey said. "And one day I came across this tiny cottage. It was empty. I found out who owned it. It was a farmer. I went to see him. Farmers also get up very early. He was milking his cows. I asked him if I could rent his cottage. 'You can't live there!' he cried. 'It's got no conveniences, no running water, no nothing!'"

"'I want to live there,' I said. 'I'm a romantic. I've fallen in love with it. Please rent it to me.'

"'You're mad,' he said. 'But if you insist, you're welcome to it. The rent will be ten pence a week.'

"'Here's one month's rent in advance,' I said, giving him 40p. 'And thank you so much!'"

"How super!" Matilda cried. "So suddenly you had a house all of your own! But how did you pluck up the courage to tell the aunt?"

"That was tough," Miss Honey said. "But I steeled myself to do it. One night, after I had cooked her supper, I went upstairs and packed the few things I possessed in a cardboard box and came downstairs and announced I was leaving. 'I've rented a house,' I said.

"My aunt exploded. 'Rented a house!' she shouted. 'How can you rent a house when you have only one pound a week in the world?'

"'I've done it,' I said.

"'And how are you going to buy food for yourself?'

"'I'll manage,' I mumbled and rushed out of the front door."

"Oh, well done you!" Matilda cried. "So you were free at last!"

"I was free at last," Miss Honey said. "I can't tell you how wonderful it was."

"But have you really managed to live here on one pound a week for two years?" Matilda asked.

"I most certainly have," Miss Honey said. "I pay ten pence rent, and the rest just about buys me paraffin for my stove and for my lamp, and a little milk and tea and bread and margarine. That's all I need really. As I told you, I have a jolly good tuck-in at the school lunch."

Matilda stared at her. What a marvellously brave thing Miss Honey had done. Suddenly she was a heroine in Matilda's eyes. "Isn't it awfully cold in the winter?" she asked.

"I've got my little paraffin stove," Miss Honey said. "You'd be surprised how snug I can make it in here."

"Do you have a bed, Miss Honey?"

"Well not exactly," Miss Honey said, smiling again. "But they say it's very healthy to sleep on a hard surface."

All at once Matilda was able to see the whole situation with absolute clarity. Miss Honey needed help. There was no way she could go on existing like this indefinitely. "You would be a lot better off, Miss Honey," she said, "if you gave up your job and drew unemployment money."

"I would never do that," Miss Honey said. "I love teaching."

"This awful aunt," Matilda said, "I suppose she is still living in your lovely old house?"

"Very much so," Miss Honey said. "She's still only about fifty. She'll be around for a long time yet."

"And do you think your father really meant her to own the house for ever?"

"I'm quite sure he didn't," Miss Honey said. "Parents will often give a guardian the right to occupy the house for a certain length of time, but it is nearly always left in trust for the child. It then becomes the child's property when he or she grows up."

"Then surely it is your house?" Matilda said.

"My father's will was never found," Miss Honey said. "It looks as though somebody destroyed it."

"No prizes for guessing who," Matilda said.

"No prizes," Miss Honey said.

"But if there is no will, Miss Honey, then surely the house goes automatically to you. You are the next of kin."

"I know I am," Miss Honey said. "But my aunt produced a piece of paper supposedly written by my father saying that he leaves the house to his sister-in-law in return for her kindness in looking after me. I am certain it's a forgery. But no one can prove it."

"Couldn't you try?" Matilda said. "Couldn't you hire a good lawyer and make a fight of it."

"I don't have the money to do that," Miss Honey said. "And you must remember that this aunt of mine is a much respected figure in the community. She has a lot of influence."

"Who is she?" Matilda asked.

Miss Honey hesitated a moment. Then she said softly, "Miss Trunchbull."

The Names

"Miss Trunchbull!" Matilda cried, jumping about a foot in the air. "You mean *she* is your aunt? *She* brought you up?"

"Yes," Miss Honey said.

"No *wonder* you were terrified!" Matilda cried. "The other day we saw her grab a girl by the pigtails and throw her over the playground fence!"

"You haven't seen anything," Miss Honey said. "After my father died, when I was five and a half, she used to make me bath myself all alone. And if she came up and thought I hadn't washed properly she would push my head under the water and hold it there. But don't get me started on what she used to do. That won't help us at all."

"No," Matilda said, "it won't."

"We came here", Miss Honey said," to talk about *you* and I've been talking about nothing but myself the whole time. I feel like a fool. I am much more interested in just how much you can do with those amazing eyes of yours."

"I can move things," Matilda said. "I know I can. I can push things over."

"How would you like it", Miss Honey said, "if we made some very cautious experiments to see just how much you can move and push?"

Quite surprisingly, Matilda said, "If you don't

mind, Miss Honey, I think I would rather not. I want to go home now and think and think about all the things I've heard this afternoon."

Miss Honey stood up at once. "Of course," she said. "I have kept you here far too long. Your mother will be starting to worry."

"She never does that," Matilda said, smiling. "But I would like to go home now please, if you don't mind."

"Come along then," Miss Honey said. "I'm sorry I gave you such a rotten tea."

"You didn't at all," Matilda said. "I loved it."

The two of them walked all the way to Matilda's house in complete silence. Miss Honey sensed that Matilda wanted it that way. The child seemed so lost in thought she hardly looked where she was walking, and when they reached the gate of Matilda's home, Miss Honey said, "You had better forget everything I told you this afternoon."

"I won't promise to do that," Matilda said, "but I will promise not to talk about it to anyone any more, not even to you."

"I think that would be wise," Miss Honey said.

"I won't promise to stop thinking about it, though, Miss Honey," Matilda said. "I've been thinking about it all the way back from your cottage and I believe I've got just a tiny little bit of an idea."

"You mustn't," Miss Honey said. "Please forget it."

"I would like to ask you three last things before

I stop talking about it," Matilda said. "Please will you answer them, Miss Honey?"

Miss Honey smiled. It was extraordinary, she told herself, how this little snippet of a girl seemed suddenly to be taking charge of her problems, and with such authority, too. "Well," she said, "that depends on what the questions are."

"The first thing is this," Matilda said. "What did Miss Trunchbull call *your father* when they were around the house at home?"

"I'm sure she called him Magnus," Miss Honey said. "That was his first name."

"And what did your father call Miss Trunchbull?"

"Her name is Agatha," Miss Honey said. "That's what he would have called her."

"And lastly," Matilda said, "what did your father and Miss Trunchbull call *you* around the house?"

"They called me Jenny," Miss Honey said.

Matilda pondered these answers very carefully. "Let me make sure I've got them right," she said. "In the house at home, your father was Magnus, Miss Trunchbull was Agatha and you were Jenny. Am I right?"

"That is correct," Miss Honey said.

"Thank you," Matilda said. "And now I won't mention the subject any more."

Miss Honey wondered what on earth was going on in the mind of this child. "Don't do anything silly," she said.

Matilda laughed and turned away and ran up the path to her front-door, calling out as she went, "Good-bye, Miss Honey! Thank you so much for the tea."

The Practice

Matilda found the house empty as usual. Her father was not yet back from work, her mother was not yet back from bingo and her brother might be anywhere. She went straight into the living-room and opened the drawer of the sideboard where she knew her father kept a box of cigars. She took one out and carried it up to her bedroom and shut herself in.

Now for the practice, she told herself. It's going to be tough but I'm determined to do it.

Her plan for helping Miss Honey was beginning to form beautifully in her mind. She had it now in almost every detail, but in the end it all depended upon her being able to do one very special thing with her eye-power. She knew she wouldn't manage it right away, but she felt fairly confident that with a great deal of practice and effort, she would succeed in the end. The cigar was essential. It was perhaps a bit thicker than she would have liked, but the weight was about right. It would be fine for practising with.

There was a small dressing-table in Matilda's bedroom with her hairbrush and comb on it and two library books. She cleared these things to one side and laid the cigar down in the middle of the dressing-table. Then she walked away and sat on

the end of her bed. She was now about ten feet
from the cigar.

She settled herself and began to concentrate,
and very quickly this time she felt the electricity
beginning to flow inside her head, gathering itself
behind the eyes, and the eyes became hot and
millions of tiny invisible hands began pushing out
like sparks towards the cigar. "Move!" she whispered, and to her intense surprise, almost at once,
the cigar with its little red and gold paper band
around its middle rolled away across the top of the
dressing-table and fell on to the carpet.

Matilda had enjoyed that. It was lovely doing it. It had felt as though sparks were going round and round inside her head and flashing out of her eyes. It had given her a sense of power that was almost ethereal. And how quick it had been this time! How simple!

She crossed the bedroom and picked up the cigar and put it back on the table.

Now for the difficult one, she thought. But if I have the power to *push*, then surely I also have the power to *lift*? It is *vital* I learn how to lift it. I *must* learn how to lift it right up into the air and keep it there. It is not a very heavy thing, a cigar.

She sat on the end of the bed and started again. It was easy now to summon up the power behind her eyes. It was like pushing a trigger in the brain. *"Lift!"* she whispered. *"Lift! Lift!"*

At first the cigar started to roll away. But then, with Matilda concentrating fiercely, one end of it slowly lifted up about an inch off the table-top.

With a colossal effort, she managed to hold it there for about ten seconds. Then it fell back again.

"Phew!" she gasped. "I'm getting it! I'm starting to do it!"

For the next hour, Matilda kept practising, and in the end she had managed, by the sheer power of her eyes, to lift the whole cigar clear off the table

about six inches into the air and hold it there for about a minute. Then suddenly she was so exhausted she fell back on the bed and went to sleep.

That was how her mother found her later in the evening.

"What's the matter with you?" the mother said, waking her up. "Are you ill?"

"Oh gosh," Matilda said, sitting up and looking around. "No. I'm all right. I was a bit tired, that's all."

From then on, every day after school, Matilda shut herself in her room and practised with the cigar. And soon it all began to come together in the most wonderful way. Six days later, by the following Wednesday evening, she was able not only to lift the cigar up into the air but also to move it around exactly as she wished. It was beautiful. "I can do it!" she cried. "I can really do it! I can pick the cigar up just with my eye-power and push it and pull it in the air any way I want!"

All she had to do now was to put her great plan into action.

The Third Miracle

The next day was Thursday, and that, as the whole of Miss Honey's class knew, was the day on which the Headmistress would take charge of the first lesson after lunch.

In the morning Miss Honey said to them, "One or two of you did not particularly enjoy the last occasion when the Headmistress took the class, so let us all try to be especially careful and clever today. How are your ears, Eric, after your last encounter with Miss Trunchbull?"

"She stretched them," Eric said. "My mother said she's positive they are bigger than they were."

"And Rupert," Miss Honey said, "I am glad to see you didn't lose any of your hair after last Thursday."

"My head was jolly sore afterwards," Rupert said.

"And you, Nigel," Miss Honey said, "do please try not to be smart-aleck with the Headmistress today. You were really quite cheeky to her last week."

"I hate her," Nigel said.

"Try not to make it so obvious," Miss Honey said. "It doesn't pay. She's a very strong woman. She has muscles like steel ropes."

"I wish I was grown up," Nigel said. "I'd knock her flat."

"I doubt you would," Miss Honey said. "No one has ever got the better of her yet."

"What will she be testing us on this afternoon?" a small girl asked.

"Almost certainly the three-times table," Miss Honey said. "That's what you are all meant to have learnt this past week. Make sure you know it."

Lunch came and went.

After lunch, the class reassembled. Miss Honey stood at one side of the room. They all sat silent, apprehensive, waiting. And then, like some giant of doom, the enormous Trunchbull strode into the room in her green breeches and cotton smock. She went straight to her jug of water and lifted it up by the handle and peered inside.

"I am glad to see", she said, "that there are no slimy creatures in my drinking-water this time. If there had been, then something exceptionally unpleasant would have happened to every single member of this class. And that includes you, Miss Honey."

The class remained silent and very tense. They had learnt a bit about this tigress by now and nobody was about to take any chances.

"Very well," boomed the Trunchbull. "Let us see how well you know your three-times table. Or to put it another way, let us see how badly Miss Honey has taught you the three-times table." The Trunchbull was standing in front of the class, legs apart, hands on hips, scowling at Miss Honey who stood silent to one side.

Matilda, sitting motionless at her desk in the

216

second row, was watching things very closely.

"You!" the Trunchbull shouted, pointing a finger the size of a rolling-pin at a boy called Wilfred. Wilfred was on the extreme right of the front row. "Stand up, you!" she shouted at him.

Wilfred stood up.

"Recite the three-times table backwards!" the Trunchbull barked.

"Backwards?" stammered Wilfred. "But I haven't learnt it backwards."

"There you are!" cried the Trunchbull, triumphant. "She's taught you nothing! Miss Honey, why have you taught them absolutely nothing at all in the last week?"

"That is not true, Headmistress," Miss Honey said. "They have all learnt their three-times table. But I see no point in teaching it to them backwards. There is little point in teaching anything backwards. The whole object of life, Headmistress, is to go forwards. I venture to ask whether even you, for example, can spell a simple word like *wrong* backwards straight away. I very much doubt it."

"Don't you get impertinent with me, Miss Honey!" the Trunchbull snapped, then she turned back to the unfortunate Wilfred. "Very well, boy," she said. "Answer me this. I have seven apples, seven oranges and seven bananas. How many pieces of fruit do I have altogether? Hurry up! Get on with it! Give me the answer!"

"That's *adding up*!" Wilfred cried. "That isn't the three-times table!"

"You blithering idiot!" shouted the Trunchbull.

217

"You festering gumboil! You fleabitten fungus! That *is* the three-times table! You have three separate lots of fruit and each lot has seven pieces. Three sevens are twenty-one. Can't you see that, you stagnant cesspool! I'll give you one more chance. I have eight coconuts, eight monkey-nuts and eight nutty little idiots like you. How many nuts do I have altogether? Answer me quickly."

Poor Wilfred was properly flustered. "Wait!" he cried. "Please wait! I've got to add up eight coconuts and eight monkey-nuts . . . " He started counting on his fingers.

"You bursting blister!" yelled the Trunchbull. "You moth-eaten maggot! This is *not* adding up! This is multiplication! The answer is three eights! Or is it eight threes? What is the difference between three eights and eight threes? Tell me that, you mangled little wurzel and look sharp about it!"

By now Wilfred was far too frightened and bewildered even to speak.

In two strides the Trunchbull was beside him, and by some amazing gymnastic trick, it may have been judo or karate, she flipped the back of Wilfred's legs with one of her feet so that the boy shot up off the ground and turned a somersault in the air. But halfway through the somersault she caught him by an ankle and held him dangling upside-down like a plucked chicken in a shop-window.

"Eight threes," the Trunchbull shouted, swinging Wilfred from side to side by his ankle, "eight

threes is the same as three eights and three eights are twenty-four! Repeat that!"

At exactly that moment Nigel, at the other end of the room, jumped to his feet and started pointing excitedly at the blackboard and screaming, "The chalk! The chalk! Look at the chalk! It's moving all on its own!"

So hysterical and shrill was Nigel's scream that everyone in the place, including the Trunchbull, looked up at the blackboard. And there, sure enough, a brand-new piece of chalk was hovering near the grey-black writing surface of the blackboard.

"It's writing something!" screamed Nigel. *"The chalk is writing something!"*

And indeed it was.

"What the blazes is this!" yelled the Trunchbull. It had shaken her to see her own first name being written like that by an invisible hand. She dropped Wilfred on to the floor. Then she yelled at nobody in particular, "Who's *doing* this? Who's *writing* it?"

The chalk continued to write.

Agatha, this is Magnus
This is Magnus

Everyone in the place heard the gasp that came from the Trunchbull's throat. "No!" she cried, "It can't be! It can't be Magnus!"

It is Magnus
And you'd better
believe it

Miss Honey, at the side of the room glanced swiftly at Matilda. The child was sitting very straight at her desk, the head held high, the mouth compressed, the eyes glittering like two stars.

Agatha, give my Jenny back her house

For some reason everyone now looked at the Trunchbull. The woman's face had turned white as snow and her mouth was opening and shutting like a halibut out of water and giving out a series of strangled gasps.

Give my Jenny her wages
Give my Jenny the house
Then get out of here.
If you don't, I will come
and get you
I will come and get you
like you got me.
I am watching you
Agatha___.

The chalk stopped writing. It hovered for a few moments, then suddenly it dropped to the floor with a tinkle and broke in two.

Wilfred, who had managed to resume his seat in the front row, screamed, "Miss Trunchbull has fallen down! Miss Trunchbull is on the floor!"

This was the most sensational bit of news of all and the entire class jumped up out of their seats to have a really good look. And there she was, the huge figure of the Headmistress, stretched full-length on her back across the floor, out for the count.

Miss Honey ran forward and knelt beside the prostrate giant. "She's fainted!" she cried. "She's out cold! Someone go and fetch the matron at once." Three children ran out of the room.

Nigel, always ready for action, leapt up and seized the big jug of water. "My father says cold water is the best way to wake up someone who's fainted," he said, and with that he tipped the entire contents of the jug over the Trunchbull's head. No one, not even Miss Honey, protested.

As for Matilda, she continued to sit motionless at her desk. She was feeling curiously elated. She felt as though she had touched something that was not quite of this world, the highest point of the heavens, the farthest star. She had felt most wonderfully the power surging up behind her eyes, gushing like a warm fluid inside her skull, and her eyes had become scorching hot, hotter than ever before, and things had come bursting out of her eye-sockets and then the piece of chalk had lifted itself up and had begun to write. It seemed as though she had hardly done anything, it had all been so simple.

The school matron, followed by five teachers, three women and two men, came rushing into the room.

"By golly, somebody's floored her at last!" cried one of the men, grinning. "Congratulations, Miss Honey!"

"Who threw the water over her?" asked the matron.

"I did," said Nigel proudly.

"Good for you," another teacher said. "Shall we get some more?"

"Stop that," the matron said. "We must carry her up to the sick-room."

It took all five teachers and the matron to lift the enormous woman and stagger with her out of the room.

Miss Honey said to the class, "I think you'd all better go out to the playground and amuse yourselves until the next lesson." Then she turned and walked over to the blackboard and carefully wiped out all the chalk writing.

The children began filing out of the classroom. Matilda started to go with them, but as she passed Miss Honey she paused and her twinkling eyes met the teacher's eyes and Miss Honey ran forward and gave the tiny child a great big hug and a kiss.

A New Home

Later that day, the news began to spread that the Headmistress had recovered from her fainting-fit and had then marched out of the school building tight-lipped and white in the face.

The next morning she did not turn up at school. At lunchtime, Mr Trilby, the Deputy Head, telephoned her house to enquire if she was feeling unwell. There was no answer to the phone.

When school was over, Mr Trilby decided to investigate further, so he walked to the house where Miss Trunchbull lived on the edge of the village, the lovely small red-brick Georgian building known as The Red House, tucked away in the woods behind the hills.

He rang the bell. No answer.

He knocked loudly. No answer.

He called out, "Is anybody at home?" No answer.

He tried the door and to his surprise found it unlocked. He went in.

The house was silent and there was no one in it, and yet all the furniture was still in place. Mr Trilby went upstairs to the main bedroom. Here also everything seemed to be normal until he started opening drawers and looking into cupboards. There were no clothes or underclothes or shoes anywhere. They had all gone.

She's done a bunk, Mr Trilby said to himself and he went away to inform the School Governors that the Headmistress had apparently vanished.

On the second morning, Miss Honey received by registered post a letter from a firm of local solicitors informing her that the last will and testament of her late father, Dr Honey, had suddenly and mysteriously turned up. This document revealed that ever since her father's death, Miss Honey had in fact been the rightful owner of a property on the edge of the village known as The Red House, which until recently had been occupied by a Miss Agatha Trunchbull. The will also showed that her father's lifetime savings, which fortunately were still safely in the bank, had also been left to her. The solicitor's letter added that if Miss Honey would kindly call in to the office as soon as possible, then the property and the money could be transferred into her name very rapidly.

Miss Honey did just that, and within a couple of weeks she had moved into The Red House, the very place in which she had been brought up and where luckily all the family furniture and pictures were still around. From then on, Matilda was a welcome visitor to The Red House every single evening after school, and a very close friendship began to develop between the teacher and the small child.

Back at school, great changes were also taking place. As soon as it became clear that Miss Trunchbull had completely disappeared from the scene, the excellent Mr Trilby was appointed Head Teacher in her place. And very soon after that,

Matilda was moved up into the top form where Miss Plimsoll quickly discovered that this amazing child was every bit as bright as Miss Honey had said.

One evening a few weeks later, Matilda was having tea with Miss Honey in the kitchen of The Red House after school as they always did, when Matilda said suddenly, "Something strange has happened to me, Miss Honey."

"Tell me about it," Miss Honey said.

"This morning," Matilda said, "just for fun I tried to push something over with my eyes and I couldn't do it. Nothing moved. I didn't even feel the hotness building up behind my eyeballs. The power had gone. I think I've lost it completely."

Miss Honey carefully buttered a slice of brown bread and put a little strawberry jam on it. "I've been expecting something like that to happen," she said.

"You have? Why?" Matilda asked.

"Well," Miss Honey said, "it's only a guess, but here's what I think. While you were in my class you had nothing to do, nothing to make you struggle. Your fairly enormous brain was going crazy with frustration. It was bubbling and boiling away like mad inside your head. There was tremendous energy bottled up in there with nowhere to go, and somehow or other you were able to shoot that energy out through your eyes and make objects move. But now things are different. You are in the top form competing against children more than twice your age and all that mental energy is being

229

used up in class. Your brain is for the first time having to struggle and strive and keep really busy, which is great. That's only a theory, mind you, and it may be a silly one, but I don't think it's far off the mark."

"I'm glad it's happened," Matilda said. "I wouldn't want to go through life as a miracle-worker."

"You've done enough," Miss Honey said. "I can still hardly believe you made all this happen for me."

Matilda, who was perched on a tall stool at the kitchen table, ate her bread and jam slowly. She did so love these afternoons with Miss Honey. She felt completely comfortable in her presence, and the two of them talked to each other more or less as equals.

"Did you know", Matilda said suddenly, "that the heart of a mouse beats at the rate of *six hundred and fifty times a second*?"

"I did not," Miss Honey said smiling. "How absolutely fascinating. Where did you read that?"

"In a book from the library," Matilda said. "And that means it goes so fast you can't even hear the separate beats. It must sound just like a buzz."

"It must," Miss Honey said.

"And how fast do you think a hedgehog's heart beats?" Matilda asked.

"Tell me," Miss Honey said, smiling again.

"It's not as fast as a mouse," Matilda said. "It's three hundred times a minute. But even so, you wouldn't have thought it went as fast as that in a creature that moves so slowly, would you, Miss Honey?"

"I certainly wouldn't," Miss Honey said. "Tell me one more."

"A horse," Matilda said. "That's really slow. It's only forty times a minute."

This child, Miss Honey told herself, seems to be interested in everything. When one is with her it is impossible to be bored. I love it.

The two of them stayed sitting and talking in the kitchen for an hour or so longer, and then, at about six o'clock, Matilda said goodnight and set out to walk home to her parent's house, which was about an eight-minute journey away. When she arrived at her own gate, she saw a large black

Mercedes motor-car parked outside. She didn't take too much notice of that. There were often strange cars parked outside her father's place. But when she entered the house, she was confronted by a scene of utter chaos. Her mother and father were both in the hall frantically stuffing clothing and various objects into suitcases.

"What on earth's going on?" she cried. "What's happening, daddy?"

"We're off," Mr Wormwood said, not looking up. "We're leaving for the airport in half an hour so you'd better get packed. Your brother's upstairs all ready to go. Get a move on, girl! Get going!"

"Off?" Matilda cried out. "Where to?"

"Spain," the father said. "It's a better climate than this lousy country."

"Spain!" Matilda cried. "I don't want to go to Spain! I love it here and I love my school!"

"Just do as you're told and stop arguing," the father snapped. "I've got enough troubles without messing about with you!"

"But daddy . . . " Matilda began.

"Shut up!" the father shouted. "We're leaving in thirty minutes! I'm not missing that plane!"

"But how long for, daddy?" Matilda cried. "When are we coming back?"

"We aren't," the father said. "Now beat it! I'm busy!"

Matilda turned away from him and walked out through the open front-door. As soon as she was on the road she began to run. She headed straight back towards Miss Honey's house and she reached it in less than four minutes. She flew up the drive and suddenly she saw Miss Honey in the front garden, standing in the middle of a bed of roses doing something with a pair of clippers. Miss Honey had heard the sound of Matilda's feet racing

over the gravel and now she straightened up and turned and stepped out of the rose-bed as the child came running up.

"My, my!" she said. "What in the world is the matter?"

Matilda stood before her, panting, out of breath, her small face flushed crimson all over.

"They're *leaving*!" she cried. "They've all gone mad and they're filling their suitcases and they're leaving for Spain in about thirty minutes!"

"Who is?" Miss Honey asked quietly.

"Mummy and daddy and my brother Mike and they say I've got to go with them!"

"You mean for a holiday?" Miss Honey asked.

"For *ever*!" Matilda cried. "Daddy said we were *never* coming back!"

There was a brief silence, then Miss Honey said, "Actually I'm not very surprised."

"You mean you *knew* they were going?" Matilda cried. "Why didn't you tell me?"

"No, darling," Miss Honey said. "I did not know they were going. But the news still doesn't surprise me."

"Why?" Matilda cried. "Please tell me why." She was still out of breath from the running and from the shock of it all.

"Because your father", Miss Honey said, "is in with a bunch of crooks. Everyone in the village knows that. My guess is that he is a receiver of stolen cars from all over the country. He's in it deep."

Matilda stared at her open-mouthed.

Miss Honey went on, "People brought stolen cars to your father's workshop where he changed the number-plates and resprayed the bodies a different colour and all the rest of it. And now somebody's probably tipped him off that the police are on to him and he's doing what they all do, running off to Spain where they can't get him. He'll have been sending his money out there for years, all ready and waiting for him to arrive."

They were standing on the lawn in front of the lovely red-brick house with its weathered old red tiles and its tall chimneys, and Miss Honey still had the pair of garden clippers in one hand. It was a warm golden evening and a blackbird was singing somewhere near by.

"I don't want to go with them!" Matilda shouted suddenly. "I won't go with them."

"I'm afraid you must," Miss Honey said.

"I want to live here with you," Matilda cried out. "Please let me live here with you!"

"I only wish you could," Miss Honey said. "But I'm afraid it's not possible. You cannot leave your parents just because you want to. They have a right to take you with them."

"But what if they agreed?" Matilda cried eagerly. "What if they said yes, I can stay with you? Would you let me stay with you then?"

Miss Honey said softly, "Yes, that would be heaven."

"Well, I think they might!" Matilda cried. "I honestly think they might! They don't actually care tuppence about me!"

"Not so fast," Miss Honey said.

"We've got to be fast!" Matilda cried. "They're leaving any moment! Come on!" she shouted, grasping Miss Honey's hand. "Please come with me and ask them! But we'll have to hurry! We'll have to run!"

The next moment the two of them were running down the drive together and then out on to the road, and Matilda was ahead, pulling Miss Honey after her by her wrist, and it was a wild and wonderful dash they made along the country lane and through the village to the house where Matilda's parents lived. The big black Mercedes was still outside and now its boot and all its doors were open and Mr and Mrs Wormwood and the brother were scurrying around it like ants, piling in the suitcases, as Matilda and Miss Honey came dashing up.

"Daddy and mummy!" Matilda burst out, gasping for breath. "I don't want to go with you! I want to stay here and live with Miss Honey and she says that I can but only if you give me permission! Please say yes! Go on, daddy, say yes! Say yes, mummy!"

The father turned and looked at Miss Honey. "You're that teacher woman who once came here

to see me, aren't you?" he said. Then he went back to stowing the suitcases into the car.

His wife said to him, "This one'll have to go on the back seat. There's no more room in the boot."

"I would love to have Matilda," Miss Honey said. "I would look after her with loving care, Mr Wormwood, and I would pay for everything. She wouldn't cost you a penny. But it was not my idea. It was Matilda's. And I will not agree to take her without your full and willing consent."

"Come on, Harry," the mother said, pushing a suitcase into the back seat. "Why don't we let her go if that's what she wants. It'll be one less to look after."

"I'm in a hurry," the father said. "I've got a plane

to catch. If she wants to stay, let her stay. It's fine with me."

Matilda leapt into Miss Honey's arms and hugged her, and Miss Honey hugged her back, and then the mother and father and brother were inside the car and the car was pulling away with the tyres screaming. The brother gave a wave through the rear window, but the other two didn't even look back. Miss Honey was still hugging the tiny girl in her arms and neither of them said a word as they stood there watching the big black car tearing round the corner at the end of the road and disappearing for ever into the distance.

"Every parent needs this incredible book! So much of your child's character hangs on the hinge of what happens during the middle school years. And this wise book reveals all the insider information you need to make these years count. Do yourself and your child a favor—read *Middle School: The Inside Story* today."

—Drs. Les and Leslie Parrott
Authors, *The Hour that Matters Most*

"Middle school involves some really tough, confusing years for today's kids . . . that demand our hearts and attention. Tobias and Acuña give us the inside story, which provides parents with practical advice and expert insight on what their kids need—even when their middle schooler isn't able to tell them."

—Dr. Tim Clinton
President, American Association of Christian Counselors
Executive Director, Center for Counseling and Family Studies,
Liberty University

"I wish I'd had this book when my sons were going through adolescence and I was a middle and high school music and English teacher. Far too often I was frustrated at home and in the classroom. I'm the grandmother of a middle schooler now. After reading *Middle School: The Inside Story*, my heart is more tuned to my grandchild's needs during this wacky and wonderful transition. Thanks to Cynthia and Sue, and this great book, I will soar through this season on a high note!"

—Babbie Mason
Award-winning recording artist, songwriter, TV talk show host
Author of *This I Know For Sure*

"I personally call the condition Tobias and Acuña write about 'middle school trauma.' This ailment can actually begin in elementary school and progress (unfortunately) through adulthood in the more at-risk students. For these very sensitive children, it can be one of the most devastating experiences of their entire lives. . . .

"Treating the resulting emotional complications that develop can be very difficult, especially if the child has to return to the toxic environment day after day. I think taking a preventative approach is the best strategy. *Middle School: The Inside Story* is an outstanding resource for parents to use to fortify themselves and their children in preparation for what may be coming down the pike. I will recommend that my patients' parents begin reading this book when their children enter kindergarten.

"Thank you so much, Cynthia and Sue, for writing this book. It will have far-reaching positive effects in every family where the parents take your comments and recommendations seriously."

—SHARON A. COLLINS, M.D., F.A.A.P
Pediatrician, Cedar Rapids, Iowa

"You don't know how bad it is or how good it can be for your middle schooler—until you grab this book to decode that mysterious world. Do it for the insights, how-to's, and absolute do's and don'ts to motivate and encourage your child. Any page on any day brings the *aha* you need through deep and rich counsel from Tobias and Acuña, who've been there, done that, and pave the way for success! Wisdom of the twenty-first-century sages—yours, now, here!"

—PHYLLIS WALLACE
20-year host of *Woman to Woman* radio show
Award-winning middle school guidance counselor

"Here's a thought: For every parent with a child entering middle school, a must read is *Middle School: The Inside Story*—a positive preparation for the transformation that is coming your way. Here's another thought: For every middle school teacher, you will find exceptional insights and strategies bringing peace to your soul and sleep-filled nights. Cynthia and Sue have hit the middle school 'Bubble' out of the park. You will be equipped for your middle school experience 'where nobody has gone before.' Simply excellent!"

—FORREST TURPEN
West Coast Regional Director, Christian Educators Association
Former middle school teacher

MIDDLE SCHOOL:
The Inside Story

WHAT KIDS TELL US, BUT DON'T TELL YOU

CYNTHIA TOBIAS
Best-selling author of *The Way They Learn*
SUE ACUÑA

Tyndale House Publishers, Inc.
Carol Stream, Illinois

Library of Congress Cataloging-in-Publication Data
Tobias, Cynthia Ulrich, 1953-
   Middle school, the inside story : what kids tell us, but don't tell you / Cynthia Tobias, Sue Acuña.
      pages cm
   "A Focus on the Family book."
   Includes bibliographical references and index.
   ISBN 978-1-58997-777-8 (alk. paper)
   1. Preteens. 2. Middle school students. 3. Adolescence. 4. Parent and child. 5. Parenting.
I. Acuña, Sue. II. Title.
   HQ777.15.T63 2014
   305.234—dc 3
                                        2014009332

Printed in the United States of America
2 3 4 5 6 7 / 20 19 18 17 16 15 14

Dedicated to my twin sons, Mike and Robert—
who not only survived middle school, but are
now grown up enough to understand why.
—Cynthia

Dedicated to my three sons—Matt, Jon,
and David, who experienced middle school
as students in Mom's classroom. We not only
emerged with positive relationships intact,
but they are also my biggest supporters!
—Sue

Contents

Acknowledgments

We want to thank our families for their support and encouragement—especially our husbands, Jack and Paul, who patiently endured having us spend all those hours writing and working away from them.

Thank you also to our editor, John Duckworth, who often challenged us to think outside of our comfort zone and pushed us to do our best.

Sue extends a special thank-you to Cynthia for her willingness to risk taking her under her wing and mentoring her. Co-authoring this book has been the realization of a lifelong dream!

Most of all, we will always be grateful for the dozens of middle schoolers who were so open and honest. They inspired us with their eagerness to find ways to share their world and deepen their relationships with those who love them.

What's Going On?

"I know it wasn't always fun when we were in, like, second grade, but now when I look back it seems like we always had good times. School was easy, and we got to do fun projects, like grow flowers and finger paint."
—A middle schooler

Five-year-old Jason is up before 8:00 A.M., even though it's Saturday. He cheerfully wriggles into his parents' bed to snuggle for just a minute, then races out to the living room to start his favorite animated movie while he waits for Mom to fix breakfast. All morning he happily interacts with his mom, sings along with his movie, and plays energetically with his toys.

Sometime between 11:00 A.M. and noon, Jason's older brother, Zach, appears sleepily in the kitchen doorway with his head bent over his cell phone and a frown on his face. When Mom asks if he wants something to eat, Zach shrugs and grunts without looking up. When Jason runs up and hugs his brother's leg, Zach shakes him off and says, "Quit bugging me, you little brat."

Mom objects: "Zach, don't talk to your brother that way! He's just showing you he loves you. You used to love it when he hugged you."

Still staring at the cell phone screen, Zach mutters, "Whatever," and walks back into his bedroom.

Zach's mom has just experienced one of the most obvious differences between her young elementary-aged child and his just-became-a-middle-schooler brother. And this is only the beginning.

Many parents are caught off guard by the change in their children when they begin the transition out of childhood and into adolescence. As a parent, you may have thought you had more time—but suddenly your 10-year-old is beginning to be less like a child and more like someone you don't even recognize. Welcome to middle school.

If you're thinking 10 years old is way too soon for early adolescence, you're not alone. It used to be that many of the issues this book talks about didn't show up in most children until at least the sixth grade. Now we're finding that signs of puberty and the beginning of adolescence can start as early as the *third* grade. So "middle school" has become a strange and wonderful world of transition captured between the bookends of elementary school and high school—and it often doesn't bear any resemblance to either.

We asked a group of experienced teachers to help us highlight some of the most distinct differences between elementary and middle school so parents can recognize when the transition is happening. If you have a child between the ages of 10 and 14, you're probably seeing many of these transformations right before your eyes:

Elementary School Student	Middle School Student
Cheerful, playful, easygoing	Moody, often unexpressive
Gets up early in the morning, even on weekends	Almost always wants to sleep in
Life is directed by adults	Expected to multitask and plan ahead

Elementary School Student	Middle School Student
Discipline and correction are direct and immediate by parents and teachers	Expected to be more self-correcting
Focused on whatever grade he or she is in	Expected to think beyond to high school, college, and career
Learns primarily through worksheets and objective tests	Required to complete long-term projects and engage in thoughtful class discussions
Acquires concrete, straightforward knowledge	Expected to think critically and deeply
Free to dream that anything's possible	Begins to judge aptitude and limits self based on perceived shortcomings
Accepts and follows parents' religious faith	Begins to ask for evidence to back up beliefs
Not really burdened by pressure of good grades	May resort to deception to maintain high grades
Takes trusted adults at their word	Challenges authority
Adopts parents' worldview and value structure	Interested in exploring other worldviews; value system is in flux

There are many books and articles by professionals who have presented compelling research on—and a myriad of ways to deal with—this mysterious stage of development known as early adolescence. But most of us still don't really know what's "normal." We can't quite figure out how these no-longer-a-child-but-not-really-a-teenager creatures think, or why they do the things they do. One minute they act like young adults; the next they resort to childish behaviors. So how can parents provide a safe and loving environment, a stable and positive relationship, and a strong launching pad into the real world? There doesn't seem to be a standard guidebook or reliable source of knowledge for how to deal with these young but complex human beings.

We decided to go straight to the source. After all, most of these kids are trying to figure *themselves* out, too. Maybe talking to us would help everyone improve at coping with change and not driving each other crazy. So we started asking middle schoolers questions, and they started talking to us. Boy, did they talk! Responses poured in from parents and teachers when we asked them to get feedback from their students. It wasn't unusual for Sue (a full-time eighth grade teacher when we started this book) to ask her class one question like, "How do you wish your parents would act?" and type four pages of notes as they replied.

I can remember my boys, at age 13 and in the seventh grade, complaining almost daily. Most complaints were along the lines of "I don't have any real friends," "I just feel dumb," "I hate everything."

I would quickly reassure them: "Almost all kids your age feel that way."

"No, they don't."

"Yes, they do."

"No, they don't."

"Yes. They do!"

When they were graduating from high school, I reminded the boys of our conversations. They both nodded. "You were right, Mom," Rob said.

Mike added, "Seventh grade was the worst year of my life."

—Cynthia Tobias

It turns out middle schoolers *do* want to be understood. But they don't have any better idea than their parents do about what's going on with their bodies, their emotions, or pretty much anything else in this stage of their lives. These are critical years; teens who don't have good relationships with their parents during middle school are going to have a very tough time in high school, when it's almost too late to establish the trust and rapport necessary to stay connected.

This book will give you dozens of valuable insights and practical strategies for handling life with a middle schooler. But the most important thing it offers is solid, tried-and-true ways—many directly from students themselves—to help you build and keep a strong and positive relationship with your child through what is often one of the most difficult stages of life.

When they were very young, your kids looked to you for guidance in their eagerness to learn how to walk, talk, and deal with the world. They used to love snuggling, confiding in you, and having you with them as much as possible. Now they're often embarrassed to be seen with you, resistant to your hugs and affection, and constantly looking for ways they can spend time with friends or just be alone. They may even make you believe that your parenting skills are hopelessly inadequate.

In some ways, it's a test of endurance—but not the kind you might expect. Instead of just barely hanging on and riding out these middle school years, this stretch of your lives together can be a time that enriches and deepens your relationship in ways you never thought possible. We guarantee it's worth the effort. The important thing to remember is that this stage is temporary; believe it or not, smoother roads are ahead if you can hang on. As the old saying goes, "When you're going through the tunnel, don't jump off the train!"

Before you start down the track into Chapter 1, though, pause for a moment to take the following true-or-false quiz. You might be surprised to learn how much—or how little—you really know about your middle schooler:

Test Your Middle School IQ

Common beliefs about middle schoolers:

T___ F___   1. Most of them just want their parents to leave them alone.

T___ F___   2. By the time kids are 12 years old, they're pretty much grown up.

T___ F___   3. It's important to make good grades a high priority during middle school.

T___ F___   4. Parents should make time for a sit-down talk about "the facts of life."

T___ F___   5. Friends should never be more important to kids than parents and family.

T___ F___   6. Parents should do everything they can to be considered "cool."

T___ F___   7. Middle schoolers don't need much supervision with homework and school activities.

T___ F___   8. Middle schoolers are self-centered and believe the whole world revolves around them.

T___ F___   9. Kids this age no longer want to be part of any family activities.

T___ F___   10. When middle schoolers struggle in school, it's usually because of a learning disability.

Every answer is "false."

As you read this book, we'll explain why; get ready for the inside story.

Here's a Thought:

As you're reading this book, try sharing parts of it with your own middle schooler. Ask, "Are these authors right? Is this how you feel sometimes?" You may be surprised at how much your child will share with you when you make it clear you really want to listen!

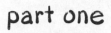

part one

CHANGES

one

Where No Body
Has Gone Before

~~~~~~~~~~

*"I wish my mom knew that I'm struggling
with a lot of things right now."*
—A middle schooler

*"I wish my parents could understand the things that go
on when they aren't around. Also that I may not always
want to share what struggles I am going through . . ."*
—A middle schooler

~~~~~~~~~~

"I think I might be raising a narcissist."

The statement came from a dad sitting in a room full of parents of middle school students. Heads were nodding in agreement all over the room as he continued. "She's so self-absorbed! It seems like she's always in the bathroom. I don't know what she's doing in there, but she spends *hours* in front of the mirror!"

Of course she does. Think about how much her looks have changed in the last six months. As adults, we usually don't find many drastic physical differences from one year to the next. We may get grayer hair or lose or gain a few pounds, but not much else. For an adolescent, though, six months is like a lifetime—almost like translating dog years into human years!

Between the ages of 10 and 14, middle schoolers may gain as much as six inches in height (and a few inches in other places). They might sprout new hair in spots they won't show their parents, grow broader shoulders, and lose the roundness in their faces. About this time many students acquire braces or contacts, both of which bring new challenges of their own. The smallest pimple can cause a major meltdown. The mirror is the object of a new love-hate relationship—and it's hard to tear themselves away.

During this time when your teen exhibits these rapidly changing physical characteristics, it might help to remember this: You're not the only one who doesn't recognize this new person in your home. Your middle schooler is struggling to get to know the kid in the mirror, too.

Middle School Guys

What makes somebody cool?
"Being able to embarrass yourself
without being embarrassed."
—A middle schooler

This is a good time for parents to stay alert for changes in body shape and size. It's not unusual for a gap to suddenly appear between the top of a seventh grade boy's shoes and the bottom of his pants. Longer arms need longer sleeves, and broadening chests need bigger shirt sizes. If your son can't be persuaded to go shopping, you can spare him a lot of embarrassment by discreetly buying clothes for him and returning whatever doesn't fit or meet with his approval.

Boys are constantly wondering if they're normal. They keep sneaking looks at each other in the locker room, comparing themselves to the other guys. Boys who suddenly shoot up several inches early in seventh or eighth grade often have an advantage; deservedly or not, they're looked up to in more ways than one. They're also more likely to be the object of the girls' interest.

For those who hit their growth spurts later, this can be an excruciating time. Classmates may keep calling attention to their short stature, and they may act out in anger as a result.

Middle School Girls

~~~~~~

What makes somebody cool?
"Having the right clothes, especially if
people compliment you on them."
—A middle schooler

~~~~~~

"Jenny, I need to talk to you for a minute."

Mrs. Walker was a young and popular middle school teacher, and Jenny quickly came up to her desk. Smiling, Mrs. Walker said, "Let's go out into the hallway for some privacy." When they were alone, Mrs. Walker gently pointed out that Jenny's new shirt (which was what every cool girl was wearing this fall) didn't quite measure up to the dress code.

Jenny was surprised. "Why? Most of my friends are wearing shirts like this, and they don't get in trouble."

Mrs. Walker nodded and lowered her voice. "Jenny, have you noticed that your shirt tends to . . . show a little more of your maturing body than the other girls' shirts do?"

Jenny blushed, but was unconvinced. "So?"

Her teacher sighed. She didn't really want to have this discussion here in the hallway, but Jenny didn't seem to have any idea how the cleavage shown by her shirt was affecting the boys in her seventh grade classroom. As she briefly explained why Jenny's shirt was a problem for young teenage boys, Jenny got a horrified expression on her face. Tears welled up in her eyes.

"*What?*" the girl shrieked. "*Eww!* Can I go get my sweatshirt?"

A girl's body shape will change even more dramatically than the physique of the boy who sits next to her in class. This is a good time to have a discussion about modesty—and to gently explain that two friends can't always wear the same styles. What looks good on one girl's figure might not be very flattering on her friend.

Another important point parents need to make to their middle school daughters: The boys are *noticing* these changes. Often innocently, girls wear necklines that expose cleavage or tight, short clothing that reflects current fashion trends. What they may not realize is how it affects developing teenage boys. Middle school teachers repeatedly share stories about quietly pointing out to a student how her clothing is influencing a boy's thoughts and raging hormones; almost always the young lady is horrified to find out how she's being perceived. Frequently the idea hasn't even occurred to her. As a parent, you can help tremendously by making your daughter aware of and sensitive to what's going on.

Girls also need adult women who'll discuss the issues that accompany her menstrual cycle, and the need for proper hygiene during this time. If there's no trusted adult who will do that, many girls seek out advice from their girlfriends—and what they hear isn't always accurate or helpful.

The Talk

"I never really had The Talk because I learned it in school. So one day my dad told me on the way to school that if I ever want to talk about that kind of stuff, I could ask. But I probably never will because it's too awkward."
—A middle schooler

"I was in the car with my mom when she turned down the radio and said, 'Alan?' And I said 'What?' and she started singing, 'Let me tell you 'bout the birds and the bees . . .' And I was like, 'Mom! No! I really don't want to talk about this in the car. I'm not comfortable with this right now.' And she was like, 'Okay. Well, just let me know if anything in your life is going on that you have any questions about.'"
—A middle schooler

What about having "The Talk" with your middle schooler?

This is something many parents dread. Even if they work up the courage to bring up the topic, their middle schoolers may be so uncomfortable that it just doesn't go well. Parents who are calm and matter-of-fact about the subject of sexuality, or who have honestly answered questions long before middle school, will have an easier time. But a parent who springs it on a middle schooler out of the blue can expect some reluctance and awkwardness from both parties.

A better solution is to address topics as they come up, or to use what's being shown on TV or sung about in the music they listen to as a jumping-off point. Most students will receive information in health or science classes, but it often isn't given through a filter of morals and values. It's important that parents use even short chats as opportunities to reflect their beliefs and to point out how they differ from those of the world around them.

Even if your efforts are awkward or don't seem well received, make your point—keeping it short and tackling the difficult issues. For example, many parents of sixth grade girls are asked if they want their daughters vaccinated against HPV (a sexually transmitted infection which can cause cervical cancer). Regardless of how a parent feels about the vaccination, this can be a time to talk about the risks of sexual promiscuity and God's plan for sexual purity.

Many middle schoolers prefer to get information from someone just a little older than they are. They say they're too embarrassed to ask their parents, so they go to an older sibling or even an aunt or uncle with their questions. They don't appreciate parents who overreact: "If I'm texting and my mom sees me, my mom will think it's a boy, so she will tell me that I don't need to be texting boys. It's like if I'm texting a boy, it obviously means that I'm pregnant or something."

If you're blessed to have someone you trust in your child's life who can be the go-to person for questions about these issues, that's great. If not, be sure you stay in tune with what's going on with your teen. Look for opportunities to bring up sensitive topics in as casual and natural a way as possible.

For guidelines and practical advice from physicians and other professionals about how and what you need to know and communicate to your children about sex, puberty, and related issues, you'll find that *The Focus on the Family Guide to Talking with Your Kids about Sex* is very informative and helpful.

A Healthy Relationship Makes "The Talk" Easier

"My mom and I are really alike, so I'll say stuff without even thinking. One time I asked her something about sex, and she told me I was a pastor's daughter and shouldn't even be thinking about that stuff. She asked me how I knew about it, and I said 'I'm 13; I know about stuff.'"
—A middle schooler

"My aunt will sometimes talk to me, and since she's in her twenties and closer to my age, it's not as awkward. She'll just say, 'You know what this is, right? And you know not to do this and this?' And I'll say yes and we'll go back to what we're doing. I like talking to her because she just keeps it between us."
—A middle schooler

"My mom told me where babies come from and she was calm about it, so we still have talks and it's just conversation. So it's not embarrassing or anything to either of us."
—A middle schooler

You are often the best potential teacher for your son or daughter when it comes to dealing with these awkward yet life-changing issues. Prepare for this as well as you can; talk to professionals or other parents or mentors, and read relevant and trusted resources. Keep the lines of communication open with your middle schooler. Admit it when you just aren't sure what to say and offer to help your son or daughter look up answers to questions.

Hygiene Matters

"I always wondered what B.O. [body odor] smelled like, and then my teacher told me it's kind of like onions. Now I smell it on boys all the time, and sometimes on girls. Why doesn't everyone just wear deodorant like they're supposed to?"

—A middle schooler

"Smell ya! Shouldn't have to tell ya!"

This obnoxious cry from childhood more than applies when puberty strikes. Even the most expensive or stylish shoes can hide stinky socks. And that's not all that can cause some pretty foul odors on a middle schooler.

As kids develop more adult-like bodies, they also develop more adult-like smells. Unfortunately, they don't yet have adult-like hygiene habits. In some ways they get dirtier than they did when they were little, but parents no longer have the option of undressing them and plopping them into the bathtub.

Eventually peer pressure may be enough motivation for middle schoolers to take care of their own hygiene. In the meantime, it's up to parents to insist on a daily shower, clean hair, clean teeth (emphasize fresh breath), clean armpits, and clean socks—and clean-everything-else that goes under their clothes. Don't assume this will happen every day automatically; you'll probably have to ask.

The topic may be uncomfortable at first, but many others will thank you—especially if you find ways to help your child smell socially acceptable within the confines of a small classroom, car, or family room at home.

What Teachers Told Us About Physical Changes of the Middle School Years

- Hygiene is important. As early as third grade, some kids begin to smell. At the beginning of fourth grade, some students should start wearing deodorant.

- Puberty seems to be happening earlier. Girls are developing. It catches parents and teachers unaware.

- One boy's body odor was so strong that the teacher had to open doors or kids would feel sick. His grandma owned a restaurant and cooked everything with onions and garlic; it seemed to be coming out of his pores. The teacher would intercept him in the morning and hand him deodorant. Then she'd meet him at lunch and tell him, "Reapply."

- P.E. uniforms should be washed regularly. So should other school clothes or uniforms.

- What teachers used to see in grades six, seven, and eight is now showing up in grades three, four, and five. Girls are developing earlier, and are either embarrassed by it or "loud and proud" about it.

To prevent too much awkwardness or embarrassment, you might consider creating a code word to discreetly let your middle schooler know it's time for an armpit freshening. Sue had a student whose mother had died when he was nine years old, so he was being raised by his elderly grandmother. He often wore nylon jerseys but seldom wore deodorant. After a heart-to-heart talk, they agreed that their code word would be "secret." If Mrs. Acuña told him she "had a secret," he would immediately head to the restroom to wash and reapply deodorant (which she supplied and he stored in his gym locker). If he told *her* he had a secret, she would know he needed to be excused for a few minutes to freshen up.

For a parent, the code word might be "pits"—as in, "Hey, Bud, wasn't last night's football game *the pits?*" accompanied by a smile and a raising of eyebrows. The middle schooler may be slow to catch on at first, but eventually it will sink in: "Oh! *Oh!* I'll be right back." The result: a graceful exit from the room to apply deodorant or change a shirt.

Here's a Thought:

This is a case when you can do something positive with a middle schooler's fear of doing the wrong thing. Kids don't want to find out that their classmates were talking behind their backs about how bad they smelled. If nothing else works, try telling a story about a student you remember from seventh grade who always smelled so bad that nobody wanted to sit by him. Or use the one we've already mentioned about the boy whose grandma ran a garlic-and-onions restaurant. Chances are good that the fear of being "that" student will be all the motivation it takes to get your middle schooler to shower more often.

two

The Good, the Bad, and the Gangly

~~~~~~

"I'm always bumping into things and knocking stuff over. Sometimes I can't walk through a doorway without banging my shoulder on the side. One time I even tripped up the stairs! It's so embarrassing, and then my parents yell at me and call me clumsy."

—A middle schooler

~~~~~~

Mrs. Baker was a sixth grade teacher who had a great idea. Why not make the classroom more warm and inviting by using table lamps instead of just those harsh fluorescent lights? She purchased two ceramic lamps and placed one on the corner of her desk and the other on a counter just across the room.

When the principal asked her how the plan worked, she told him: "They lasted five months. The first died when a student caught the cord with his foot, sending it smashing to the floor. The second met a similar fate when a student's elbow caused it to fly off the counter. I learned my lesson, and I no longer have lamps of any kind in my room."

Remember "child-proofing"? Your child is now at the age where you must once again guard the valuable or fragile possessions in your home. It's not because those items are in danger of being taken—they're in danger of being broken.

At this stage, middle schoolers have almost the same raging curiosity they had when they were toddlers. "Oooh, what's this?" they say as they grab for the delicate object that catches their eye. They must squeeze, shake, and fiddle with items in order to explore and discover. It might be a good idea to do some modified child-proofing for a little while: Move your breakables to a safer spot and fasten pictures securely to walls.

The other thing you'll notice is that middle schoolers tend to be clumsy; they drop things, knock them over, and crash into them on a regular basis. When teens hit a growth spurt, some parts of their bodies get ahead of other parts. It begins in their hands and feet, much as it does with puppies. The arms and legs soon follow, and then the torso stretches.[1] The most challenging part for a self-conscious adolescent is that he can grow as much as half an inch in 24 hours—literally waking up with new hands and feet. (If you want to experience how difficult that makes life, try spending tomorrow in oversized gloves and shoes.)

With longer legs, arms, and hands, middle schoolers crash into things because they literally no longer know where their bodies end. The good news is that it's a temporary condition with a sound physiological reason. The bad news is that these growth spurts can keep parents buying new clothes and shoes every six months—and groceries every other day.

Amazing Gracelessness

"Whenever I drop something, my dad yells, 'Save the pieces!'
Like I'm not already upset because I spilled stuff again!"
—A middle schooler

*"Whenever I drop something, my mom says, 'You need
to focus!' It's not that I'm not focusing; it just happens!"*
—A middle schooler

As a parent, you may find this new clumsiness merely disconcert-ing—but your middle schooler is absolutely mortified. Each year Sue surveys her middle school class: "Anybody finding you can't clear a doorway without smashing your shoulder into the frame?" Hands go up. "How about bashing your hip on tabletops and furniture? Falling down unexpectedly?" This leads to cries of "*Yes*! That happens to me *all* the time!" Then come the stories: "I broke my mom's favorite lamp, and I wasn't even *close* to it!" When they hear that this is normal and is due to growing, there's great relief, followed invariably by pleading: "Would you *please* tell my parents this? They just think I'm clumsy and careless!"

It may have been cute to point out this awkwardness when they were little, but the best thing you can do now is try to pretend you don't notice. You'll be a hero if you can anonymously help middle schoolers avoid situations that will make them look awkward or embarrass them-selves. When they're not looking, move soda cups away from the edge of the table (and flailing elbows). Sit at the end of the row in church or a movie theater to minimize the number of people they have to climb over. You can't prevent every accident (sometimes they appear to trip over their own shadows), but you can do your part to help lessen the chance of public humiliation.

Whatever you do, don't point out their clumsiness or smile when they stumble. You can't laugh *with* middle schoolers because they're too busy squirming with embarrassment to laugh at themselves. And never discuss their new awkwardness in front of them, especially with other adults. Do whatever you can to help preserve their dignity, even if that means resisting the urge to ask if they're okay. Being able to save face is *everything* in a middle schooler's world—especially when it doesn't take much to make them feel self-conscious.

What Teachers Told Us About Clumsiness

Clumsiness is beginning at an earlier age. Fourth graders are tripping and falling; teachers may think it's for attention, but it usually isn't.

So Crabby!

"My parents don't get that I'm tired. A lot. They think I'm lazy, but sometimes I just get sleepy."
—A middle schooler

"I get annoyed easily . . ."
—A middle schooler

"Every morning when my alarm goes off, I keep hitting the snooze button. And then my mom comes in every five minutes and says, 'It's time to get up! Time to go take a shower!' I'm just a little slow in the morning."
—A middle schooler

Sudden growth spurts can cause episodes of fatigue; after all, it takes a lot of energy to grow that quickly. Tiredness can lead to crankiness, which an unsuspecting parent may blame on something else

("How can you be *tired*? You slept until noon and you haven't even *done* anything!").

When a middle schooler seems grouchy or out of sorts for no reason, it's a good idea for a parent to take a quick look for any recent physical changes. Is he taller? Did you just have to buy her new shoes or clothes because the old ones didn't fit? It could be that all of it's related to the bad mood (and yawning) you're seeing. That irritability might just disappear with a well-timed nap—much as it did when he was six months old!

Middle schoolers are also tired because of a physical change in their brains. Melatonin is a chemical in our brains that rises in the evening, making us tired—and then lowers in the morning, helping us to wake up. During adolescence, for reasons scientists have yet to discover, the timing of melatonin's rise and fall changes, rising later in the evening (closer to midnight), and not lowering until mid-morning.[2] Unfortunately, just as all this is happening, we're asking kids to start school earlier and get out later. It would be ideal if middle and high school days started *after* elementary school instead of before, but school districts who've tried it have found there are too many conflicts with after-school sports and jobs.

Here's a Thought:

Ask your middle schooler to let you know when she's just too tired to face homework or chores. She agrees to take a break for no more than an hour before she starts working on the required task—and you agree not to bug her about doing nothing for that hour.

three

How They See (and Don't See) the World

"I want to pray for my grandma; she's having surgery."
  "What's the surgery for?"
  "I'm not sure."
  "When is her surgery?"
  "I don't know."
  "Will she have to stay in the hospital?"
  "I have no idea."
  "How do you know she's having surgery?"
  "My mom said I'd have to ride home with my friend on the day of the surgery."
  —Conversation between middle schooler and teacher

It's typical for middle schoolers to hear only the part of the story that applies to them. We like to call it The Bubble—as in, "You need to get out of your bubble." Parents should get used to it, because it's not going away any time soon. The Bubble is a survival technique that gives middle schoolers time and space to deal with—well, with themselves.

The physical changes are what we can actually see. But big changes are happening inside, too. Emotionally, kids feel they have little control over their mood swings. Intellectually, they're thinking all sorts of new thoughts about who they are and where they fit into the big picture of life. Spiritually, they're beginning to question so much of what they used to take for granted. Between studying themselves in the mirror and reflecting on all that's going on inside their hearts and heads, is it any wonder they barely notice the rest of us?

It's Not All About You!

As an incentive in our school's fundraising campaign, we had a "human hamster ball" for the assembly. Once inside, you can move it all over the room, but you're insulated from everything outside; voices are muffled and things look blurry. You focus on the sound of your own breathing as you concentrate on keeping the thing upright.

Teens enter their own version of this when they hit adolescence. The hamster ball—or Bubble, as we call it—is a major source of frustration for parents. It narrows the teens' view to about two feet away from themselves. They're oblivious to anything that doesn't directly concern them.

To parents, this looks like self-centeredness in the extreme, and many fear they've raised the World Champion of the Me Generation. "It's like he doesn't even know the rest of the family exists!" they cry, as they stumble over his backpack in the middle of the room or face another accusation of, "You never told me that!"

—Sue Acuña

So are we supposed to let our middle schoolers get away with going off into their own private world and ignoring the rest of us? Not completely. And not forever. But right now it's the only real method of self-protection they've figured out. There are so many changes coming at them at once, they have to spend almost all their time trying to figure out what's happening and what to do about it. They still need us—in some ways more than ever. We can't live in their Bubble—it's strictly single-occupancy. But we definitely should be regular visitors, occasionally poking our heads inside.

When you know he's in his Bubble, don't yell at him about the mess he left behind after lunch. Invite him to join you in the kitchen and see if he can figure out why you're there. He'll probably be surprised to see the open cupboard door, the open peanut butter jar, and the open bread wrapper. Chances are good that once he does see them, he'll clean them up without further prompting.

Bubble Trouble

My mom used to pick up the grandkids after school. One afternoon she arrived in my classroom after the students had gone, her eyes blazing. "As I walked on the sidewalk, *not one* of those junior high kids would move aside to let me pass! I had to step into the *parking lot* to get by them!"

I gently explained that the sad reality was they probably hadn't even noticed her. If she'd stopped and asked them to move, they likely would've looked surprised to see her, then stepped aside.

—Sue Acuña

When you give important information ("Dad will pick you up at 1:00 for an orthodontist appointment. Don't leave school without your homework assignment, okay?"), have her repeat it to you. That way you'll know whether the words penetrated The Bubble. If she can't repeat it, you'll know they didn't make it through. You can give the information again, this time with her paying more attention.

Or when he inconsiderately interrupts your conversation, point it out with words like, "I'm sure you didn't mean to interrupt the important conversation I'm having." He'll probably be surprised to see there's someone else talking to you. But he'll get the message without being embarrassed in front of someone else.

No need to battle The Bubble; it's going to disappear in its own time and way. But your friendly visits periodically will remind your teen that you—and the rest of the world—are still there. It shouldn't be used as an excuse for being rude or inconsiderate, but you may be able to trace a lot of frustrating behavior to The Bubble. That's when you can find ways to gently point out when your middle schooler is being self-centered—or nudge her away from the mirror and back to the outside world.

What Teachers Told Us About The Bubble

Middle schoolers can't pass by without crashing shoulders into someone. It may seem rude, but it's a result of gangliness combined with The Bubble of half-consciousness many kids are encased in.

Their Greatest Fears

"Last night I started thinking about what would happen to my brothers and me if my parents die. I got so freaked out I couldn't go to sleep!"

—A middle schooler

"What would happen to us if a shooter
came on campus?"
—A middle schooler

"Everybody was dancing at my cousin's
wedding but me. I didn't know any of the
dances, and I didn't want to look stupid."
—A middle schooler

If you were asked to list the top fears of a teenager today, you might think of some very logical and straightforward responses—and there are certainly some obvious dangers. As middle schoolers' awareness of the world around them grows, so does their anxiety about the bad stuff out there that can harm them or their families. They live in a post-9/11 world, where terrorists have blown up buildings on TV, and nobody knows where it will happen next. Even closer to home, they know of schools where students have been killed, and they worry about what will happen to them. These are the thoughts that sometimes keep them awake at night. When asked, middle schoolers will readily tell you that, among other things, they fear the following:

- parents dying
- disasters, natural and manmade (earthquakes, terrorist attacks)
- being kidnapped or assaulted
- school shootings
- death at the hands of another

But there's another list, one made up of fears that middle schoolers may *not* mention to the adults in their lives. In fact, they may not even talk about it with each other, partly because they can't always put it in words and partly because they think they're the only ones who feel that way. Even though there are several items on this hidden list, the top one receives a virtually unanimous vote among middle schoolers everywhere: *looking stupid.*

Adults don't always remember that in middle school the fear of looking stupid, of being ridiculed by friends, of not being welcomed into the crowd, is one of the scariest things of all. It is a fear strong enough to keep them from going to their best friend's party because it's at a skating rink and they can't skate. It will keep them from trying out for choir or soccer or the school play, and it can make their stomachs hurt every day before lunch. They've all seen instances where somebody is suddenly and without warning ostracized by peers, and they are terrified that they may be the next victim. They know that terrorist attacks and school shootings are scary—but rare. But not fitting in at school? That could happen to them tomorrow in the lunchroom!

In fact, many of the other items on the hidden list climb much higher than you might think:

- getting in trouble
- failing in school
- not making the team
- letting parents, friends, or teachers down
- childhood fears, such as thunderstorms, darkness, and getting lost
- being rejected by a group without knowing why

Parents are often surprised to learn that being a social misfit can be scarier than facing a terrorist attack, and they don't know where to begin to address it. First and foremost, don't downplay it. It really is a paralyzing force in a middle schooler's mind. Keep in mind that middle schoolers want what adults want when they voice their fears: to be heard and understood. When your middle schooler balks at trying out for a team, acknowledge her fears and explain that those are normal feelings. You might even compare them to a beaded curtain that you just have to push through to get to the other side. Reminding her to breathe may sound too simple, but don't overestimate its capacity to calm anxiety.

Many adults remember their junior high years as so painful that "you couldn't pay me enough money to go back." Genuine empathy helps middle schoolers know that these years can be difficult for everyone, but it will get better. Sometimes that thought alone is what will get them out of bed and out the door in the morning.

Here's a Thought:

To show that adults do remember how it felt to be a middle schooler, dig out your junior high school pictures and maybe even your report cards if your mom saved them for you. Let your kids make fun of how you looked. Gently remind them that no matter how horrible or awkward things sometimes seem in middle school, it's temporary—and your high school pictures almost always look a lot better!

Dreams and Aspirations

"I really need some space from [my parents']
thoughts about me and just need to make my own
thoughts which will prepare me for the future."
—A middle schooler

Ask an average eight-year-old what he wants to be when he grows up, and you may get answers like "a firefighter, a lion tamer, or a bus driver—just like my dad!" Throughout childhood most kids accept their parents' encouragement to dream big, and embrace the idea that nothing is beyond their reach.

But for a middle schooler, reality hits hard—harder than it probably needs to. After all, how can you believe you can do anything you set your mind to when you can't even figure out who you are or what you want to do? There's nothing like puberty to make you acutely aware that you may not be that big a deal.

Doubts, insecurities, self-consciousness—so many things make it difficult to believe big dreams can come true. Middle schoolers may begin limiting themselves because of what they think they can't do. If no one intervenes, those feelings can keep them from pursuing even activities they enjoy.

Many times students who enjoyed sports or music in elementary school will worry so much about not being able to keep up with their peers that they will forgo tryouts or auditions, claiming, "I'm not good enough." At this point they're torn between wanting their parents to encourage them and resenting it when their parents push too hard.

What Teachers Told Us About Dreams and Aspirations

Encourage your kids to discover what they like and what they're good at.

If you sense your teen is giving up on his dream because he feels inadequate or discouraged, you might suggest he talk to someone who's already doing the job he dreamed about. This may be a good time for an informal chat or even a short job-shadow exercise. Remember, if you're the only one encouraging and complimenting him, your middle schooler will probably think you're saying it because you're his mom or dad and you have to. A more objective adult can often have a stronger influence in this situation.

Still Love Me?

"I wish my parents could understand that I turn away when they're mad, not because I don't want to listen, but that I wanna hide my tears."
—A middle schooler

Many years ago a popular psychology book asked this question: "Why am I afraid to tell you who I am?"

The answer: "Because you might not like who I am, and that's all I've got."

It's a fact that you won't always like your child's behavior, attitude, and actions during this unpredictable and constantly changing phase of life. But the one thing you must communicate is the rock-solid commitment that reassures your child you'll always love the person he or she is—at any given time.

And while you're maintaining high standards of behavior and insisting on accountability, give some space and grace—and leave room for saving face. This child who has been entrusted to you is a gift that you will pass on to the world at large in a very short time. One thing is for sure—*your* life will never be the same!

Here's a Thought:

If you want to talk about family matters, current events, or other topics that don't seem to interest your middle schooler, try starting at the end with "Here's what this has to do with your life" or "Your day may change tomorrow because of what I'm about to tell you." Do it in a light-hearted manner, avoiding a tone that sounds like criticism.

part two

PARENTING

four

What Your Child Needs Now

~~~~~~~~~~

"My parents want to control everything about my life.
They tell me what to wear and what to eat and when to
go to bed. Why can't I make any of my own decisions?"
—A middle schooler

~~~~~~~~~~

The fact that your children will always need you will not change. But *how* they need you constantly changes, especially during their journey from childhood to young adulthood. And the beginning of the biggest changes happens when children reach the age of puberty.

Some parenting experts recommend that parents start operating more in the role of consultants than managers when their kids hit middle school. Think about the parallel: From the time your kids are born to well into their elementary grades, you need to manage most things for them. Bedtimes, menus, wardrobe—most of these decisions are made by parents. Once children reach 10 or 11 years old, this is no longer acceptable to them—which is why so many power struggles begin by the fifth or sixth grade, and often continue through high school.

If you can step out of a hands-on management role and into more of an advising role, those battles may be fewer and far less heated. You're still in charge as a parent, but how you communicate authority can make all the difference in how much cooperation you get. Instead of delivering commands or ultimatums, try asking questions and making gentle suggestions. For example, "You're not wearing that to school!" will lead to a battle. Instead, try asking: "You haven't worn that in a while, have you? Doesn't seem to fit quite the way it used to. Go check it out in the mirror and let's talk about it." Then you might be able to ease sideways into a discussion about the appropriateness of the outfit, especially if it's gotten too tight or too small.

Sometimes a consultant has to let a client make bad choices and live with the consequences. If it's not a major issue of safety or morality, consider how much control you need to hang on to in a particular situation. Try just listening and making a suggestion or two and then stepping back and letting your "client" make the final decision.

They Need Role Models

"My mom yells at me for gossiping, but then I hear her talking to her friends about people at church. Why is gossiping okay for adults but not for kids?"
—A middle schooler

For middle schoolers, along with more adult-type bodies comes the perception of themselves as being more like adults. In order to figure out how grown-ups should behave, middle schoolers are watching the adults around them, and are quick to judge when they perceive even a hint of hypocrisy.

To a middle schooler, a double standard—whether it's an issue like language or an even larger one like dishonesty—is not only unfair, it's also confusing. Are they supposed to believe that what you *say* is true, or are they supposed to follow what you *do*?

Teachers frequently hear their middle school students parroting what they've heard at home. Parents should realize that while their kids may not seem to be listening or to care about what's being said, they're absorbing every word—and storing it up for an opportune moment to share. For example, teachers almost never have to guess at a parent's political stance, especially around election time. Middle schoolers eager to engage in an adult conversation will talk freely about political issues as if they have an opinion of their own, but when pressed for evidence or details, they'll admit they just overheard their parents discussing it.

You may get called out by your middle schooler for what he or she perceives as hypocrisy. If you can't give a valid reason for why you're not following your own rules, you'll lose a lot of credibility unless you confess your guilt and apologize instead of getting defensive. In so doing, you can model for your child the proper way to respond when you've been caught doing something wrong. That's important, because they really are always watching!

Don't Rush to Rescue

"If I forget my assignment, I can always call my mom and she'll bring it to school for me. Same with my basketball uniform or my lunch. She'll yell at me, but at least I'll have my stuff."

—A middle schooler

"I ate my daughter's lunch today!"

The middle school student's mom was standing at the teacher's desk after school, looking quite pleased with herself. "It was hard, but I stuck to my guns and didn't rescue her today!" The teacher smiled. Sarah had complained in class about the fact she'd forgotten her lunch yet again, but this time her mom had refused to bring it to her at school. Sarah's mom had just made a big step toward shifting some much-needed responsibility to her daughter—no more automatic rescues. And now there was a pretty good chance Sarah would remember to bring her lunch tomorrow.

Teachers call them "helicopter parents." They're the ones who walk their children into the classroom every day, help them unpack their things, and tell the teacher what their child is thinking. At the end of the day they come in, talk to the teacher about their latest concern, find out what the homework is, and pack up and carry their child's belongings out to the car. If their child forgets anything during the day, they'll retrieve it and take it to school—even if it means taking time off work to do so.

Sadly, these parents think they are doing what's best for their children by monitoring them so closely, but they can't see how in the long run they're creating more problems. This becomes painfully true in middle school, when parents should be shifting more responsibility to the students.

Besides being unhelpful in the long run, helicopter parents can also be a cause of embarrassment for their middle schoolers. Parents who show up in a classroom unannounced may make their children uncomfortable, because they're sure nobody else's parents are as weird as theirs.

It's important for parents to let their middle schoolers suffer the consequences of irresponsibility, even if it means a missed game or a low grade. Following through and remembering to bring what you need are both life skills that have to be practiced before they can be mastered. Overprotective parents often serve the needs of their children best when they land their helicopters and let their children learn to fly on their own.

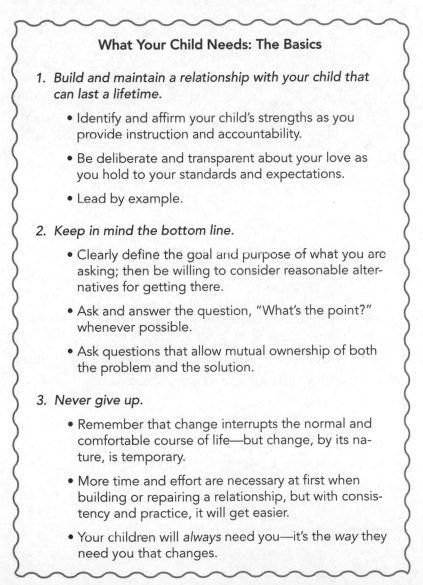

What Your Child Needs: The Basics

1. *Build and maintain a relationship with your child that can last a lifetime.*

   • Identify and affirm your child's strengths as you provide instruction and accountability.

   • Be deliberate and transparent about your love as you hold to your standards and expectations.

   • Lead by example.

2. *Keep in mind the bottom line.*

   • Clearly define the goal and purpose of what you are asking; then be willing to consider reasonable alternatives for getting there.

   • Ask and answer the question, "What's the point?" whenever possible.

   • Ask questions that allow mutual ownership of both the problem and the solution.

3. *Never give up.*

   • Remember that change interrupts the normal and comfortable course of life—but change, by its nature, is temporary.

   • More time and effort are necessary at first when building or repairing a relationship, but with consistency and practice, it will get easier.

   • Your children will *always* need you—it's the *way* they need you that changes.

Here's a Thought:

Find a place to post end-of-day feedback—such as a white board, sticky note on the fridge, or text message. Ask every family member to share one good thing about today and one not-so-good thing. If advice or help is needed, include the letter "A" at the end. Otherwise, keep it a safe place to simply share or vent.

five

Behind Closed Doors

~~~~~~~~~

*"My parents don't get that after school
I kinda want to be left alone. When
I'm in my room doing homework, they
barge in and tell me to do chores."*

—A middle schooler

~~~~~~~~~

"It's like one day they're your best buddies and they want to tell you everything, and then the next day they just disappear into their rooms and don't want to be around you anymore!"

This frustrated parent has discovered what almost every parent of middle schoolers experiences—an unexpected physical and emotional distance.

For middle schoolers, self-consciousness and a sudden increase in modesty create a keenly felt need for more privacy. Sometimes they just want time alone to think about what's going on in their hearts and heads. Childhood days of having parents involved with every aspect of their lives—bathing, dressing, eating—are in the past. Their journey to independence has begun.

Why Is the Door Closed?

"Why is it so hard for my parents to understand the words, 'I want to be left alone'? They just keep bugging me and wanting to know my business!"
—A middle schooler

"Should I enjoy the peace and quiet, or barge in and see what he's up to?"

These are the words of a concerned parent dealing with one of the big dilemmas of adolescence: The Closed Door. It forces parents of middle schoolers to stop and think about how much they trust their children—and how much they *should* trust them. After all, this may no longer be the child they thought they knew.

Parents should respect a closed door when their child is getting dressed; closed bathrooms, under normal circumstances, are off limits, too. But what about a door that hides a middle schooler who's unhappy—or engaged in a texting or Internet conversation with someone you may not even know? How does a parent stay involved without violating a middle schooler's privacy?

Many middle schoolers experiment with shutting themselves away in their bedrooms. After all, they've figured out this is their only personal domain at home. As soon as this begins to happen, parents need to be able to distinguish between normal privacy needs and situations that might be cause for concern.

Besides dressing rooms and bathrooms, there are general boundaries that should always be observed. For example, if a member of the opposite gender is visiting in the room, the door should be open. But there are many other situations that aren't quite so obvious. Unless it grows suspiciously quiet within, a door closed behind two good friends is probably not an issue, unless they're on the Internet.

A middle schooler who wants to be alone much of the time is not necessarily cause for alarm. Sometimes it's a personality issue. Introverted kids who've spent the school day surrounded by dozens (or even hundreds) of other people may need time alone to recharge. Sometimes it's because privacy is something new and worth exploring. Maybe a middle schooler no longer has to share a bedroom, or a wise parent has allowed "privacy hours" when siblings aren't allowed to disturb. Teens relish time to themselves. It gives them a chance to think deep thoughts, dream big dreams, or wallow in their misery—real or imagined.

Middle schoolers with creative gifts can be insecure about their unfinished music, art, or writing projects and will be irate if they're interrupted in the middle of their masterpieces. Those involved in relationships may be embarrassed to have their words of endearment (or their giggles) overheard by others who might tease them. Conscientious students may need the peace and quiet for finishing homework.

Of course the middle school years are also full of new discoveries about their bodies, and your middle schooler may be looking for ways to experiment with sexual activity behind those close doors. If you're prepared to talk about it, you can usually handle these situations in a calm and reasonable manner. One great resource for anticipating and dealing with this is *The Focus on the Family Guide to Talking with Your Kids about Sex.*

Parents need to be alert without being paranoid. Keep your radar on; trust your instincts when you decide whether the current need for privacy is normal and nothing to worry about, or whether it needs a closer look. Be open with your middle schooler. If you're not comfortable with her spending so much time behind closed doors, sit down with her and tell her. Outline the house rules you'd like to put into effect. Be prepared to justify your reasons and involve her in the process of determining when it's okay to close the door and when it's not. Remember, you're still the final authority—but you'll get dramatically improved cooperation if you calmly and openly discuss your concerns.

Striking a Balance on Privacy

"I wish my parents would understand that I still love them—I just want some time to myself."

—A middle schooler

"Why can't you just trust me?"

Middle schoolers can be a little sensitive about how much control their parents seem to exercise over their lives at a time when they're flexing their wings and testing new boundaries. Parents need to acknowledge and accommodate a middle schooler's need for privacy, but they're wise to still encourage (and sometimes insist on) balancing it with family time.

Point out that you'd like to trust your child until he gives you reason not to, but you want to be involved in the process of helping him discover and use the right ways to be more independent. Do your best to give your middle schooler room to figure out how to balance privacy and participation with the rest of the world. Try not to overreact to the closed doors—remember that the forbidden becomes more desirable. Choose your battles.

Your teen's need for "alone time" is not usually a sign of rejecting you. Instead, try to see it as another phase of development and a step toward one day living away from the family.

When to Investigate

When my son was a teen, I'd walk past his room and see him sitting sideways on the bed, leaning against the wall. I'd stop in his doorway and ask, "Am I supposed to be giving you your space, or am I supposed to be expressing my concern?"

"No, I'm okay," he'd say. As I'd turn to leave the room he'd continue, "It's just that I don't get why some people act the way they do . . ."

I'd ease my way back into the room and often wind up sitting on the floor listening as he unburdened his heart of whatever was bugging him.

—Sue Acuña

There are some closed-door situations that should raise a red flag for parents. A hibernating teen who is visibly unhappy for an extended period of time (more than a couple of days) or without an obvious reason may need to be watched more closely. Parents may want to check in every half hour or so, *knocking first* and asking if everything is okay. Don't be put off by a hostile response; it may not be aimed at you personally.

It's okay to ask, much as Sue did with her son, "Am I supposed to be leaving you alone, or would you like somebody to talk to?" Sometimes the answer may be, "I *said* I wanted to be left alone." But once in a while you may find that your comforting presence and your helpful advice are both needed and wanted.

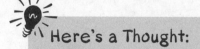

Here's a Thought:

Suggest that your middle schooler—and other kids if you have them—make their own PRIVACY sign that can hang on their doorknob or work area when they want to keep siblings out of their space. On the flip side of the sign could be something like READY TO PLAY OR TALK. Encourage each child to use *both* sides of the sign.

six

Technical Difficulties

〜〜〜〜〜

*"If I'm texting, my parents always want to know who
I'm talking to, and if I say 'my friend,' they want to
know which friend. If I tell them I'm helping someone
with a problem, they ask like a thousand questions
about stuff that's none of their business!"*

—A middle schooler

〜〜〜〜〜

The Internet introduces another type of privacy parents must watch for and monitor: the *virtual* closed door. Too much privacy online can create a whole new set of problems if it allows a middle schooler the freedom to make bad choices.

Wise parents will not allow computers or video games in bedrooms, because they know monitoring their use in there is almost impossible. Insist that computers and game consoles be in a more open and public area. It's also a good idea to have a household rule that cell phones are left in the living room or other public area at bedtime to discourage middle-of-the-night texting. You might even set up one central charging area for everyone's phone or tablet.

If you ever want to start an animated discussion among parents of middle schoolers, ask this question: "Should parents have access to and/or read their children's text messages and e-mails?" Many parents have strong opinions on this matter, while some wouldn't know how to read such correspondence even if they wanted to.

Rule Number One when your kids are old enough to own electronics should be this: *Parents must be familiar with the operation of their children's electronic devices.* It's amazing how many parents will say, "I don't even know how to work that thing." Being unable to access your child's phone or computer is like allowing a locked room in your house to which only your child has the key—but it's worse, because strangers can have the key and get in there without your knowledge.

Don't buy your children anything you can't figure out how to use. Even if you don't know every detail, you need to at least know enough to convince your child you can access information that's stored there if you have a reason to do so.

Where Do You Draw the Line?

"[My parents] are constantly trying to help or know everything about me. But if they are always trying to make my decisions for me, I have no independence."
—A middle schooler

"I wish my parents would understand that school, society, and friends have changed from when they were a kid."
—A middle schooler

Let's say you *do* know how to turn on and use your daughter's phone. Should you read her text messages?

Not necessarily—but you should have the *ability* to read them if you need to. Middle school is a particularly difficult time as far as relationships go, and many vicious words have been transmitted over cell phones and through cyberspace. Most parents, when confronted with nasty e-mails sent by their own children, are shocked that they would do such a thing.

Should you demand your children give you all their passwords? We handled the password issue in two different ways, each equally acceptable. Sue required all passwords be given to her as they were created and changed. Cynthia didn't ask for passwords up front, but made it clear that they were to be given upon demand. In both cases our teens knew we would be checking up on them if necessary—which was the main point.

Social media changes rapidly, and new sites are constantly being introduced. It's hard for parents to keep up, but it's vital that they do. Even though parents don't need to see everything posted by their middle schoolers, an occasional surprise check-in can keep things from getting out of hand. Cynthia's rule with her boys was that they could be on Facebook as long as she was one of their Facebook friends (so she could see what they were posting). They also had to tell her, if she asked, how they met each of their Facebook friends (to protect against strangers and predators).

Some parents will not allow their middle schoolers to be on any social media site, which is certainly up to personal discretion. Just remember our earlier tip: What is forbidden becomes more desirable.

It's important to sit down and have an open discussion with your middle schoolers about expectations and rules for use, as well as consequences if they break the trust you're placing in them. It's best to do this from the very first computer or smartphone purchase, but it's not too late to catch up—and there's no excuse for not trying!

As the twenty-first century progresses, these social media and Internet issues are going to multiply at an even more astounding rate than we've seen so far. The issue of virtual privacy will continue to get more and more complicated—and it's not going away. But good parenting doesn't go away either. It just becomes more technologically savvy with every passing year and new invention. It's one more reason this job of parenting is always a new adventure!

Setting Limits

"As soon as I turn on the Xbox my brother complains that I've been playing too long, and he tells my mom, and my mom tells me to get off. It's so not fair!"
—A middle schooler

No matter how many other activities you offer middle schoolers, a large majority of them will think all free time is a chance to log more "screen" time (TV, computers, video games, tablets, anything with a screen). If you have these electronic devices in your home, spend some time discussing and setting reasonable limits with your middle schooler—and agree in advance what you will do to enforce them.

The American Academy of Pediatrics recommends no more than one or two hours a day in front of any electronic device.[3] While many parents agree this is a reasonable amount of time, they don't always know how to make sure their children stick to the limits.

Most video games come equipped with parental controls which allow parents to choose how long the console is on during a 24-hour period, as well as which games kids are allowed to play. A password is needed to change the settings. A simpler solution is to disconnect the power cord from the back of the game console and return it only during approved playing hours. Video game controllers are also easy for parents to confiscate.

When it comes to Internet usage, computers also come equipped with software for creating parental controls—or you can purchase it separately. These programs can be set to allow access to the Internet only during specific hours and to limit the Web sites that can be visited. If you're not sure how to do this, you might want to ask an older teenager for assistance.

Unlimited television watching may seem like a safer option, but many programs aren't appropriate for middle schoolers. Consider reducing your channel choices on cable or satellite, as well as checking to see if your television service is equipped with parental controls. At the very least, parents should discuss with their children what programs they find appropriate and why. Without guidance, middle schoolers will watch and absorb whatever happens to be on.

When it comes to cell phones, it's not just about setting limits on the minutes your middle schooler talks or the number of texts that are sent. Most cell phones can access the Internet, and it's difficult to track sites your child visits via phone. Most middle schoolers do a lot more texting than calling, so if you're concerned about how many texts your middle schooler is sending (and who is getting them), go online and check out the usage on your carrier's Web site (you'll need to sign in to your account). Discuss with your child how many texts per day you feel are appropriate, and how many would be considered excessive. Again, come to an agreement on limits and consequences.

Do Battles over Entertainment Have to Wreck Your Relationship?

When our daughter Kelsey was in middle school, a certain R rated film came out that was *the* talk of her classmates—and the rest of the nation. As R rated films go, it was on the lighter side, but still contained enough objectionable content that we just weren't comfortable letting her see it. According to our daughter, "all" of her friends had viewed this particular movie (which of course wasn't true, but many had). She was convinced she should see it, too.

If you've dealt with a similar situation, you can imagine how Kelsey felt—that her status as a maturing young adult was on the line. She certainly didn't want a reputation for being the girl who was only allowed to watch *Cinderella*, TV Land reruns, and movies filmed in the 1940s and '50s.

I'd love to say this challenge had a happy ending at the time. But it didn't. Even though many, many Christian parents were allowing their kids to see this one, we believed we were making the right decision by putting our foot down. There was no compromise that would make her happy and allow us to stay true to our values. The answer was no. End of story.

Well, not quite. Kelsey is in her early twenties now; recently my wife and I talked with her about her growing-up years. I asked her to describe the most difficult "media moment" in her upbringing. She recalled the situation I've just described. Then I asked, "Knowing what you know now, what would you change if you had to live this time all over again?"

"Not a thing," she replied. Chuckling, she recalled how badly she'd wanted us to let her see that film. But she's glad now that we drew a line in the sand and didn't waver. Whew! It took almost a decade to discover that even from our daughter's perspective we made the right decision.

Setting healthy entertainment boundaries in your home may mean you won't see much buy-in from your kids—at least in the present. But stay the course. Don't waver. A better time probably is coming.[4]

—Bob Waliszewski
Plugged-In Parenting

Here's a Thought:

Start designing a family contract for your middle schooler to sign in exchange for use of a cell phone, tablet, or computer. Agree to reasonable limits and outline your requirements in writing; then discuss the agreement before both of you sign it.

seven

The Missing Links: Relationships and Communication

"I just wish my dad would stop watching football when I'm trying to talk to him."
—A middle schooler

"My parents say I don't tell them anything, but whenever I try they tell me they're too busy or it's not a good time."
—A middle schooler

"Sometimes I want to tell my parents something, but they tell me to wait. Then when they ask me later what it was, I don't want to say, because I think they're not going to listen anyway."
—A middle schooler

Remember how many changes are happening to your children—not only physical, but mental, spiritual, and emotional. Their thoughts are becoming deeper and more introspective, and when they express those thoughts they speak from the heart. Parents who struggle to carry on a conversation often don't realize they're still talking to their kids as if they were eight years old. Not surprisingly, this can cause middle schoolers to clam up around their parents and go find someone who will really know what they're talking about.

When it comes to talking to middle schoolers (and everyone else, for that matter), there are three basic things to remember:

1. They want to be listened to.

2. They want to be understood.

3. They want to be taken seriously.

The bottom line is that when it comes to how you communicate, your middle schooler wants to be treated as you treat your adult friends and co-workers. That means speaking respectfully, using empathy, and avoiding anything that would embarrass or belittle. Try saying, "I respect your opinion, but what about this?"

That word "respect" speaks volumes to middle schoolers. Remember, they may want to share with you what they're thinking. But if you insist on treating them like they're still young children, you can expect them to either respond as children or react to you as adults who've been insulted.

Middle schoolers are trying to figure out how to work toward being grown-ups, and grown-ups are trying to figure out how to get their children to listen to them. After all, parents need to help their children learn what it takes to become mature and independent. So how can that be done with the least tension and misunderstanding?

Most adults expect teens to stop whatever they're doing, make eye contact, and respond in a way that shows they're listening. Just think for a moment about how many times parents say, "Are you listening to me?" or "Do you hear what I'm saying?" Yet sometimes these adults don't return the same courtesy to their children. To encourage more communication from your middle schooler, try muting the TV, turning your chair away from the computer screen, putting down the phone, and adopting a position that communicates, "I'm listening, and I'm interested in what you're saying."

Sometimes We Miss the Obvious

One dad told us he'd been eager to try these communication techniques with his 10-year-old child. "I had fixed him his favorite meal," he said, "but he wouldn't eat it. I tried listening to him and tried to understand and take him seriously—but he just got more irritated with me. I finally said, 'Hey—I'm trying to take you seriously here. Don't you want to be taken seriously?'

"My son shook his head and replied, 'No—I want to be taken to McDonald's!' "
—Cynthia Tobias

Don't Interrupt

"Why is it that parents can interrupt us whenever they want, but we can't ever interrupt them without getting yelled at?"
—A middle schooler

"When I try to talk to my mom, my big sister keeps interrupting. But if she's talking to my mom, I don't ever get to interrupt; my sister just yells at me to be quiet."
—A middle schooler

The complaint, "You never listen to me!" comes as often from middle schoolers as it does from parents. As kids cast about for the right words to explain how they're feeling, they're often interrupted by impatient or busy parents who just want to tell them something and move on. Since the parent usually has the busiest schedule, the middle schooler feels quickly dismissed instead of being given the opportunity to genuinely communicate important information and feelings.

What parents don't realize is that their middle schooler is just as frustrated as *they* are when their children interrupt *them*. Middle schoolers are emotional and impulsive, and they can't always separate important details from unimportant ones. This means they're good at making short stories long. If you really want to hear what's in your child's passionate heart or busy brain, you'll need to exercise patience and maybe even pinch your lips together to keep from interrupting. Or you can try saying something like, "I really want to hear this story, but I'm pressed for time. Can you just tell me the most important part, or would you rather wait until I have more time?"

Once again, modeling the behavior you expect from your middle schooler is critical. "Don't do as I do; do as I say" is a philosophy that not only isn't fair, but will drive your middle schooler away to find someone who will listen without interrupting.

Use Empathy

*"I feel like my parents don't understand
my friends or how I feel."*
—A middle schooler

*"They think they know what I'm feeling, but they
won't let me explain how I'm really feeling."*
—A middle schooler

When faced with an emotional teen, your best response is usually an answer wrapped in empathy. Let's say your child declares, "That stupid teacher gave us a *hundred* questions in history, and they're all due tomorrow! She's the meanest teacher in the whole school!"

You might respond, "Oh, that's so frustrating, to have that much homework in one night!" End of response. Don't offer suggestions, and don't point out the obvious (that getting started *now* might be a good idea). Just use empathy to show that you get it: Your child is frustrated. Try to figure out the feelings behind the outburst and show that you understand. Remember, it's a basic emotional need to be understood.

Let's say your empathetic response leads to another flare-up: "No kidding! And I still have a math test to study for *and* a stupid paper to write!"

Just answer with more empathy: "Wow! That *does* sound like a lot!" This is harder than it appears, because your first instinct may be to get your teen to calm down, or to suggest a solution to the problem. But try simple empathy a few times, and you might be surprised at the results. In the best-case scenario, you'll get a calmer middle schooler who's able to be more realistic and to come up with a game plan to deal with the problem. Best of all, you might be seen as a parent who actually understands.

Keep It in the Family

"Parents shouldn't be telling everyone your business."
—A middle schooler

When children are little, parents can get away with talking about them as if they aren't there. But somewhere along the line, children start to listen—and by the time they get to middle school, this can pose a serious barrier to parent-child communication.

Middle schoolers suffer from extreme self-consciousness; even a small lapse in judgment can be cause for embarrassment. To have a parent broadcasting that to adult friends—or worse, to mention it to the middle schooler's friend or parent, especially in the child's hearing—will leave a middle schooler writhing in agony or seething in anger. Just as parents trust spouses, co-workers, and friends to keep confidences and not embarrass them, middle schoolers want to trust their parents to do the same. If parents want their children to confide in them, their children have to know that what they say will be just that—confidential.

The No-No List

"When my parents are mad at me, they give me these long lectures and act annoyed with me and then they make snarky comments in my direction."
—A middle schooler

"My parents don't listen to my side of the story because they think they already know what I'm going to say. So they cut me off before I get to the end."
—A middle schooler

If you find communicating with your middle schooler to be less than satisfying, check out what we like to call the "No-No List." These are 10 common mistakes parents inadvertently make in talking to their kids. Often just recognizing them will take care of at least half the problem.

1. *Interrupting.* Cutting them off before the end of their story. Or predicting how the story will end and finishing their sentences. Even worse: interrupting an emotional story with questions about chores or homework.

2. *Downplaying feelings.* Saying something like, "You think that's a big deal? You should try living *my* life!" when middle schoolers are excited about something or really angry at someone.

3. *Yelling.* Considered "going off" by middle schoolers, it usually causes them to stop communicating. Note: To a middle schooler, yelling has less to do with volume and more to do with attitude and tone of voice.

4. *Using "always" and "never."* Pointing out faults with language about how he *always* forgets to be responsible or how she *never* treats you with respect. As with most adults, the moment "always" or "never" is inserted into a discussion, the listener gets defensive and starts looking for ways to justify the behavior.

5. *Criticizing.* Complaining frequently about such things as clothes, hair length or style, and friends. Expressing disappointment in behavior, attitude, grades, etc.

6. *Using half an ear.* Saying "Uh-huh" and "Hmm" to make it sound like you're listening even though you're not. Not making eye contact while the middle schooler is speaking (how many adults will allow their *kids* to get away with that?).

7. *Belittling in front of others.* Telling friends and family members about their children's faults and mistakes when they're standing right there. Or describing a situation that really embarrasses them, and then expecting them to laugh along.

8. *Being judgmental.* Asking "What were you thinking?" or "Why are you so . . . ?" or pointing out how immature your middle schooler is.

Assuming it was his or her fault before getting all the facts straight. Or continuing to blame the middle schooler even if it wasn't his or her fault: "You must've done *something* to make him act that way toward you."

9. *Solving their problems.* Making them feel inferior by telling them what they should do. Interfering with the growth in self-confidence that comes with persevering through a problem on one's own.

10. *Being sarcastic.* Using a tone of voice that makes you sound serious, but choosing words whose meaning is unclear: "Sure, buy anything you want; I've got plenty of money," or "No, I'm *kidding*." Being clever without considering the collateral damage.

Deciphering the Code

Politicians and diplomats could take a lesson from middle schoolers when it comes to being noncommittal. Translating the hidden meaning behind the words teens speak is like an art form. Here's what parents need to know:

Question: "Are you doing (homework) (chores) (the weeding)?" Answer: "I was just about to start!"

Translation: No.

Question: "Are you finished with (homework) (chores) (the weeding)?" Answer: "Almost!"

Translation: No.

Question: "Did you kick your brother?" Answer: "He spit at me!"

Translation: Yes.

Question: "Did you wear that to church?" Answer: "Dad didn't say anything about it."

Translation: Yes.

Question: "Who broke this glass?" Answer: "It was an accident!"

Translation: I-did-but-please-don't-be-mad-at-me.

Question: "Do you love me?" Answer: (shrug) "I guess."

Translation: Yes-of-course I do-but-I-just-can't-say-it-back-to-you-right-now.

Question: "Will you do this job for me just because you love me?" Answer: "You're the best mom ever!"

Translation: No.

The truth is that despite how it appears sometimes, middle schoolers like to avoid drama with their parents when they can. By providing noncommittal answers, they hope to head off a lecture or a tirade—or to buy some time to complete those tasks they managed to avoid until they heard the reminder.

When you find yourself on the receiving end of a noncommittal response, answer with a casual comeback or comment like, "I know that means 'No'!" Your middle schooler will probably laugh, pleased that you get the joke.

Translation: "Thanks for understanding me!"

Scheduling Family Time

"My parents tell me to get off my phone and spend time with the family, but all they're doing is watching TV! How is that considered family time? It's not like we're playing a game or going somewhere together or anything that might actually be fun."

—A middle schooler

In the midst of their hectic schedules, middle schoolers still need to stay connected with their families. Parents are sometimes surprised to learn that their kids actually *want* to spend time with them, though how that time is spent might look different from the way it did several years ago.

Family-friendly activities can include sitting down together to watch a movie (which the kids have helped select). Everyone should agree that laptops, phones, and tablets be put away while the movie is on. Families also can have fun playing games together; video games using devices like a Kinect or a Wii can get everyone off the couch and moving in friendly competition. (Bonus points if Mom or Dad tries out some moves during a dance game!)

Card games are still popular at this age, as are classic games that involve team play, such as Apples to Apples. You can pick an all-family Game Night once a week and make sure everyone agrees to keep that evening open. Even if family time only lasts an hour or two before everyone scatters, every minute of the time you invest will reap immeasurable benefits in terms of the relationship you have with your children.

Sibling Skirmishes

"My sister is a senior, so my parents are focused on helping her find a college—so they talk about that a lot. But if they talk to me, my sister cries and says they never pay attention to her."
—A middle schooler

"Parents should give equal punishments to all three of us. With my sister, they just give her a look—but with me I get a lecture. They should lecture her, too, or not lecture me."
—A middle schooler

Want to get a roomful of middle schoolers wound up? Just ask them what their siblings do that drives them crazy.

What Eighth Graders Told Us About Siblings

"If I'm lying on my bed trying to take a nap, my little brother will come and jump on me. When I tell my mom, she says he just wants to hang out with me. But when I go back to my room he has messed it all up."

"If I have friends over, I try and hang out in one place with them. If we don't send my sister away, she'll sit there with us and listen to us, or she'll be really mean to my friends. She'll make rude comments or be like, 'Oooooooh.' She doesn't understand that I want to hang out with my friends; it's okay if she's there for a little bit, but not the whole entire time."

"Whenever my little brother feels like getting me in trouble, he just shouts, 'Mom!' at the top of his lungs. And so my mom calls me into the room where she is and asks me what I did."

"I'll be doing something by myself, and my little sister will want to do it with me. She always has to do something with me; she never wants to be by herself. We share a room, so I can't get away from her, so sometimes I just lock myself in the bathroom."

"I hate when my brothers get something that I want but I don't get it. If I want a video game, my parents will say no, but they will get my brother whatever he asks for."

Those with younger siblings complain about invasion of privacy and how the younger ones want to be with them wherever they are. They'll tell you they have to do the chores that their little brothers and sisters neglect, and that the younger kids in the family get special privileges. They'll complain about how unfair their parents are, and how easily their siblings get them into trouble.

Those with older siblings? As you may have guessed, they complain about *exactly the same things*. Go back and read that last paragraph and substitute "older" and "big" for "younger" and "little" and you'll get a pretty accurate picture.

The key for parents is to be sensitive to the *perceived* unfairness, whether it's justified or not, without obsessing over keeping everything balanced. It's a fact that life really *isn't* fair, and parents can do a great service for their children by helping them recognize and deal positively with it.

You will rarely be able to convince your middle schooler that you're doing your best to treat every child fairly. However, you greatly increase your chances when you listen with empathy and say something like, "It doesn't seem fair, does it?" Acknowledge their frustration, but don't feel that it's always your job to do something about it.

It will also help to insist that siblings respect each other's privacy as much as possible. No one gets to go through their brother's or sister's room or belongings without asking, and a reasonable request to be left alone should not be ignored. Just as parents sometimes need a little space between them and the kids, kids need a little distance from each other.

Is It Possible to Be a "Cool" Parent?

Heidi was an eighth grade student whose mom was very youthful. Mom both talked and dressed like her middle school daughter, and Heidi often expressed her displeasure to me during class. "I want my mom to be my mom, not my friend," she said. "I have friends to be my friends. I hate it when my mom tries to act all cool to impress my friends. She just embarrasses herself and me."

—Sue Acuña

It's hard for parents of middle schoolers to realize that they're no longer their child's favorite playmate. Cries of, "Come play with me, Mommy!" have given way to complaints of, "Do you have to stand so close to me?"

In an attempt to win back their child's affection, some parents will try to become more like their middle schooler and friends by dressing or talking like them, or by spending lots of time just being with them. The urge to separate from parents begins as young as fifth or sixth grade, and parents need to carefully let it happen. Adolescents create their own language and adopt their own style of dress for just that purpose—to be different from adults, who are not welcome inside their world.

"Cool parents are the ones who don't treat you like a little kid who doesn't understand."
—A middle schooler

"My friend's parents are cool because they don't freak out over little things that she does wrong; they save the freaking out for big stuff, like bad grades."
—A middle schooler

According to middle schoolers, the "cool" parents are the ones who take them seriously, who talk to them as if they were on the same level. They don't talk down to middle schoolers or point out how much they don't know; instead, they let them participate in discussions and never make them feel stupid for not understanding something.

"Cool" parents know how to joke around with middle schoolers without embarrassing them by being too weird. They also know that while a short visit is fine, they're not welcome to linger at a middle school sleepover or party; they may be visitors but not residents. "It's kind of hard to explain," said one wise young lady. "But the coolest parents don't seem to care whether they're cool or not. They just *are* without trying hard to be."

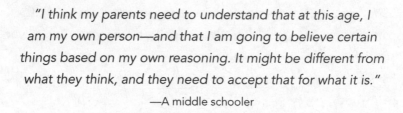

"I think my parents need to understand that at this age, I am my own person—and that I am going to believe certain things based on my own reasoning. It might be different from what they think, and they need to accept that for what it is."
—A middle schooler

"I pretty much believe what my parents have always taught me about right and wrong. I don't really think about rebelling or anything."
—A middle schooler

But cool parents are wise, too. They don't fall for the accusation that they're the only parents who don't allow their kids to do the latest fun thing. Popularity isn't something they strive for, at least in the middle school world. They ask other parents in an effort to confirm some of the more outrageous things their middle schoolers tell them, and they stay connected to other parents in order to more easily compare notes. Middle schoolers don't respect parents who make unreasonable rules, but neither do they respect parents who are easily manipulated. They want "cool" parents who are fair and can be trusted to hold their ground when necessary, but who also know when to relax and have fun with the kids.

Nobody gets it right all the time, and parents who aren't very intuitive will struggle more than parents who are. The important thing is to admit when you've messed up, and to apologize if necessary. You're not apologizing for expecting good behavior—only for the way you asked for it. Remember, it's not *what* you say that matters as much as *how you say it*. If you find yourself at a total loss because you've misunderstood what your middle schooler is trying to tell you, it's okay to say so and to ask for a "do-over," just like you did on the playground back in grade school.

Now *that* would make you a pretty cool parent!

Here's a Thought:

Once a week after a family meal or other gathering where you're all in one place, take turns having an "It's All About You" session. One family member gets to talk, uninterrupted, for up to five full minutes, followed by a time where everyone can ask questions, make comments, or give advice (if it's asked for).

eight

Too Late to Discipline?

"I wish my parents wouldn't yell so loud at me. It doesn't make me want to do whatever it is they want me to do."
—A middle schooler

Another important change during the middle school years is how parents discipline their children. The Time-Out Chair turns into Being Grounded, and Counting Down usually gets left behind entirely. Parents may find themselves frustrated because they can no longer pick up a child and carry him to his bedroom. They may even harbor a secret fear that their middle schooler will stand his ground in defiance, refusing to comply—and then what will the parent do?

This is not a time to be fainthearted. When you discipline your middle schooler, chances are good she's not going to be happy about it. Don't be like the parent who asked for help in issuing a consequence for her daughter's disobedience but balked when the suggestion was made to take away the girl's phone for a few days. "Oh, I couldn't do that," the mom said in dismay. "She'd be so mad!"

Middle schoolers are smart. If they know their parents fear their anger, they'll use it to keep from getting into trouble. A better tactic is to offer to make the consequence worse if your child continues to react with so much disrespect. Then be sure you follow through and do what you say.

This is also not the time to be a tyrant, looming over your middle schooler with an attitude of "You will obey me—or else!" When you're faced with inappropriate behavior or a refusal to follow directions, it's important that you stay calmly in control.

One Mom's Regret

A frustrated mom came up to me after a seminar to tell me about her rebellious teenage daughter. "I've been the boss her whole life," she said, "and my daughter has no doubt who's in charge. She's had to obey me without question or the consequences are drastic."

Before I could reply, she pointed to a sullen, angry-looking girl waiting just outside the door. "See that girl?" she asked. "That's my daughter. She leaned closer, with tears in her eyes. "She hates me. Do you have anything that could make her love me again?"

—Cynthia Tobias

In her book *You Can't Make Me (But I Can Be Persuaded)*, Cynthia teaches parents strategies for sharing control with their children without compromising parental authority. For example, if you told your middle schooler to take out the trash before going to bed and it didn't get done, don't barge into her room and yell at her. Wait until the next morning and let her know that since you had to take out the trash yourself, she will not be allowed to stay after school and watch the volleyball game. It's even more effective if you can come up with natural consequences and make the punishment fit the crime. In the trash-before-bed example, a more natural consequence could be to assign extra chores for the next week.

Every consequence should come with instruction, such as, "Sharing the household chores is an important part of belonging to this family, and everyone is expected to help out." If you can explain why the consequence is necessary or appropriate, you'll get much better results. Remember, kids don't have to agree with your reasons—but their cooperation will improve if you at least have some.

Keep in mind that it's not necessary for your middle schooler to be angry at a consequence for it to be effective. In fact, some young teens enjoy the power of *not* showing their parents how upset they are. They adopt an attitude that says, "Is that the best you can do?" or "Punish me all you want; I don't care." Don't be fooled; they *do* care. It's just that they don't want to give you the satisfaction of seeing how much. Don't let them ruffle your feathers; stick to your consequence. Nothing frustrates a middle schooler like an adult who stays calm and reasonable despite his or her best efforts to make you mad.

When Wills Collide

"My dad says I'm just like my mom; we're both really, really stubborn."
—A middle schooler

Once you start practicing, you'll find it becomes easier to communicate with your middle schooler without as much tension and frustration. In her book *You Can't Make Me (But I Can Be Persuaded)*, Cynthia offers insights on communicating with strong-willed kids of all ages. Here are a few ideas you can try right away:

- Keep your voice calm and steady. If you're the first one to get angry and begin to shout, you lose.
- Quietly say something like, "I can't believe you just said that." Then walk away from the conflict if you need a moment to calm down and regroup.
- Remember how important it is for your middle schooler to save face. Instead of immediately criticizing or punishing, ask a question like, "Are you sure you want to do this?" or "Is that really what you think?" You may still have to do things the hard way—but sometimes your child will seize the opportunity to gracefully back down.
- If you have to repeat the same consequence multiple times, do so; stronger or more drastic punishment will not necessarily give you better results. Prove that you have more "staying power" and that you will remain calm and consistent.
- Resist the temptation to ask questions that will escalate the battle, such as, "What were you thinking?" or "What's the matter with you?" Try to avoid using "why" and "you" in the same sentence.
- Don't be afraid to delay dealing out consequences until you're both calmer. Say, "I'm too angry to be reasonable right now. We'll talk about this later."

Are You Sure They're Arguing?

"I always get yelled at for talking back, but to me we're just having a conversation."

—A middle schooler

*"I was trying to explain something, but my mom said
I was talking back, and she took my phone."*
—A middle schooler

Middle schoolers are trying hard to learn the rules of the adult world, so they ask as many "why" questions as they did when they were toddlers. Unfortunately, they don't always ask their questions in a respectful tone of voice, or they choose the wrong time to ask a question—so it sounds like they're challenging their parents' authority. Attentive parents will listen to the tone and take note of the circumstances before dismissing questions and arguments as "talking back."

If you can't come up with a good answer to a question right away, it's okay to say so, but assure your middle schooler that you'll think about it and get back to him or her. And remember: "Because I said so!" is sometimes a necessary answer, but it isn't the most satisfying. If there's a good reason—safety, maybe, or consideration for others— then state it. If there isn't a good reason, it's okay to say so, but "I don't know why; it's just important to me right now" is better than "Just do what I say!" It's also okay to say you're just too mad to talk about it right now, but you'll explain later, when everybody's calm.

Dealing with Disrespect

*"I feel bad sometimes after I've yelled
at my dad. I don't know why he makes
me so mad, but he does."*
—A middle schooler

"I wish that my stepdad would understand the things he does wrong, like hypocrisy, and I wish when I ask him to stop then he actually would try to stop and fix it. Like, just 'man up.'"
—A middle schooler

"My parents still talk to me like I'm six years old! When will they figure out I'm not a little kid anymore?"
—A middle schooler

When your middle schooler is disrespectful, make sure your response doesn't sound like it's disrespectful in return. Raising your voice to match theirs or returning name calling for name calling ("You're such a spoiled brat!") won't help your cause. In fact, you'll get better results if you *lower* your voice. Your goal, remember, is to deal with your young person on an adult level. Model the tone and manner you want your child to use with you.

An effective technique is something we call "The One." Simply hold up one hand with your forefinger pointing to the ceiling (as if you're counting). Don't say anything like "Stop" or "That's enough." Just hold up your finger and wait. It's less threatening than pointing *at* someone, but signifies that this would be a good place to stop.

When there's a pause, repeat what you just said in a calm and reasonable tone. Or invite your middle schooler to repeat her last words: "How about if you try that again—only more respectfully this time?" (This is also a useful technique to stop a middle schooler from interrupting.)

Another helpful technique is to use one-word prompts. For example, say "hostile" when an unfriendly comment is made, or "manners" if someone is being too demanding. "Language" is good when someone says something inappropriate, as is "volume" when someone speaks too loudly. These are gentle, non-threatening reminders that allow middle schoolers to change their behavior without losing face. Your words are especially effective when accompanied with a smile. Don't be surprised, however, if they use the same one-word prompts on you!

If your middle schooler tries to sidetrack you, avoid the new topic altogether, or point your finger up in the air and call it as it is: "You're trying to change the subject, but we need to talk about these grades." This may cause the middle schooler to seek a new path on which to lead the parent, one more likely to get a rise out of her, such as "You just hate me!" or "You're never satisfied! You don't care about me!" This time, instead of being angry, a parent may be hurt and feel the need to defend herself. Don't fall for it; stick to the subject at hand and remain as calm as you can. Eventually your middle schooler will give up—or if not, you can simply say this obviously isn't a good time and refuse to discuss it until later.

Incentives vs. Crime and Punishment

"My parents take away my phone if my grades are bad, but they never give me a way to earn it back."

—A middle schooler

"I've taken away everything he cares about and he doesn't even respond when I ground him! How else can I make him do what I tell him to do?"

This is a familiar refrain among parents of middle schoolers. It often happens when there have been many frustrating incidents, one after another, and you're so irritated at your child you can't think straight. You're certainly not alone. But slow down, take a breath, and consider some good alternatives.

Let's say the problem is a failing grade. It's late in the semester and your student doesn't seem to have any desire to dig in and bring the grade up—he's just eager to take a vacation and start over next semester. You might try this approach: Tell your middle schooler that you remember how hard it was to put your best effort into school when you knew that vacation was right around the corner. Ask about upcoming tests or projects, and then ask what it would be worth to work hard enough to get a passing grade instead of simply writing off the whole semester. If the suggested reward is out of the question ("a trip to Disneyland"), be prepared to negotiate: "I was thinking more along the lines of dinner at your favorite restaurant."

Some parents may object because this sounds suspiciously like bribery. But maybe it's just another way of looking at incentives. Whatever you call it, it usually works better than simply increasing the punishment. After all, what gets most parents out of bed and off to work on a cold winter morning? Sometimes teenagers need a "paycheck," too.

Chores for Middle Schoolers

"Why do parents give you more chores to do before you've finished the first ones?"
—A middle schooler

"I hate it when I just get home from school and want to take a break and my mom tells me she has a list of chores for me to do."
—A middle schooler

"No matter how much I clean the bathroom, my mom complains and then cleans it herself. Why do I even have to do it?"
—A middle schooler

~~~~~~~~~~~

"I finally just gave up and decided to do all the housework myself," the exhausted mom complained. "I get so tired of the battles, the attitude, the halfhearted job they do. It's so much easier to do it all myself."

"I only have a few hours to spend with them when I get home from work," said another parent. "I don't want to spend that time fighting about chores."

The complaints and resistance by your middle schooler can wear you down until you're tempted to skip the battle of assigned chores altogether. But the benefits of taking responsibility for completing household tasks are many—including better self-esteem, learning important life skills, and practicing a strong work ethic.

Parents get the most cooperation when they involve their kids in decisions about who will do what when. Whenever possible, present compelling problems to be solved instead of simply a list of chores to do. For example, "We need to have the trash can at the curb by 8:00 A.M. on Fridays. Dad's already gone to work by then, and Mom's making lunches and getting kids ready for school. What are our options?" Be prepared to negotiate and adapt. Here's how Sue handled it:

> I called a family meeting and explained that we needed a system to make sure daily chores got done. I listed the tasks that needed to be done on a daily basis: unloading and loading the dishwasher, setting and clearing the table, and taking care of the kitty's food and litter box. We discussed how often they wanted to switch off (every week), and I let them choose which day to switch (Saturday is the first day of the new chore week).

Next we discussed consequences for failure to comply. Grounding from screen time was an obvious choice, but the boys also came up with the idea that offenders would have to be at the beck and call of Mom and Dad for the *entire weekend*, and Mom and Dad would be sure they worked *really hard*. (I remember enforcing this only once.)

The chore chart lived on the refrigerator; I made it by printing out a simple chart and strengthening it with adhesive photo laminate. I bought some little wood pieces and painted them, then glued them onto strong magnets. Every Saturday somebody (usually the guy on dishes) switched the magnets. Later we revised the list: The table guy also did trash and re-cycle, and the guy on cat duty also helped with food prep. After washing his hands, please.

Chores are important, but keep in mind that middle schoolers have other pressures on them from homework, sports, and other activities. That doesn't mean they get out of doing them; it means you need to let them know you're aware of how busy they are and help them learn to manage their time. The house will be cleaner, the kids will be more independent, and the parents will be less frustrated.

Reasonable Expectations

Your middle schooler should be able to do the following basic chores:

- unloading and loading the dishwasher
- washing dishes by hand
- packing a lunch
- washing and vacuuming the car
- sweeping and vacuuming floors
- dusting furniture

- washing windows
- emptying the trash
- feeding and bathing pets
- making beds
- sorting and organizing drawers and closets

With your instruction and involvement, these more advanced chores can be added:

- sorting, washing, and folding laundry
- weeding and mowing the lawn
- planning and cooking a meal
- mopping floors
- babysitting younger siblings for short periods
- changing bedsheets
- cleaning shower, tub, and toilet
- ironing clothes
- setting alarm and getting up on time

Here's a Thought:

On the subject of discipline, try this: During a calm time, when nobody's in trouble, ask your middle schooler what form of discipline would be most effective with him or her. Offer choices such as extra chores, loss of phone or gaming privileges, and grounding; be open to reasonable suggestions. Be prepared to negotiate and compromise until you find something agreeable to both of you.

As for chores, make a list of heavier-duty weekend tasks, leaving room for family members to sign up by the ones they're volunteering for. Have Mom and Dad sign up, too (let the kids sign up first). Rotate the chore duty periodically.

nine

Verbalizing Values

~~~~~~

A parent sought me out at church, wanting advice on how to get her daughter to be more polite. "She interrupts me all the time, and she never says 'please' or 'thank you' unless I remind her to." She continued, "My husband just laughs and says she's me all over again. Which is actually true!"

I cautioned her not to say that in front of her daughter, because it would seem to give the girl permission to continue being rude. Sometimes when we don't like our middle schoolers' behavior, we need to ask ourselves where they picked it up.

—Sue Acuña

~~~~~~

Parents often complain that since today's youth culture seems to dismiss any sort of parental boundaries, it makes it harder for them to teach about and expect moral and spiritual values without seeming hopelessly out of touch with the rest of the world. But almost all the middle schoolers who shared with us reinforced the idea that reasonable boundaries make them feel more secure, and growing up with clear moral and spiritual beliefs helps them make better decisions. Of course, even when parents do their best to transfer their beliefs and values to their children there's no guarantee their kids will follow their path.

But middle schoolers want to believe in something, and they want to know their parents have solid reasons for acting the way they do. This is why it's so important for parents to start building a strong and positive relationship with each child as early as possible. Don't be afraid to instill strong values as your child grows—learning good manners, respectful behavior, and spiritual truths will be a plus the rest of your child's life. No matter how far your child may stray from what you believe, there will always be a solid foundation and a place he or she will love coming home to.

Jack's story is a great illustration of this:

In junior high, I didn't know the word "identity." Two things happened in eighth grade. I looked around and I realized that I was one of only a very few in the class that had a crew cut. I felt out of place, so I grew out my hair. Then I realized I had a choice of how long and that how long I grew it depended on which group I was trying to get into. I thought about that. I thought it would be cool to get in the druggie group, but I didn't know how, and I had to cut my hair in order to play basketball. When you're an athlete, you don't have the druggie look.

I went to church because it was important to my mom. I was in a youth group—even became president of the junior high group. But in the eighth grade I was walking home and mulling over a section of text in my science book discussing theories of the formation of the earth. There were a couple theories and I remember thinking that there is no need for God here—that I believed in the gaseous theory of the particles forming from gases. Then I made a decision. I knew it was a conversion decision and that I was an atheist. I said out loud,

"I'm an atheist." I didn't talk to anyone about it or ask anybody, and I stayed at church as president of the youth group—no one knew I was an atheist.

I remember walking home with a church girl (I didn't really know what a Christian was, but I knew there was something different about her). She told me that God loved me which I thought was the weirdest thing I'd ever heard. In her house it felt different—she was nice to me and I liked walking with her. I went to Sunday school for two reasons—donuts and pretty girls. Once I got there I would argue with the Sunday school teacher, especially about the creation stories.

I was an argumentative, analytical teenager—but being in that environment eventually brought me back to God.

When you get right down to it, everything comes back to relationship—our relationship with God, our spouse, our children. If we can get the basics of a good relationship down, over half the battle is already won.

Spiritual Growth Spurts

Our "identical" twin boys were only six the Easter they each made a special card for Mommy. Robert, the compliant, easy-to-please son, had drawn a beautiful picture of the cross with a Bible and lily and the words: "To Mommy—Christ is Risen. Happy Easter!" Michael, our wonderful strong-willed son, presented a card that was plain on the outside, but inside there was a colorful Star Wars character and the words: "Happy Easter from Jabba the Hutt." These two boys were the same age with the same parents growing up in the same household, and yet they were so different in their outlooks and perspectives! It's been a fascinating journey as we've watched their physical, emotional, and spiritual development.

—Cynthia Tobias

Middle schoolers have physical, mental, and emotional growth spurts, so you shouldn't be surprised when they hit a *spiritual* growth spurt. No longer content with just "Jesus loves me this I know, for the Bible tells me so," they are beginning to ask questions such as, "How do I know God is real?" "How do we know our religion is the right one?" "Why do we go to this church?" "When do I get to decide whether I want to go to church or not?"

"I don't like getting up early on Sundays for church, and most of the time the sermon is boring. But I like being able to hang out with my friends, and sometimes we talk about some good stuff in Sunday school."

—A middle schooler

As Christian parents we dedicated our children to God, who created and designed them with all their uniqueness. Part of that uniqueness may involve times of doubt, which is when children need their parents to guide them in navigating the choppy waters of uncertainty over what they believe.

Remember, middle schoolers are right in the middle of some of the most intense self-discovery they'll ever experience. Their whole world is beginning to shift and re-settle, and it's natural to develop questions and doubts about the faith they may have simply taken for granted when they were young children.

Wise parents will welcome the questioning as a sign that their children are beginning the process of personalizing their faith, of making it their own rather than merely that of their parents. If parents don't feel equipped to answer the tougher questions, they can seek help and advice from youth pastors, who are specially trained to deal with the inquiring minds of kids who are searching for answers.

"I know I should be able to find answers to all my questions in the Bible, but I don't even know where to start looking."
—A middle schooler

Because they are still making the leap from concrete thoughts to more abstract reasoning, some middle schoolers will see Christians as "good" and non-Christians as "bad." They'll find it hard to understand how people who call themselves Christians can ever do mean or unlawful things. Parents should explain that Christians aren't perfect, but we can be thankful knowing grace is available for the asking. Just like adults, middle schoolers struggle with the idea of grace, and parents should be prepared to engage in many conversations on this topic alone. Other topics that fascinate this age group include sin, baptism, communion, and heaven. Parents shouldn't be afraid to share their own doubts or confusion over certain faith topics; in fact, they can suggest looking for answers together.

This is a good time to continue (or begin) times of personal Bible study and devotions, and to encourage middle schoolers to do the same. Talk about your own prayer life, speaking in a casual manner:

"In my prayers today I mentioned your test." Model the faith life you want your child to have.

Some parents grow concerned because their children treat youth group or Sunday school as a social occasion rather than a time of spiritual growth. No need to worry—it's perfectly okay for them to attend because they want to spend time with their friends. God uses many means to get us where He wants us to be, and He can certainly use youth group activities as a way to get a message to your middle schooler.

Involve your middle schoolers in decisions regarding their worship life, but retain the right to make final decisions. For example, you might tell them you'll be willing to discuss their church attendance when they reach the age of 16—but don't promise them they won't have to go to church then, unless you really mean it.

Consistently model for them what a life built on faith in God looks like. What happens when we run into challenges to our faith? How do we handle concern about finances or unexpected setbacks?

We can't force our children to choose our spiritual path or to follow our beliefs. It's not uncommon to have children who grow up with a solid faith and a strong foundation in the church to walk away when they grow older. Don't panic. Build the strongest foundation you can while you have your children under your roof.

It's been said that God is the perfect Father—and even He has wayward children. Far from losing hope or giving in to despair, He loves them when they don't love Him back, accepts them as they are, opens His arms when they weep, and keeps the table set for their return.

Lead by your example, and admit your mistakes when they happen. Share more instruction than sermons, more grace than blind justice, more love than retribution. As your middle schooler seeks to find his own way, make sure he knows there are two things he can always count on: God's unconditional love, and yours.

Love in Earthen Vessels

We have love
contained in an earthen vessel,
and we pour it out
with as much care
and in the greatest abundance
we can,
even though we can't always tell
how it is received
or the good it has done.

And God,
in His infinite love and understanding,
keeps our earthen pitchers full,
directs the flow of love,
and pours the contents
directly from His own pitcher
onto the places
we may have missed.

—Cynthia Ulrich Tobias

Letting Kids Take Spiritual Responsibility

*How can you build self-discipline and self-control in middle
schoolers?*

*With no encouragement from me, some of my stu-
dents decided to practice both of these qualities for Lent.
Giving up something for Lent is fairly common, but the
idea of adding something was relatively new to me.*

*I took a quick survey, and my students were giving up
Facebook, Twitter, tomatoes, soda, sweets, salty foods,*

and sugar. When I asked what kinds of activities they'd added (or pledged to do more often), the answers were "working out," "walking the dog," "stretching and push-ups," "spending more time with the family," helping "Dad more in Sunday school," and "being active for at least an hour every day." I was so inspired I decided to spend 30 minutes on my treadmill every night.

We've had discussions in class about the difference between self-discipline and self-control, and we came up with this: Self-discipline is making yourself do something you don't want to do, while self-control is keeping yourself from doing something you shouldn't do. When you get right down to it, adding or subtracting things for Lent (or any other time) is all about those two qualities. My middle schoolers proved they could take that challenge.

—Sue Acuña

Does Anyone Still Teach Manners?

While discussing how to improve classroom relation-ships, one girl said she didn't feel the need to be friendly to girls she didn't like. "That would be like faking nice," was her argument. I explained that the world revolved around people "faking nice" to each other. In the adult world, "faking nice" is another term for courtesy, tact, and manners.

It can be tough to teach middleschoolers manners, especially if they think it's all about being phony. Help your young person understand the difference between dishonesty and doing the right thing even when we don't feel like it.

—Sue Acuña

~~~~~~~~~~

While inconsiderate behavior may be common, there are no excuses for rudeness. Good manners can—and should—be taught to middle schoolers. When they realize it actually makes them appear more grown up, they're usually more willing to learn and use them.

They should be expected to:
- shake hands when meeting someone new for the first time
- look people in the eye when speaking to them
- hold doors open for those coming behind them
- give up their seats to adults, especially the elderly
- wait patiently in line
- order their own food in a restaurant
- say please and thank you every time it is appropriate
- cover their mouths when sneezing or coughing
- refrain from burping and making other bodily noises in public
- keep their voices low in public places
- remove their hats in a restaurant and during the singing or playing of the national anthem
- ask, "May I please . . ." instead of demanding, "I need to . . ."
- say "Excuse me" when interrupting, or when they bump into someone
- offer to help their parents carry groceries and other objects

Parents need to remember, however, that manners should be modeled by them so their children can see that it's a grown-up thing to do. When your middle schooler spontaneously demonstrates good manners (e.g., by holding the door open for you), be sure to make a comment to indicate you've noticed. But keep it low-key, or else they'll be reluctant to do it again.

Here's a Thought:

At the dinner table or another place and time when the family is together, work on coming up with a "mission statement" that describes what your family is all about and what you seek to accomplish together. Encourage your kids to design a "family logo" as commercial organizations do. Emphasize that your mission should reflect the values and beliefs your family wants to represent to the rest of the world.

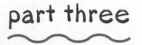

part three

FRIENDS AND OTHER PROBLEMS

ten

Finding Where They Fit

~~~~~~

"Friends will listen to you complain when your parents won't. Parents just want to rant and tell you that you shouldn't feel that way."
—A middle schooler

"One day I snapped at my friend James and I was feeling really bad. My friend Michele looked over at me and said, 'Come here; you need a hug.' My mom would've just yelled at me for being so mean."
—A middle schooler

~~~~~~

Many middle schoolers say they want to spend more time with their friends than with their families because they feel their friends understand them but their parents don't. All those feelings that keep bubbling up inside can be confusing to them, and they don't appreciate it when parents or older siblings say they shouldn't feel that way—or ask that annoying question, "What's wrong with *you?*"

It's all part of that need to be understood. Like most of us, middle schoolers gravitate toward people who express understanding, and that's usually people close to their own ages. They also complain that family members are often off in their own corners, each person doing his or her own thing; when they get together with friends, they have more fun. Just going to the mall and walking around is considered more fun than being at home, mostly because they can be loud and silly and no one tells them to stop.

One of the biggest adjustments parents have to make when their kids start middle school is having new friends enter the picture— friends the parents don't know, from families they also don't know. How can they allow their children to visit the home of someone they've never seen?

Parents worry that while they think they've raised their children with good values, those values will all be undone by a stranger. One good solution is to meet the new parents at a school event and get to know them—maybe even comparing house rules, like those governing which movies or television shows they allow their children to watch. Another is to have the new friend over for an afternoon and get a sense of what he or she is like. It's also perfectly okay for parents to refuse to let middle schoolers spend the night at new friends' houses until they've had a chance to check them out.

As hard as it is to let go, this is when it starts. Until they have reason to suspect otherwise, parents may need to trust that their lessons have stuck, and that their kids will make good choices. Middle schoolers want to spend more time with peers, because those peers are the people with whom they'll grow up to be adults. This is the time of life when they begin separating themselves from their families in order to start learning how to live apart from them. But parents should rest assured that their middle schoolers will still seek them out when major events—good and bad—occur, because at this age they are still young enough to want their parents' approval or assistance!

Who Am I Now?

~~~~~~~~~~

What makes somebody cool?
"How you carry yourself. Walking with confidence is cool;
looking down and not making eye contact is not."
—A middle schooler

"Not caring what other people think—
being okay with who you are."
—A middle schooler

~~~~~~~~~~

As they experience physical changes, middle schoolers have to figure out how that new body in the mirror reflects who they really are. Their physiques can change their identities at school, as classmates are quick to comment:

"Wow, you're *so tall!*"

"Look at those three guys—Todd looks so short compared to the other two!"

"Ha! Out of the corner of my eye, I thought you were the *teacher!*"

Middle schoolers try on new identities to see if they fit. If everyone says Justin should play basketball because he's gotten so tall, he may just take on the challenge—even if he's always professed a hatred for the game. If Danielle is encouraged to flirt with a boy because she's looking more mature than her classmates, she may feel obliged to try. These new identities can fade away almost as quickly as they arrived, so parents would do well not to get too excited or worried until they see how long an interest will last. The exception: if a teen's new identity includes dangerous or inappropriate behavior. This is the age, after all, when kids often smoke for the first time in an effort to look as "cool" as their friends. Experimentation with drinking and drugs can occur for the same reason. If you become aware of such behavior, you need to address it head-on. We'll give you some "red flags" to watch for in Chapter 12.

Middle schoolers also worry about not fitting in: *Will people think I'm too tall or too short? Too fat or too skinny? Will they hate me now that I have acne (or braces or glasses)? Is orange still a popular color, or will I look stupid if I wear an orange shirt?* Middle schoolers don't always have a strong sense of "self" because their identities are not yet formed. If, for example, two high school girls go shopping, one might pull a sweater off the rack and say, "You should buy this; it is so *you*." Middle schoolers rarely do that, because it's still too hard to pinpoint just what that "you" is like.

The Unwritten Rules

"If the eighth graders don't like you when you're in seventh grade, nobody will like you."
—A middle schooler

"When you're in sixth grade, the eighth graders like you because you're younger and cute, but not as a best friend (you're not allowed in their circle)."
—A middle schooler

Unwritten rules—ones that are already familiar to those who know the system—can be more intimidating than anything in the student handbook. Middle school social rules govern everything from which shoes are acceptable to who sits where in the lunchroom.

For example, if there's a mix of girls from different grades in the bathroom at the same time, the older girls have priority at being closest to the mirror; younger girls are expected to stand back and wait their turn. And while adults look at students in grades six, seven, and eight as being all about the same, in middle school you're expected to know your place. It's okay for an eighth grade boy to flirt with a seventh grade girl; in fact, all the girls will be flattered that he's interested in one of their own. However, it can cause all-out war if the eighth grade girls flirt with the seventh grade boys—because now the seventh grade girls feel that the older ones are encroaching on their territory.

What Eighth Graders Told Us About Unwritten Rules

"You have to be a leader."

"Try not to mess up your eighth grade year; people are looking up to you."

"It's okay to be a dork because you're the oldest, and it doesn't matter what they think."

"Don't be a narc."

"Don't annoy the older students by trying to talk to them all the time or by being overly crazy."

"To eighth graders, sixth graders are still little kids."

"It's okay to enjoy the attention of younger students, but they're not welcome at your social gatherings."

Middle schoolers also know that while older students are expected to tolerate younger ones and even be friendly to them, they're not allowed to invite them to social gatherings. An eighth grader, for instance, would never invite a sixth grader to a birthday party. And sixth graders are supposed to know when they're welcome to talk to the older students and when they should go away because they're driving their elders crazy.

There are also rules about who can get away with what. If you're pretty far up the "cool" scale, you can do silly things like break out in a chorus of "Jesus Loves Me," and everyone will either laugh or sing along. But if you're lower in social status, such an action will result in a disapproving silence or comments like, "So *immature!*"

One More Unwritten Rule

It's observed by students of all personality types and abilities. It's The Code, and it says, "You do not get your friends, or people you like, into trouble."

I used to be surprised at how even class leaders and straight-A students would adhere to The Code, until I figured out something critical: Most middle school students see it as a moral obligation, right up there with offering to share your lunch when your friend doesn't have one. It's a sign of your loyalty, a test of your friendship; you just don't rat out your friends.

Parents underestimate the power of this concept—even though it's also true in the adult world, where it's called "professional courtesy."

—Sue Acuña

Crossing an unwritten line can result in a new student receiving anything from a disdainful look to outright hostility: "Dude, what's *wrong* with you?" When you're in middle school, you're already pretty sure everyone is judging you and finding you lacking. You live in fear of real and imagined criticism and scrutiny. It's common for a middle schooler's self-esteem to take a noticeable dive during the first few weeks of school.

This is when your child may especially appreciate encouragement and empathy for what he or she is going through. It's tempting to downplay what's going on ("Oh, that's nothing—*I* didn't know anybody at all when *I* started middle school!") or reassure them with overused platitudes ("Things will look better in the morning"), but such a response won't be appreciated. Instead, a simple "Yeah, I remember how awkward I felt in junior high" will convey understanding in a way that lets kids know they're not the only ones to ever experience such pain and uncertainty.

Here's a Thought:

Ask your middle schooler what would happen if a sixth grader were invited to an eighth grader's party. Follow up with a question about what your middle schooler would do if invited to a party with older (or younger) students. The answers you get may give you some insight into the unwritten rules in your child's school.

eleven

Young Love,
Old Challenges

"*Everybody pressures you to tell them what boy you like, but I don't like any of them that way. I wish we could just go back to all being friends, because there's so much drama when people start going out together.*"
—A middle schooler

"*My mom wants to know what girls I like in my class. Like I'm going to tell my mom!*"
—A middle schooler

"*I spent most of one day interviewing over a dozen girls to get to the root of the hostile atmosphere among most of the girls in my class. It boiled down to two girls fighting over a boy they both liked, but they'd been egged on by a third girl who was playing one against the other. When the facts were revealed, the two girls were united in their anger at the third girl—and I had a whole new situation to deal with.*"
—Sue Acuña

James and Mandy are in love and plan to get married. They like to spend every minute together—hugging, holding hands, and gazing into each other's eyes. They make a cute couple—especially since they're both five years old.

When middle schoolers hear that adults view their relationships the same way seventh graders would view James and Mandy, they get offended. At the ripe old age of 12 or 13, they feel mature enough to handle "real" love and relationships.

As early as fifth or sixth grade, body shapes change, faces mature, and some middle schoolers get a whole new perspective on gender. Instead of "Boys are gross," it's now, "Do you think he likes me?" And just like that, young love starts to bloom.

What happens next greatly depends on how parents respond. Unfortunately, some parents encourage dating at an early age. They think it's cute to drive kids to a movie or out for pizza. It *is* cute when they're in the first flush of romance, but there's nothing cute about the emotional devastation after a breakup. At this age, middle school emotions are all over the place as it is. Self-esteem bounces from high to low; many relationships become sources of drama, insecurity, and possessiveness.

The middle school brain doesn't help much. Studies show that the back part of the brain, where ideas and impulses form, is way ahead of the front part, which is where reason and caution live.[5] So the voice that says, "You know what would be cool (or hilarious or awesome)?" is much louder than the voice that says, "You could get hurt (or pregnant or grounded)." This can cause a teen to quickly progress from the thrill of holding hands and touching lips to bigger thrills—without any thought to the risks involved.

Why Is Dating a Big Deal?

"We used to be best friends, all the way back to first grade. But in eighth grade everybody said we should be a couple, so we started going out. Then he started liking somebody else and we broke up, and we don't even talk anymore. I not only lost a boyfriend—I lost my best friend."
—A middle schooler

"I don't understand the point of dating in seventh or eighth grade, because it's not like you're going to marry that person. Why would you date when you're just going to wind up breaking up in a few months anyway?"
—A middle schooler

When middle schoolers date, it can lead to all kinds of complications such as abusive relationships, sexual experimentation, isolation, guilt, depression, loss of friendships, and lower grades. Even the simpler, less complicated relationships eventually end in a broken heart and a huge amount of self-doubt.

Young teens will always have crushes. Boys will dream about being seen with certain girls; girls will write their first names with the boys' last names to see how it looks. And kids will pair off and "go out." But that doesn't mean they actually need to be *going* anywhere together.

Parents can help by setting some dating guidelines early. For example: "You can go out with a group, but not on an actual date until you're 16." Parents can also avoid the temptation to make too much of a relationship. Don't encourage the exchange of personalized jewelry, for example, or spend too much time asking about the "girlfriend" or "boyfriend." If a teen does get involved in a relationship in middle school, parents should be casual about it. Trying to prevent these things usually only makes them more attractive. Pushing too hard to make them look like high school relationships creates undue pressure and can lead to disastrous consequences.

Our best advice? Take the middle road—sort of an "Oh, that's nice" approach. Ask a question or two, then let it go. Be available if advice is needed, but don't offer ideas like taking her flowers or inviting him to her birthday party.

Above all, *don't* encourage them to go out on a date. Some parents think it's "sweet" that their 13-year-old has a boyfriend, and will drop the couple off to watch a movie unsupervised. Some middle schoolers are quick to express their disapproval: "We went to a movie with Kelly and Drew, and they were all making out and stuff. It was so gross!"

If they find themselves in a dating situation, middle schoolers will feel pressure to do what's expected—or what peers are nudging them to do ("Did you kiss her yet? What are you waiting for?").

Sue handles this topic every year with her middle school students:

I teach my eighth graders that there's a continuum of physical intimacy, designed by God for marriage. It begins with holding hands, and the first time you hold hands with your boyfriend or girlfriend, your heart beats faster and you get the tingles. It's awesome! But after a while, it's not exciting anymore, and so you move on to kissing. First comes small kisses, and then deeper ones.

Now the part of your brain that controls your physical self kicks into high gear, because it knows where this is supposed to lead. Your body is ready to respond, because it doesn't know that you're not married. The moral part of your brain knows this is wrong, but it's being drowned out by the other part. From deeper kissing it's a short step to making out and then "going all the way." This is all part of God's plan for the closest two human beings can be, the strongest kind of love they can express—*when they're married.*

If you're experimenting with this kind of intimacy before you're married, where should you decide to stop before it leads to trouble?

Most middle schoolers can figure out that you have to be careful how you kiss—if you kiss at all. Wise parents will not encourage handholding or kissing at age 11 or 12, because there are still many years to wait before marriage. No need to get that brain jump-started!

If you're concerned about your middle schoolers dating, or if you fear they are already sexually active, this would be another good time to consult *The Focus on the Family Guide to Talking with Your Kids about Sex*, which offers tips on how to set rules and limits for dating.

"I think people should wait until high school to date, when it might matter more. I want to wait until my ninth grade year before I start dating, because people in eighth grade take it too seriously and it leads to too much drama."

—A middle schooler

Here's a Thought:

Middle schoolers are often pressured by friends to have boy-girl birthday parties. Parents can make it easier on children with a ruling such as, "You can have those kinds of parties when you turn 16, but for now just invite the girls (or boys)." This will take the pressure off your middle schooler and head off situations he or she isn't prepared to handle—like "Truth or Dare" games that involve interaction between couples.

twelve

Responding to Red Flags

~~~~~~~~

"Can you show me the cuts?" I asked.

Lifting up her sleeve, she showed me several parallel lines etched into her arm.

"I made them with a kitchen knife," she said.

"Have your parents seen those?"

"Yeah, but I just told them the cat did it and they believed me."

—Sue Acuña

~~~~~~~~

There's no shortage of books and Internet articles that will give you detailed lists for recognizing signs of behavior disorders, learning disabilities, drug and alcohol abuse, and much more. We just want to give you a few broad and basic guidelines for recognizing some behaviors that should raise a red flag. If you notice one or more of the following, it's worth a second look—and maybe even a visit to a qualified professional for advice and/or treatment.

How to Spot Possible Substance Abuse

"I know people my age who do drugs,
and it's weird just knowing that."
—A middle schooler

"I know a guy who did drugs in junior high, and one
time at church he tried to snort lemonade mix."
—A middle schooler

"My cousin was in seventh grade and her eighth-
grade boyfriend was smoking pot. He told her
he quit, but then he got arrested for selling
drugs when some kids got caught with drugs
and said they'd gotten them from him."
—A middle schooler

If your child is involved with substance abuse, he or she probably is displaying at least one or two of the following:

- acting especially secretive, demanding excessive privacy and avoiding eye contact
- behavior at school that's dramatically different from behavior at home
- suddenly changing close friends, or hanging out with a new group of friends you don't know
- experiencing prolonged and extreme mood swings
- using a lot of profanity or language that's out of character for the rest of the family

- acting particularly mean or cruel to siblings or friends
- uncharacteristically late with assignments or showing a sudden decline in grades

This is certainly not a comprehensive list. In fact, the most important sign that something's wrong is good old-fashioned parental instincts. Don't ignore your personal radar. If you notice a red flag or have any sense of uneasiness, start by talking to your child openly about your concerns. Then talk to others who see your child on a regular basis—teachers, coaches, or parents of their close friends. If you believe there's a real problem, look for the right professional to help you solve it. Start with a trusted pediatrician or counselor for further evaluation.

Don't automatically assume the worst—but don't ignore the obvious, either. Be sure to observe your child's reaction when you express concern. Often you'll learn more from what they *don't* say than from the responses they give you. The best idea of all is to take the time to talk to your child on a regular basis so that you'll quickly notice something different in his actions.

Depression

"I don't know what's wrong. Some days
I just want to stay in bed and I feel like
crying all the time. It's like, what's the point
of even getting up? I just don't care."
—A middle schooler

Most middle schoolers have bad days, influenced by hormones, circumstances, and lack of sleep, among other causes. How can a parent know when a middle schooler moves from a bad few days to actual depression?

If you have serious concerns, don't wait to get help. Ask your pediatrician or family doctor for referral to a therapist, or get advice from your school counselor or psychologist.

If it doesn't seem that serious yet, make a note of how long your child has been feeling blue. More than a week, especially if there's no obvious reason (such as failing grades or a breakup), may mean it's more than just moodiness. Withdrawal from close friends or loss of interest in what used to be a favorite activity may indicate depression, but then again it may mean a falling-out with a friend.

Try asking your middle schooler for insight (see our communication tips in Chapter 7). If you don't get anywhere with that (and many parents won't), check in with other adults who work with your child on a regular basis and see what kind of behavior they observe away from home. If their concern mirrors yours, it's definitely time to seek professional help.

Eating Disorders

"My friend and I just wanted to get in shape for basketball, so she found a diet and we went on it. But now she's making herself throw up and she hardly eats anything, and she's made me promise not to tell her mom. I'm so worried, but I don't want her to get mad at me."
—A middle schooler

Young people—girls *and* boys—are under tremendous pressure to have "perfect" (read *slender*) bodies. They're also experiencing some emotional issues that you probably didn't have to deal with. Those can lead to eating disorders as well.

Warning signs of eating disorders can include:

• wearing long sleeves or loose-fitting clothes, even in warm weather
• disappearing into the bathroom soon after every meal
• picking at or nibbling food
• tooth enamel erosion, especially behind the front teeth (often spotted by a dentist)
• compulsive exercising
• obsessing over diet books or Web sites
• charting weight loss or gain, or stepping on the scale several times a day

Remember, anorexia (starving oneself) is only one type of eating disorder; a person suffering from bulimia (binge eating and purging) may not look excessively thin. Neither will a young person suffering from obesity, of course; the aforementioned signs don't apply in that case, but treating the condition can be just as crucial.

There are many resources available to parents who suspect their children may suffer from an eating disorder, including the Mayo Clinic Web site or your local children's hospital. But the first step should be a complete physical with a family physician or pediatrician, especially if the doctor knows your child already.

Bullying

"I didn't tell my parents when this kid kept kicking me and stealing my stuff, because what could they do?"

—A middle schooler

"There's this weird guy on Instagram, and he keeps putting bad stuff on people's pages, like 'You go cut, you should go kill yourself,' or 'You're so ugly.' He has a fake profile, so nobody really knows who he is."

—A middle schooler

When parents hear about bullying in the news, many can't help but wonder if their child will be—or already is—a victim. Sometimes it's hard for victims to speak up because it's embarrassing to admit you're being picked on. But here are some warning signals that could indicate a bullying situation:

- withdrawal
- a loss of friends
- a drop in grades
- a loss of interest in activities he or she previously enjoyed
- torn clothing
- bruises
- a need for extra money or supplies

When parents suspect there's bullying going on in middle school, they should alert the teacher. Before demanding consequences, however, they need to wait until they get the whole picture. Sometimes it's a true bullying situation, where a stronger child is making life miserable for a younger or weaker one; but often it's a more complicated situation with at least partial blame on both sides. Teachers often wade into situations thinking they know who's guilty, only to discover the alleged victims have been doing their share of harassing. Some middle schoolers are very crafty at manipulating the situation to shift blame from themselves, especially if they have a parent who doesn't believe the child could ever cause trouble—and who has a habit of going to school to rescue the schemer.

Bully or Victim?

Two eighth grade boys came to me and said Jack had shoved Todd up against the wall in the boys' locker room and wasn't letting him go. I quickly alerted our principal, who went in to break it up. Before he suspended the perpetrator, he talked to several boys to get the whole story. As it turned out, Jack had grabbed Todd to keep him from throwing a punch at Brent—who had been calling Todd names throughout gym class.
—Sue Acuña

The Tough Guy

"When my brother was in seventh grade and I was in fourth grade, another guy called him a 'queer' for talking to the little kids. I didn't know what that was, but my teacher told me it was bad, so I felt bad for him."

—A middle schooler

Boys who are bullies are often easy to spot because they use direct attacks in the form of name calling or physical contact. Sometimes the bully is the classic bigger, tougher kid who shoves his way to the front of the line or makes derisive comments in class. But sometimes he's smaller than the other boys and uses bullying tactics to get attention or to show that he's tougher than he looks. A boy who bullies to get attention will repeatedly take things that belong to someone else. He may also provoke the students he views as powerful by telling them what other people are saying about them, whether it's true or not.

Dealing with boy bullies is a fairly straightforward issue: Warn them that if it keeps happening there will be consequences, and then empower the other students to let you know if they witness any more incidents. Victims of the bully are not likely to turn him in for fear of repercussions, so it's more effective for students who observe him in action to say something, with the assurance that they will remain anonymous.

Mean Girls

"I was in a class with a girl who was a bully, and I just tried not to make her mad because if she got mad at you she would get everybody else to be mad at you, and then there would be drama."
—A middle schooler

Unlike a bullying boy, girl bullies can be hard to spot. A girl who bullies other girls may be outspoken with her snide comments and disapproving attitude. She may intimidate other girls or call them names in front of other people. But a girl bully can be so well behaved in class that the teacher has no idea what's going on in other places—or even when her back is turned.

Girl bullies can use subtle means of communicating their dislike for another girl, including an eye roll, a toss of the head, or a meaningful look exchanged with someone across the room. These mean girls will snort or look away when their victims speak in class or walk by the lunch table; boys or adults in the same room may not pick up on it, but other girls have gotten the message.

Social media is a powerful weapon in the hands of a girl who wants to hurt other girls. Simply posting pictures of an event can be a way of communicating rejection because the pictures serve as a way of letting other girls know they weren't invited. Things can get vicious when girls make derogatory comments about another girl who may not be a member of the site; someone will always take it upon herself to inform the victim about mean things that have been said about her.

Dealing with a girl bully can be tricky because she can be so sneaky in how she attacks. It gets complex when the victim is doing her share of bullying behind the scenes, because the other girls will usually take sides and deny anything is going on—or tell only half the truth. Confrontation by an adult can lead to repercussions for the victims, who are then afraid to report continued hostilities. Still, only when victims are empowered to tell adults what's happening can anything be done. Girls are encouraged to take screen shots of any cyberbullying (Internet or phone) they experience, and to refrain from responding in kind. They should also be reminded that looking a bully in the eye takes power away from her; walking past with your head down encourages her to pick on you.

Here's a Thought:

Most schools have a plan for dealing with bullies. If you suspect your middle schooler is the victim of a bully, contact someone at the school—teacher, counselor, administrator—and ask for an investigation. Provide as much detail as you can get out of your middle schooler, and keep an open mind until you get information from third-party sources (such as students not directly involved in the situation).

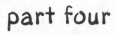

part four

SCHOOL

thirteen

Not So Brave in the New World

"Before I went to middle school, I worried about buying new clothes and hoped they would be cool enough."
—A middle schooler

There's a famous saying: "Life is what happens while you're making other plans." In middle school, it could be expressed like this: "School happens while your life is absorbed with everything else."

When we asked middle school students to tell us what they wish their parents could understand about them, dozens of topics come up—and almost none of them had to do with the academic side of school. In fact, there are only two academically oriented school topics that emerged on a regular basis: grades and homework. Other than that, school is the great big stage where your new adolescent life is on display for an audience that doesn't understand you, isn't sure when to take you seriously, and wonders why you didn't take the time to learn your lines.

This often means you'll need to help your middle schooler succeed in *spite* of school, because a major share of the drama and learning experiences that shape kids' lives will play out between the time they leave for school in the morning and the time they get home that night. That can overshadow the valuable opportunities for parents *and* teachers to help these teens figure out what they can do to succeed—sometimes in spite of themselves.

These years offer a safety net that won't be there again once they enter high school. Permanent grade records almost always begin in ninth grade. For purposes of college scholarships and transcripts that determine eligibility for any number of athletic and elective programs, ninth grade removes the safety net.

But up until then, mistakes can be forgiven and failures can be redeemed. Middle school can be the testing ground for what works and what doesn't. This doesn't mean you let your child give up caring about being a good student. This means when it comes to school, you and your middle schooler get to have the gift of trial and error without heavy consequences in order to find out what will succeed.

This section will give you practical tools and strategies for teaching middle schoolers how to make the transition from elementary school to the framework that will take them through high school and college. Since so much of the story will happen during the hours they're away from home, you as a parent have the opportunity to help them learn how to get their act together and face new academic demands with confidence.

Moving from Elementary to Middle School

"The idea of middle school and so many teachers and classes scared me. And I worried about having the right school supplies for every class."

—A middle schooler

Have you ever had to find your way around in a big, new city, driving without any kind of GPS or navigational system? That's pretty much how your child feels the first day of middle school. Not only is this a new city, but there are a lot of rules to live by if you want to fit in and not look dumb. No one hands you a map and guidebook, and most of what's been familiar to you since first grade is behind you now—never to return.

There are several things you can do before school even starts to ease your child's stress and help him or her feel a lot more confident.

1. *Go explore.* Do everything you can to make the new school feel familiar and less intimidating. Begin with touring the school before the first day. Visiting the school in the spring before your student starts in the fall means your middle schooler will have a mental picture of how the other kids look and what the classrooms and normal flow of the day feel like. If you wait to visit until summer, you'll find empty halls—which gives freedom to explore but doesn't give a realistic view of what a school day looks like.

2. *Get a schedule.* It's best when your middle schooler can get a copy of his schedule and walk the halls with it in his hand, scoping out where he needs to go before the first day arrives. Even that isn't foolproof; one seventh grader told us he knew exactly where he was supposed to go when the halls were empty, but when they were filled with kids, he kept getting lost. Some secondary schools have the youngest students start a day or two before the older ones, in order to give them a chance to learn the lay of the land. Check with the school; if they don't offer such an orientation, ask about arranging a time to make your own practice run.

3. *Ask others.* Finding someone who's spent a year at the school can be beneficial, as long as the experience was mostly positive. The best resource would be someone who can describe teachers and make them sound like real people, and who starts a lot of sentences with, "Oh,

and you know what's really great?" This person can also field questions
your middle schooler may have that she's afraid to ask you for fear of
sounding stupid.

Be sure you or your middle schooler asks lots of "whys," as in . . .
"*Why* didn't you like that teacher?"
"*Why* is his class better than the other teacher's?"
"*Why* should I hope I get third lunch?"

After the conversation, remind your child that his experience may
not be the same as anybody else's, because he is a different person with
a different personality. An eighth grader at a large public junior high
said that he was terrified of his English teacher because he'd been told
he was the meanest teacher in the school. "I actually wound up liking
him and learning a lot in his class," he says now.

Talking parent-to-parent about the school can put Mom's or Dad's
mind at ease also. Ask questions about which office staff are most helpful, and familiarize yourself with rules that may not have existed when
you went to school. For example, do you know if the school has a
"Zero Tolerance" policy, and what that might mean? Do you know the
current definition of "sexual harassment"? Even knowing the morning
drop-off and afternoon etiquette can reduce a parent's stress.

4. *Focus on the positive.* After meeting with "those in the know," be
sure to debrief with your middle schooler. Keep steering her back to the
positive stories that were shared, and then ask her to tell you the top
three things she's worried about in middle school. Address those you
can, research the others, and be sympathetic about the ones that can't
be changed (for instance, "My friend won't be at the same school with
me"). Then ask for the three things she's most looking forward to. You
might write them down and post them on the bathroom mirror, even
if the list says, "Before school, after school, and weekends."

This might be one time when your middle schooler will welcome
your stories about what you enjoyed about middle school. Maybe you

liked having so many different teachers, or perhaps you played in the pep band at basketball games. Tell stories to get your child excited about having similar experiences.

5. *Discuss the budget.* Any school year brings added costs, but entering the strange new world of middle school can bring unexpected expenses. An insecure middle schooler—or a fashion-conscious one—may insist on the latest trendy clothes. That old backpack, while still in good condition, may be unsuitable this year, along with the barely-used binder, the cartoon character pencils, and the non-scientific calculator.

Unless you have several hundred dollars to spend on each child, you'll want to do some negotiating. Declare how much you're willing to spend, and look together at the ads to see what's popular this year. Maybe you'll spend extra for the movie star binder but settle on a backpack that's cheaper but of good quality. If a graphing calculator is required, point out the impact that the extra expense may have on the clothes budget. Most middle schoolers are capable of being quite reasonable if given enough information.

Ready for the First Day

*"I couldn't sleep the night before seventh grade, because
I was worried about being bullied by the bigger kids."*
—A middle schooler

*"I had a dream that I couldn't find my classes
and the principal yelled at me. I started crying
and everybody stood around laughing. When I
woke up, I didn't want to go to school."*
—A middle schooler

By taking a few proactive steps, parents can make it possible for middle schoolers to have fewer nightmares in the days before school starts. They won't be able to eliminate all of the anxiety, but can increase their children's levels of confidence and comfort—which will in turn prepare them to deal with the unexpected.

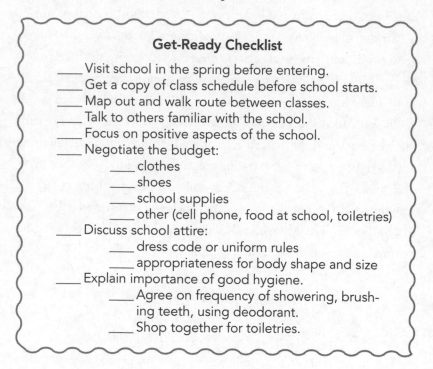

Get-Ready Checklist

____ Visit school in the spring before entering.
____ Get a copy of class schedule before school starts.
____ Map out and walk route between classes.
____ Talk to others familiar with the school.
____ Focus on positive aspects of the school.
____ Negotiate the budget:
      ____ clothes
      ____ shoes
      ____ school supplies
      ____ other (cell phone, food at school, toiletries)
____ Discuss school attire:
      ____ dress code or uniform rules
      ____ appropriateness for body shape and size
____ Explain importance of good hygiene.
      ____ Agree on frequency of showering, brushing teeth, using deodorant.
      ____ Shop together for toiletries.

A New Start

"I was excited about going to middle school, but I was sad to leave my old school where I knew everybody and the little kids looked up to us. It's hard to go from being the oldest to being the youngest kids in the school."

—A middle schooler

When we asked middle schoolers for first impressions of the new school, they said things like these:

"It was awesome!"

"It was scary."

"The gym is so cool! But I know I'm gonna get lost in all those halls!"

There are so many things they have to absorb: the physical layout of the campus, the routine of changing classes, several new teachers at once, and many new rules. And then, of course, there's the challenge of learning a whole new social order.

You can make it easier for your nervous new student by breaking things down into smaller, more manageable pieces. Let's take a look at some of the biggest ones.

What's My Next Class?

"I got my schedule on the first day, but it didn't help; I had no idea what those numbers and letters meant! I just kept asking until I found somebody in my next class and then I followed him."

—A middle schooler

For most middle schoolers, the first day or two of school will pass in a blur of noise and confusion. No sooner will they figure out which class comes next and how to get to it, when the bell will ring and it will be time to change again. Though there may be familiar faces in every class, there will be many more that are unfamiliar, and some may even belong to students a year or two older than they are. On top of that, there's no desk to call their own where they can safely stow books and papers. There's just a locker with a tricky combination, and a lot of heavy books to carry around in a backpack.

What advice can we give them for coping? Encourage them to take a deep breath and stay calm. Anxiety will only make it harder to focus and remember what comes next. Suggest they learn one or two new names every day. It may help to write them down somewhere or to practice using a method of association (such as "Brenda has braces"). If struggling with opening a locker is an issue, buy a cheap combination lock and practice at home. With or without lockers, your student will need a sturdy backpack with padded straps.

Rules and Dress Codes

"Everybody complains about having a uniform, but secretly some of us kind of like it because we never have to decide what to wear in the morning, or worry about not being cool."
—A middle schooler

Virtually every middle school has a dress code or a required uniform. Parents should check out the school's dress code for themselves and not take their middle schooler's (or a friend's) word for what it says. You don't want to spend big bucks on something only to learn it can't be worn to school. Most schools mail out their guidelines, but they can often be found on the school's Web site.

This is also a good time to discuss how your middle schooler's body may have changed in the last few months. For boys, longer legs and arms may mean their favorite shirts and jeans have to be replaced. For girls, new curves may mean low necklines are out and jeans have to be purchased in larger sizes.

Students at this age may try on different identities as often as they try on new clothes. You might want to discuss how one's choice of clothes says a lot about a person. It's a good time to encourage middle schoolers to think about how they want to be remembered: Do they want people to think of them as the kid who always wore the dirty shoes? Or as the girl who had a new weird hairstyle every week?

Middle school also opens up other new fashion possibilities, like piercings. Girls who already had their ears pierced once may want to add more holes to their ears. If the topic of piercing other body parts comes up, treat it with a light touch but hold firm to your standards. This could be a good place to set some limits, as in, "Not now, but we'll reconsider it on your sixteenth birthday!" Boys may also be considering piercing their ears or other parts of their faces. First check the dress code, and then have a discussion about your expectations.

Another added attraction for middle school girls is the use of makeup. Often it's hard to get to the bathroom sink in the girls' restroom because of the crowd at the mirror. Girls are going to experiment with each other's makeup. You may forbid it for your daughter, but you can't follow her around school all day to make sure she isn't applying her best friend's mascara. If she's expressing interest in wearing makeup, it might be time to engage the help of a friend who sells beauty products. She can be a teen girl's "consultant" and show her how to apply makeup to enhance natural beauty instead of causing people to think, "Oh, wow—look at how much makeup she's wearing."

And then there are shoes. Often costing as much as a whole outfit, shoes can make or break a middle schooler's popularity in some circles. Almost every year some teachers see students who change their shoes before going outside for fear of getting them dirty—and they're often the boys!

Policies and Procedures

"We had a flat tire on the way to school, so I was late. When I got to class, everybody stared at me and the teacher asked for my tardy slip. I had to go all the way back to the office to get one, because I didn't know I was supposed to go there first."

—A middle schooler

A new school means new rules, policies, and procedures. There will almost certainly be a dress code, even if the school requires uniforms. You'll probably need a pass to leave the classroom, and you need to know what to do if you arrive late. How do you pay for lunch? What if you get sick or have some other emergency? How does one get detention—and where is it held?

Some of the rules have words that need defining; what is "loitering" or "truancy"? It's normal for new students to feel more anxiety when they don't know what to expect. As a parent, you can help ease this by getting a copy of the student handbook and going through it with your child.

Most schools issue a copy of the handbook, post it online, or both. It helps if you look through it first, then spend a little time going over it with your middle schooler. There's no need to read every word (chances are good that your child won't have to know every detail about search and seizure) but be sure to point out rules relevant to your student's situation.

If your child is an auditory learner (see Chapter 16), he or she may need to ask questions along the way. A visual learner will need to look at the handbook with you and may even want to picture what's appropriate. Chances are good that your kinesthetic child will simply be eager to have the whole discussion over with, so try to be brief in order to cover the most ground.

Grades and Academic Pressure

"After I turned in my math test, I looked at the paper of the boy next to me and realized I'd done one of the answers wrong. I went back up to get my test, but the teacher knew what I was doing and wouldn't let me have it. I was so embarrassed that he knew I was cheating, but I was afraid that if I got a B in the class my parents would kill me!"
—A middle schooler

"Sometimes if I don't get my math assignment done, I'll get the answers from a friend. It's not exactly cheating, because I would've gotten the same answers if I'd done it. But I can't get a low grade in math because my parents will go off on me and make me quit track!"
—A middle schooler

Ask a seven-year-old what grade he's in, and he will proudly proclaim, "I'm in second grade, and my teacher is Miss Roberts!" All he thinks about is what's going on in second grade, giving little or no thought to what will happen the next year or the year after that.

Middle schoolers, on the other hand, are only too aware that high school is just around the corner; they know they need to get their act together now. But there's a lot going on in their lives—physical changes, emotional changes, and the shedding of so many things that made them feel secure during childhood. Now they have to adjust to a more difficult academic schedule with multiple classes and teachers, and from where they stand, life looks a lot harder and scarier. In second grade there were concrete questions and straightforward tests about what they learned, but now they're expected to think critically and express those thoughts on paper. Oh, and they get graded on all of it.

Sometimes parents—and even teachers—insist that middle school students buckle down and hit the books and start preparing for college, career, and the adult life that's headed their way. But the typical middle schooler is struggling just to deal with why he is a stranger in his body or why she suddenly feels so uncertain about what she wants to look like.

If you put a lot of pressure on your middle schooler to get high grades, it can increase the temptation to use deceptive means to measure up to expectations. Add the strong influence of peer pressure, and even good students can be tempted to cheat. It's certainly not unusual for middle schoolers to lend each other their notes. If they get caught "sharing information," they will claim—and believe—that they weren't cheating; they were only *helping!*

As we've mentioned, middle school offers a safety net where grades are concerned. Permanent records—important for college scholarships and other purposes—don't start until ninth grade. Instead of pressuring middle schoolers to get good grades or even straight A's, parents should focus more on helping them polish their study skills. The "tuition" for lessons learned in middle school is lower than in high school, and there is still time to improve before grades really count.

In elementary school, a child's day is shaped by the whims of parents and teachers. At home, decisions about what to eat and what to wear are made for the younger ones, as well as what time to leave for school and what's inside the lunch box. A middle schooler, on the other hand, may skip breakfast, agonize over what to wear, spend a long time in front of the mirror criticizing her appearance, worry over whom to sit next to on the bus, and struggle over whether to work on homework or hang out with friends. While kids treasure every bit of this newfound independence, they also experience anxiety over whether or not they're managing their time well. Many of them have to balance a busy schedule of classes, homework, practice, and social events, and they can find it all overwhelming.

The earlier middle schoolers learn to motivate themselves, the better off they are—and the more likely it is that the lesson will stick. As parents we will always be needed, but *how much* we are needed will change. The middle school years provide parents and children with opportunities to shift more responsibility for learning to the students—giving them a chance to prove they can be responsible for their own success.

Here's a Thought:

Go back through this chapter and read your child some of the quotes from students about starting middle school. If your child is about to start middle school or is in the first year, ask which of the quotes he or she can identify with, and why. If your student is already an "old hand" at middle school, ask the same question about his or her feelings regarding the move to high school; did he or she learn any lessons from starting middle school that could be applied to the next transition?

fourteen

The Hassles of Homework

~~~~~~~~~~

*"I wish my parents would help me more with homework.
[I wish they'd realize] that I don't have as many friends
as I say I do. [That they] would want to bond with me
more. That I don't have it as easy as they think."*

—A middle schooler

~~~~~~~~~~

"Jason!" His mom's voice was full of frustration. "I just can't understand why you lose your assignments! I made you that beautiful notebook with all those folders and dividers. Each subject has its own color and its own pocket for loose papers. You don't even have to open the rings; all you have to do is put your papers in there! Why isn't this working?"

Jason hung his head sheepishly. "I can't find the notebook."

Organized parents of disorganized middle schoolers often run into this sort of problem. As a parent, you've invested a lot of time and energy making sure your child has the best possible system for keeping up with the new school year. But you might be forgetting the most important thing of all: Without input and involvement, your student won't be invested in the success of *any* method. There is no ideal, one-size-fits-all system. Every student needs a personalized plan that he or she has helped create.

The key to a successful organization technique lies in asking and answering the most important question: *What's the point?* What does your middle schooler want to accomplish? Once you answer that, you can figure out what needs to be done.

For example, let's say you've determined the point of organization is to help your daughter find what she needs. How will you know you've succeeded? When she can locate whatever you ask for in 60 seconds or less—no matter what the notebook or organization system looks like.

Technology and Homework

"I had an app on my phone to keep track of my homework, but I gave it up because I didn't like it. However, I use my iPod for a calculator and a dictionary, and I use my tablet to look up Web sites for math help."

—A middle schooler

Students in the twenty-first century have some creative options available to them, from tablets to smartphones. While the education system struggles to figure out how to use technology in the classroom without enabling cheating, some of these devices can be useful outside the classroom right now. If you decide to buy your middle schooler a laptop or tablet, make it a point to find features and programs that can help organize information needed for school.

Many schools now have online resources that allow teachers to post assignments with due dates, grades, and information for parents. Work with your student to figure out how to keep up with news from the school's Web site as well as in e-mail from teachers. Again, involving your child in this process will help both of you develop effective methods of staying current with assignments. Just don't forget to have a backup plan in case the Internet isn't working or a site isn't accessible. Sometimes it still helps to write assignments down or keep the phone number of a classmate nearby.

Keeping Kids Motivated

"When my parents nag me about my homework, it doesn't help me get it done. It just causes us to fight more."
—A middle schooler

To take more responsibility for their own success—in school and in life—middle schoolers need to know their strengths. If we teach them to master this, they'll be prepared with skills that can last them the rest of their lives. Later in this book you'll get insights and strategies for identifying and using learning styles. But the fact is that kids encounter situations in and out of school that won't accommodate those learning styles. It's critical that they adjust in order to overcome in less than ideal circumstances.

So this next step, accountability, may be the most important one of all.

As we teach children what it takes to keep themselves motivated and competent, it will be meaningful and lifelong only if they can prove it works. This may sound daunting, but you'll be surprised at how well even the most basic strategies can start working right away. There's no better place to start than middle school.

One of the most common areas that begs for accountability is that of homework—doing it, keeping track of it, and turning it in on time. You can bug your kids about it, dog their footsteps until they do it, and hover over them until it gets delivered to school. Or you can teach them to motivate *themselves* to get it done. It's not as hard as you think. Have them brainstorm ideas for what might help them concentrate and get their work done. You can use a lot of the tips in this chapter to offer suggestions.

One frustrated mom came up after a seminar with a complaint about her sixth grade daughter. "She tells me that on Thursdays she can only do her homework between 8:00 and 8:30 while she watches her favorite TV program. I think that's just a big fat excuse."

Location, Location, Location

During the fourth grade, my twin boys did their homework in completely opposite environments. Mike, the more analytic one, insisted on being alone at the dining room table clear of everything except neat, well-organized books and materials. He needed a quiet room and plenty of uninterrupted time to finish his assignments.

Robert, on the other hand, quickly discovered he was most productive when he was lying on his stomach, either on the floor in front of the fireplace or actually on top of the big coffee table in the living room. He wanted to have something to eat or drink nearby, and he took frequent breaks to try to stay inspired enough to finish the homework by bedtime.

The bottom line? Both boys got their homework done.
—Cynthia Tobias

Our advice is pretty simple: As long as you approve of the television show, this Thursday let her do her homework while she watches it. But at 8:30, collect the homework. If it's done and done well, you tell her, "Wow—I could never do it this way, but for you it obviously works." If it's not done well, you get to say, "Nice try. We won't be doing it this way again."

Don't underestimate the importance of finding the right environment—even if it includes some elements that would make you uncomfortable if *you* were studying. Every child is going to be different. Remember the most important question to ask yourself: *What's the point?* If the point is to get the homework done, let your child propose how he wants to do it, and—as long as it doesn't violate serious rules in your household—simply require proof that it works.

We aren't going to let kids get by with excuses—we won't tell them they don't have to do homework if they don't want to. We tell them what needs to be done, and we give them a chance to prove that doing it their way will work.

Should Parents Be Checking Homework Assignments?

"My dad didn't understand what we were supposed to do on that math worksheet last night.

"Then my mom wanted to know if we can use plaster of paris on my science model. I don't even know what that is!"

—A middle schooler

It's natural for parents to want to help their children succeed in school. But where's the line between a reasonable amount of help and too much?

Fortunately, parents don't need to check every line or every problem on homework assignments. It's okay to spot-check a few problems, or to skim a writing assignment and check for glaring spelling and grammar errors. But don't rewrite any papers or redo any projects to rescue a student who is careless or late.

In middle school, parents should start phasing themselves out of the helper role and into the guidance position. If your child is college-bound, that transition isn't too far down the road—so for the next four or five years you need to work toward more independence, especially regarding homework. When problems occur or a middle schooler doesn't understand the assignment, it's time for the student—not the parent—to make the initial contact with the teacher.

Deadlines

"My brother always bugs me by playing Twenty Questions, and I wish my mom would tell him to just go away while I'm doing my homework."

—A middle schooler

If a parent learns that homework isn't being completed on time, it's time to sit down and discuss strategy. Start by asking some important questions (and be prepared to negotiate):

- What grade do you want to earn?
- What do you think it would take to get that grade?
- Would you like any help?
- How will I know your homework is being done?
- How do you want to be reminded?

Keep in mind that your middle schooler is the one who knows the teacher and the expectations. You may think he should get A's in history, but he may feel a B is the best he can do.

Here's a Thought:

Suppose your daughter has a big science test this week. You could try nagging and threatening: "You'd better be studying for that test! If you get another low grade, I'm going to ground you until the end of the quarter!"

Or you could try a less pushy, more subtle approach: "How are you going to celebrate when your science test is over?" or, "Guess I'd better start saving my dollars for your A in biology, huh?"

By using a less threatening approach, you may not get the immediate response you'd like: "Hey! I'm off to study for my biology test!" But you will have planted a seed and allowed your daughter to saunter off and pretend she was planning on studying all along.

Mission accomplished; conflict avoided.

—Sue Acuña

fifteen

Getting Teachers
on Your Team

~~~~~~~~~~

*"Sometimes I think that all the teachers give us homework
on the same night just to make us miserable."*
—A middle schooler

~~~~~~~~~~

Finding your way around school and getting into a daily routine may take your child only a day or two. But adapting to multiple teachers might take a whole semester.

There are so many different rules and expectations to learn: One teacher allows open seating while the other has a seating chart; this one welcomes active discussions; that one expects kids to raise their hands.

Students have to adjust to teachers who give handouts for every assignment as well as to those who simply write a note on the board and expect everyone to copy it. One teacher may have a box where students are expected to hand in their work; another will manually collect every paper. It can be overwhelming to remember all those assignments *and* the proper way to hand them in. Then there's the worst-case scenario: when students receive an assignment from every teacher on the same day—and they're all due tomorrow!

Making Teachers Your Allies

"Parents want to know that teachers love their kids and that they will go to bat for them."

—A teacher

Check out your options regarding teacher availability. Most teachers welcome an occasional e-mail asking about a student's progress. Be specific, though: "Does he have any missing or late assignments?" will get you a quicker response than the vague "How's he doing?"

Most middle schools send out progress reports as often as every three to six weeks. Progress reports don't always become part of a student's permanent record; rather, they're used to let parents know how things are going at a particular point in time. This can be a good indication of whether a middle schooler's organizational system is working, and it can also serve as a good jumping-off point for a parent-teacher discussion.

So how can you get teachers on your child's team? With the input of dozens of trusted colleagues who are classroom teachers of all grades, here are some practical and effective ideas for communicating with your middle schooler's teachers. They're adapted from Cynthia's book *Every Child Can Succeed: Making the Most of Your Child's Learning Style.*[6]

- *Presume the best and treat the teacher as an expert.* Be positive and upbeat in your attitude and approach.
- *When discussing your child, start many of your questions with the same four words: "What can I do?"* For example, "Jenny's learning style seems very different from your teaching style. I think it's great that she's learning how to deal with lots of different approaches. I'm wondering, though, *what can I do* to

help her understand the way you teach? *What can I do* at home that might help her succeed better in your classroom?" Let the teacher know that you and your child are taking the responsibility for learning and coping with classroom demands.

- *Recognize that there are practical limitations on what the teacher can do for your child.* Try to make it as easy as possible for the teacher to accommodate your child's learning style while still meeting bottom-line outcomes. For example, if you've discovered that your child needs to follow a certain system for recording and keeping track of homework, make up the necessary assignment sheets so that the teacher would only need to fill in a couple of blanks and sign the bottom.

- *Know that teachers become more aware of active and interested parents.* A teacher will often make an extra effort to watch out for that parent's child—not because of favoritism, but out of a heightened sense of awareness and personal appreciation for the child.

- *Make contact with the teacher under ordinary as well as extraordinary circumstances.* If you only show up on the radar when crises hit, it can put the teacher on "red alert" at the sight of you, triggering a defensive response.

- *Don't rely solely on the information you get from your child about a particular teacher, since each person sees the world from his or her own perspective.* Naturally, your personal loyalty rests with your child. But do your best to look at the situation objectively before talking to the teacher.

- *Avoid phoning the teacher right after school.* There are many details demanding the teacher's attention, and it may have already been a hectic or exhausting day. If possible, call or e-mail in the morning, leaving the message that you'd like to hear from the teacher as soon as it's convenient.

- *Whenever possible, start and end your communications with the teacher on a positive note.* Look for the best in the situation and build on strengths as you find them. For example, can you tell that the teacher is genuinely concerned? Reinforce that by mentioning how much you appreciate that concern in the first place.

- *When you're communicating with the teacher, keep your child in the loop as much as possible.* Discuss your conversations with the teacher honestly and positively. Don't make them a secret, or your child may feel you and the teacher are teaming up against him. Emphasize the positive aspects that both you and your teacher discussed about your child. Talk about how to use those strengths to overcome areas of possible weakness or limitation.

When to Stand Up for Your Middle Schooler

One day a mom showed up in my classroom doorway after school, fire in her eyes. She told me her son had climbed into the car and complained that I was accusing him of using bad language at school.

She knew her son better than that, she said, and was sure he never lied to her. In fact, he'd gotten teary about the whole matter, and when she asked him if he wanted her to talk to the teacher, he'd said yes. "Do you think," she said to me, "that he would send me in here if he were guilty?"

Yes, as a matter of fact, I did. What better way to convince your mother of your innocence than to work up some tears and agree to having her confront the teacher?

The reality was that other students had told me about this young man's language—and I'd seen it myself in intercepted notes. He was guilty, all right.

Standing up for your middle schooler is often the right thing to do—when you've heard both sides of the story.
—Sue Acuña

- *If you want to make sure the teacher knows about learning styles, you can avoid getting a defensive response by simply letting the teacher know what you've read and asking for feedback.* Perhaps even ask if you can loan the teacher a copy of *The Way They Learn*[7], thereby encouraging the teacher to give you some ideas for further reading, too.

- *Remember, every teacher is a lesson in learning for your child.* The more variety your middle schooler experiences in the classroom, the more opportunities there will be to discover and develop strengths and to use them to cope with uncomfortable demands. Instead of resenting a different teaching approach, do your best to help your child understand and value a variety of methods. By helping children discover and appreciate their teachers' unique styles, you can be preparing them to face a world of differences with the confidence of knowing they can use their strengths to cope with almost anything!

Here's a Thought:

Teachers told us that parents often don't follow procedures for finding things out on the school Web site or via e-mail. If you don't want to keep in touch with your child's teachers electronically, check the student handbook, call the school office, or ask a more "connected" parent. Once you know the procedures, take a moment to send an encouraging message to one of your student's teachers.

sixteen

Learning Styles and Learning Disorders

~~~~~~

When Travis fell out of his chair for the umpteenth time, Serena threw up her hands and asked nobody in particular, "How does this happen? Can't he figure out what he's doing?"

Brad called out, "Hey, that was awesome! Maybe we should all fall out of our chairs, and then he wouldn't feel so bad!"

—Sue Acuña

~~~~~~

Even when kids exhibit "typical" middle schooler behaviors—clumsiness, extreme self-consciousness, immature emotional reactions—each of them is wired uniquely with his or her own combination of learning style traits. That means the reason for *doing* the behaviors can be completely different. Understanding those reasons can help you reduce a *lot* of tension.

Everyone has every piece of the learning styles puzzle—but those pieces aren't all the same size. We're fearfully and wonderfully made, and the diversity *within* each individual (let alone *among* individuals) is truly amazing. You don't need to learn a lot of new terminology or have a degree in psychology to figure out some obvious and practical learning-style puzzle pieces.

Take, for example, the three basic modes of remembering: auditory, visual, and kinesthetic.[8]

How We Remember Information

"It's hard to stay focused on one thing because the noises that surround me are a distraction and instead of memorizing my work, I remember the noise."
—A middle schooler

Learners with a large auditory piece need to *hear* and *talk*. They naturally put a high value on verbal communication, and rely on it to help them understand and evaluate information. Until they've heard themselves ask questions or talk through what they're thinking, it's hard for them to process and remember what they're learning. Once you know that, it's not hard to figure out which ones are the more auditory learners. They may frequently interrupt you to ask a question or add to what you're saying, and they usually expect you to respond verbally right away (when you can get a word in edgewise!). They often use auditory phrases, such as, "Let me ask you a question," "Can I just tell you one thing?" and "Could I talk to you a minute?"

Learners with a bigger visual piece need to *see*—not just physically, but also to be able to visualize what you're talking about in order to understand and remember what you mean. While auditory learners need to talk about it, the visual ones need to take a look—or at least picture things in their mind. They're often not much on the spoken word, but writing, drawing, and watching are all high on their list of favorite things. They often prefer observation over talking through what to do. You'll hear them say things like, "I see what you mean," "I can't see that happening," and "Could you look at this for a minute?"

Learners who are more kinesthetic need to *move* and *do*, and for their minds to be in motion their bodies have to follow suit. In fact, if they're required to be quiet and sit still while they learn, often all they think about is moving. They listen best when it's in short spurts with at least tiny breaks in between (even if it's just shifting positions or turning in their seats). Kinesthetic learners remember best when they're *doing* something with the information, or at least recognizing why it's important to learn it. They're frequently overheard saying things like, "Can I just try it?" "I got it," or "I'll get back to you."

As your child enters the middle school years, identifying these learning styles can help both of you figure out how to use related strengths to overcome frustrations and limitations. You may be surprised to find out what a difference it can make when kids have to cope with situations that may not match their natural strengths and preferences.

How We Think

"I'm analytic, and it drives me crazy when we all have to read directions together in class. I'd rather just read them on my own."
—A middle schooler

In addition to the auditory, visual, and kinesthetic learning styles, two other puzzle pieces will provide useful information as you and your middle schooler are figuring out how this new world works.

All of us have minds "pre-wired" from birth. When it comes to how we interact with and understand information, one of the most reliable research models puts the population into two general categories: *analytic* and *global*.[9] (These are not the same as *personality* traits.) Again, no one fits neatly into any one category—but there are distinct differences that can explain a lot, especially when you need to turn conflict into cooperation.

Those who are wired to be more *analytic* naturally take in information in a more specific, linear manner, looking for details right away. Analytic learners need time to put things in order, figure them out, and focus on one task at a time. They thrive with structure, predictability, organization, and right-or-wrong answers. Middle schoolers who are highly analytic will appreciate teachers who post schedules and rarely deviate from them.

On the other end of the spectrum are more *global* learners, who have a natural bent to be more intuitive—and who constantly look for ways to pull separate details into a bigger picture. These global learners need context, consensus, and team effort. They thrive with spontaneity, flexibility, and the inspiration of the moment. Global middle schoolers will light up at the words, "We're going to do something a little different today."

It's not hard to imagine some of the conflicts that can happen when two opposite styles live or work or learn together.

What's Normal; What's Not

Christine's parents were alarmed at her teacher's insistence that she had an attention deficit disorder. She had always been an animated, loving, social little girl. The final straw for the school was the cold winter day when Christine found another child's coat and was given permission to take it to the office. When she didn't return for over 25 minutes, punishment was swift and the referral to a pediatrician was promptly issued.

But when Christine's parents listened to her explanation, they heard a different story. It turned out she'd been concerned that the owner of the left-behind coat was going to be too cold, so she'd gone from class to class trying to reunite the coat with its owner before outdoor recess.

—Cynthia Tobias

Middle schoolers can do the most irritating and frustrating things—but the fact is, many of their behaviors are a result of learning styles, and don't rise to the level of being a learning disorder or deficit. If you happen to have a middle schooler who's annoying you and you're wondering if perhaps there's some cure for this, we'd like to give you a gentle reminder. Sometimes what irritates you most about your child is going to turn out to be one of his most valuable traits as an adult. He's practicing on you right now.

Middle schoolers exhibit their learning style strengths in ways that can be misunderstood—even when their behavior is completely normal.

Take auditory learners. They need to *talk*. As soon as they think of something, it shoots right out of their mouths. In fact, until they're mature enough to know how to manage it, auditory kids talk *while* they think—in a sense saying things they haven't even thought of yet. Weary parents protest the constant stream of chatter that covers so many subjects so rapidly and so randomly. Exasperated teachers send messages home warning that these students are socializing inappropriately in class. They're not supposed to talk in class, but they just *have* to tell *someone* what they're thinking, so they talk to the person next to them.

Visual learners need to *see*—they remember what they can *picture*, so they spend a lot of time doing so. Often when they appear to be totally lost in thought, they're just trying to get a mental image of what you're talking about. Active visual imaginations can quickly take "picture detours" when something triggers an image in their minds that sends them off the trail and into less-traveled scenery. Parents (especially the more auditory ones) can say the same thing multiple times without their visual kids ever quite tuning in. Teachers complain that these students frequently daydream, "spacing out" during an important lecture.

Kinesthetic learners need to *move* and *do*—they're curious, restless, hands-on. In order to really understand something, they have to touch it, hold it, or use it. Parents notice their short attention spans when those kinesthetic bodies simply can't be still for more than a few seconds. Something is always moving—a foot tapping, a head bobbing, a body shifting positions. Teachers are constantly telling them, "Get your feet off the person's desk in front of you!" or "Sit back down—you've sharpened your pencil three times already!"

Analytic learners need to make sense of information *in order*, and they struggle when the person talking to them seems vague, unspecific, or unpredictable. Parents who prefer to "go with the flow" frustrate these analytic kids, whose minds long for structure and clearer, more concise instructions. Teachers (especially those who are not particularly analytic) can get irritated with analytics' questions that seem so detailed and picky—"Where do you want me to put my name? Should I abbreviate the date or spell it out? Should I use blue or black ink?"

Global learners understand information best when it connects to something they already know or care about; they struggle when they have to learn facts one at a time, without any seeming connection to their own lives. Parents (especially the more analytic ones) can lose patience dealing with the thought processes of their global kids. You can't just tell them something without inviting another dozen questions about seemingly unrelated topics. Teachers discover their global students can rarely work alone; they're constantly comparing notes and working together on projects.

With all the changes middle schoolers are going through, how will you know when your child has a problem that goes beyond normal boundaries? One of the best reasons to work hard at keeping a strong, positive relationship is to make sure you'll notice if something starts to go wrong. There will be common behavior issues—unpredictable emotional episodes, angry outbursts, resistance to authority. But no two middle schoolers are the same, and some won't even go through a rebellious stage. It's important that parents stay alert for signs that may indicate their one-of-a-kind middle schooler could be headed for serious trouble.

Involve the Learner

"Before I knew my learning style, I would take notes with lots of pictures and colors because everybody else did. But then I found that words in plain pencil worked better for me, because I'm not that visual, and I'm analytic."

—A middle schooler

When it comes to getting organized for school, don't automatically assume you know what the best system will be for your child. Chances are good that you and your child don't share a lot of the same learning style strengths. It's more important that you both agree on the purpose of having the system. It may take more patience on your part, and more than a little trial and error, but in the end success can last for a lifetime. If you take into account your child's learning style, the following tips might help.

- Talk to your auditory learner. Ask him to discuss ideas that might work for setting up a system that accomplishes the goal. If he just keeps shrugging and saying, "I don't know," ask him if he'd like a couple of suggestions—but resist the temptation to just tell him what to do.

- Your visual child may want to show you different organization systems that appeal to her. You may even go shopping together and browse through the possibilities. Keep reminding each other that she'll have to prove it *works* no matter how wonderful it *looks*.

- Your kinesthetic learner, wired for action, may just want to try the closest thing and then move on to more interesting parts of life. Stay focused on what he needs to accomplish; be prepared for two or three experiments that may or may not work.

- Analytic learners tend to be naturally drawn to organizing. They usually want a more structured system; when it comes to planners or assignment sheets, they prefer to have spaces for more detailed information. They may even have two different pencil pouches—one for pencils, one for markers and pens— and perhaps even a three-hole punch and calculator in their notebook.

- Global learners usually prefer a more general system of keeping track of their papers and materials. Chances are good they'll be stuffing papers into a notebook, not hole-punching them and neatly putting them in the right section. They need something with folders or pockets, something that doesn't depend on taking time to put things away in specific places.

Remember, your child is not usually trying to drive you crazy on purpose. Keep asking yourself, *What's the point?* as you help your middle schooler search for the best way to stay organized.

Help Them Focus on Their Strengths

"I record myself reading my notes out loud and listen to them before going to bed. My mom thinks that's weird, but it really works."
—A middle schooler

Creating a good learning environment at home is vital. So is remembering that the needs for each type of learner vary greatly.

• For auditory learners, sounds are important—and the lack of sound can sometimes be just as critical. Give them a chance to talk about what they need to do. Ask brief questions, and be patient with long answers. The more they talk it through, the more likely it is they will get their homework done.

Then help them figure out the best environment for doing homework; challenge them to find the least distracting place. When they're working, do your best not to interrupt them, and keep outside noise to a minimum.

"If I put stuff on my calendar, I remember it without ever having to look at it again. I can just picture what's there on that day."
—A middle schooler

• Help visual learners create pictures in their minds of what their tasks should look like. Ask to see their homework assignment; sometimes just looking through it again will help them remember what they're supposed to do. Offer to provide a visual homework reminder: a calendar, whiteboard, or pop-up reminder on their computer or cell phone. Remember, just giving them verbal reminders probably won't have much effect.

"I learned I'm kinesthetic, so I write my notes over and over, two or three times, and then I can remember it better for the test."

—A middle schooler

• For kinesthetic learners, the greatest challenge can be sitting still long enough to *do* their homework. For these active and restless learners, spending more than five or ten minutes on something that seems like just another pesky chore can be perceived as torture. Their best chance for achievement often involves taking frequent short breaks and keeping some part of their body moving. Having something handy to eat or drink will also help them focus. Keep in mind that the point is not to have them sitting still to do their homework; the point is to get the homework *done*.

"My teacher isn't as analytic as I am, so she doesn't care what the date is on the board. But she says I can change it every day, so I do, and then I can focus better."

—A middle schooler

• For learners wired to be analytic (step-by-step, detail-oriented, predictable), it's important to find the best place for concentrating. They tend to thrive in a quiet, uncluttered space where they can be alone and uninterrupted. They often like to do their homework on a predictable schedule and rarely request help. Make sure they're clear about the assignment deadline. Don't hover or nag, but get their cooperation in coming up with a method of accountability. One thing analytics really like is having a list; that way they can cross things off as they finish them.

"If I don't think a teacher likes me, I have a hard time in that class. It's important for me to have my teacher know who I am and to care about me."
—A middle schooler

• For learners wired to be global (big-picture, intuitive, contextual), it may be easier to study when they're *not* alone. Globals are naturally drawn to working cooperatively with others; if they sit alone, they may struggle to concentrate on the task. One tried-and-true solution is to make sure everyone works while the global works. If your whole family can do something quiet and productive (reading, working on the computer, etc.) while your global child is studying, it's easier for him or her to stay focused.

Puzzled by Your Middle Schooler?

Take a few moments to check all of the descriptions below that apply to your middle schooler. It should give you some good insight into who they are and why they do what they do!

Auditory Learners . . .
_____ need to talk.
_____ often interrupt.
_____ blurt information without thinking.
_____ give out a constant stream of chatter.
_____ get in trouble for socializing.

Visual Learners . . .
_____ need to see.
_____ get a mental picture.
_____ watch more than talk.
_____ see an example before doing.
_____ seem like they're not tuning in.

Kinesthetic Learners . . .
_____ need to move and do.
_____ are curious about the unknown.
_____ are restless and easily bored.
_____ need to have hands-on experiences—"Hold it, touch it, use it."
_____ would rather just try something than ask how to do it.

Analytic Learners . . .
_____ make sense of information in order.
_____ need specifics and details.
_____ prefer structure and predictability.
_____ ask more detailed questions.
_____ prefer to work alone.

Global Learners . . .
_____ tend to think more about the big picture than the details.
_____ are easily distracted and driven by inspiration.
_____ enjoy mixing up the routine.
_____ need to see how information applies to their lives.
_____ work best in groups or with a "study buddy."

Here's a Thought:

Thinking about your own learning style, jot down a couple of sentences that describe what someone needs to know about you in order to understand you better. Share it with your middle schooler and ask him or her to do the same thing.

seventeen

Finishing Strong

~~~~~~~~

*"I'm getting a D in algebra?" Doug looked close to tears.
"My dad's gonna kill me! How could I get a D?"*

*I asked him if he knew how many assignments he'd
missed recently.*

"Uh—a couple, I guess."

*"Try six late assignments in just the last two weeks.
That may explain why you got an F on the last test, and
why you have a D right now."*

—Sue Acuña

~~~~~~~~

By the time spring rolls around, it's been a long year. Students are tempted to just let the clock run out until summer break. Those who've been trying to adjust to middle-school changes are struggling to find the energy to keep it up. Even high-achieving students are ready for a break. With only a couple of months left, how can parents motivate their students to finish the year strong instead of giving up too soon?

It may help to think about your middle schooler's learning style. An analytic learner could be motivated by concentrating on the value of having good grades all the way through the year. Ask her to imagine how that last report card will look if the grades for the first three quarters were good but those in the fourth quarter were a grade or two lower. Remind her that whether or not it goes on her permanent record, everything she does this year is an opportunity to prepare for the future—even assignments at the end of the year.

The global learner, on the other hand, isn't that concerned about letters on paper or what will matter two months from now. A global learner can be motivated by appealing more to his sense of loyalty and relationship. Have him imagine how disappointed his teacher will be if his grades take a dive. The teacher may even take it personally and assume it's her fault that he wasn't able to learn the material.

The most important thing to remember is that you must first get your middle schooler to agree that finishing strong is important. Then challenge her to think about what will motivate her to accomplish that.

Setting the Example

"What kids observe in our lifestyles as parents and teachers is the most powerful thing."
—A teacher

It's tempting for parents to slack off as the school year wears on, too. But letting your middle schooler sleep in a little later or growing careless about getting the homework done on time can take more of a toll than either of you realizes.

Awareness is at least half the battle. If you see that things are starting to slip, talk about it. Ask your student for ideas. "Hey, I think we're all getting a little tired of this homework routine. What do you think it would take to get us motivated again?" Encourage your child to remind you to use more positive words if you forget, and do your best to notice and reinforce good behavior.

Remember, your example will always be noticed, often be followed—but seldom be acknowledged.

Hitting the Reset Button

"If I get a lot of bad grades on my report card at once, it makes me want to just give up because I don't feel like I can ever catch up."

—A middle schooler

The first half of every school year is a period of adjustment. The first half of a year of middle school is often a period of *drastic* adjustment. Take this chance to evaluate progress at the halfway point. The goal is not to punish your child for low grades or unmet expectations. Instead, figure out together what worked and what didn't. Talk about realistic solutions for improvement. Resolve to finish strong in the first half and then set new goals for the second half.

Don't try to tackle everything at once. If your middle schooler is getting D's and F's in three classes, they can't all be fixed at once. Discuss what the root causes might be.

Is it a problem with organization? It may be time to try a new system.

Is it a lack of sleep? Consider eliminating some activities or changing the evening routine.

Is it a problem with the teacher-student relationship? Schedule a face-to-face conference and see if together you can resolve the issues.

This is not a decision the parent should make alone. It's critical to get your middle schooler's insight into what's gone wrong—and what needs to change. Resist the temptation to jump in and declare what *you* think needs to be done. The only solution that will work is one that the student has helped to create.

Once you have a grasp on a solution, break it up into manageable pieces and work on one thing at a time. Consider it a success if the grade in one class can improve, and then focus on the next one.

Remind your student that the new semester is a fresh start—and there *is* a reset button.

Staying Positive

It's not always cool to like school too much. In middle school it may not be cool to like anything too much, lest you bring upon you the scorn of your peers.

But sometimes kids just can't help wanting to tell you what happened at school. Value those rare moments. The best thing you can do is sound interested in whatever is shared with excitement. Try to show you understand why it was so funny or dumb or irritating, and you'll be sure to hear more stories about fire drills and spewing food!

—Sue Acuña

Sue takes a large group of teenagers on a 10-day mission trip every summer—usually about 60 of them, along with several other adults. Her experience has always been that the hardest day tends to happen a little over halfway through the trip. But she's figured out a great way to get over the hump and restart the momentum:

Our schedule was challenging—from breakfast at 8:00 A.M. to bedtime at 11:00 P.M., with a lot of Vacation Bible School and soccer camp in between.

Because this was my sixth year on this trip, I knew Wednesday would be a tough day. The newness was wearing off, fatigue was setting in, and Friday seemed far away. I gathered my team of 28 around a picnic table and explained why this day might be the hardest. Then I said, "I have some words for you: drowsy, yawning, fatigue, exhaustion, sleepy, tired . . ." At this point Kai, one of my college-aged leaders, hunched over and quietly rolled off the bench. As everyone laughed, I thanked him for helping me make my point.

"Let me give you some new words," I continued. "Energy! Enthusiasm! Excitement! Pushing through! Stamina! Peppiness!" The students got into the spirit and called out more words: "Fun! Happiness! Joy!" Their eyes got brighter, they sat up straighter, and most began to smile.

I told them that if they dwelled on how exhausted they were and kept thinking, *I'm so tired; when can we leave?* they'd make themselves truly miserable. But if they thought in more positive terms—*I'm having a good time; I can do this*—and focused on what they were doing rather than how they were feeling, they'd be surprised at how much better the day would go.

They took the lesson to heart, and we had a great Wednesday. In the heat of the afternoon, a red-faced and sweaty Erika, age 15, kept repeating one of our camp songs: "I'm alive . . . awake . . . alert . . . enthusiastic . . ." She wasn't singing loudly or energetically, but neither was she complaining. I smiled at her effort.

Positive words make a big difference for middle schoolers—on a mission trip or at home.

You may be surprised how effective this strategy can be with your discouraged or frustrated middle schooler. You may even want to make a game of it or develop a code word or phrase—something like "Up word!" with a smile right in the middle of conversation. No additional explanation or reminder will be necessary. Encourage your child to keep *you* accountable, too, with reminders or the use of the code.

Sometimes just switching the sentence around to a positive statement instead of a negative one can make a huge difference, too. Instead of saying, "If that homework isn't done by dinner, you're not playing any video games tonight," you could say, "As long as your homework is done before dinner, you can feel free to play that new video game afterward."

Or instead of saying, "You'd better be out of that shower and ready to go in 15 minutes," you could say, "Will you have enough time to take a short shower if we need to walk out the door in 15 minutes?"

Too often we underestimate the power of being positive. But with a little practice you'll find it makes more of a difference than you thought possible!

Here's a Thought:

If your child brings home a bad grade, rather than just threatening punishment if the grade doesn't improve, try asking her what grade she wanted. Wait for her to answer (because she'll be surprised you asked). When she tells you the grade she wished she had, ask her what she thinks it will take to earn it. This involves her in the process and can avoid a lot of anger and defensiveness.

eighteen

After School and Out of School

"I think my parents don't understand how hard homework is when I have my football practices and other things that I do."

—A middle schooler

You hear it from parents: "I'm picking my son up early from basketball practice so I can get him to his piano lesson so he can still get to his soccer game."

And you hear it from students: "Please don't give us homework tonight! I have to go to volleyball practice after school, then to my dance practice, and then I have youth group. And I didn't get last night's homework done because right after school I had tae kwon do and then our game went late."

How much is too much? How do you decide where the breaking point is when you want your middle schooler to learn new skills, make friends, be involved, and belong somewhere?

This isn't just a problem for parents of teens; the scheduling nightmare can begin with kids as young as five or six. But when the middle school years begin, the pace can start picking up faster than you realize. It's more important than ever to help your child develop good time management practices that can last the rest of his life. Now is the time you and your child can both learn how to strike the right balance.

At the beginning of the year, new and exciting activities beckon—and some students will be tempted to try them all. Before your middle schooler signs up to participate in a sport or club, get specific information regarding the time commitment. Unlike elementary school, middle school athletic teams practice almost every day, and practices can last into the early evening. Games involve traveling to and from other schools, which means team members may not get home until late. Doing homework on the bus sounds like a good idea, but it's a rare middle schooler who can ignore the social opportunities and other distractions provided by a long bus ride. School clubs may not require the initial time commitment for meetings and practices, but later in the year there may be major conventions or competitions that can take up entire weekends.

Involvement in school activities has many benefits. However, when your middle schooler is still adjusting to a new building, new teachers, and a new schedule, a wise parent will keep a lighter schedule of extra-curricular activities.

Keep Your Balance

"I wish my parents would understand that sometimes I have too much on my plate and that I'm not Superman and I can't do everything."
—A middle schooler

Some psychologists recommend that teens be involved in only two major extracurricular activities, such as one sport and one musical or fine arts program. While that sounds reasonable, parents often want their kids to be involved in school sports with friends, in club sports for competition, in music lessons for cultural enrichment, and in church activities for spiritual growth. How do you find a balance?

One thing to watch for is how many nights a week your middle schooler isn't home. More than three or four nights can create major interference with homework. The lateness of the activity also matters. To be successful in class, middle schoolers should get about nine hours of sleep each night. If they have to get up for school at 6:30 A.M., that means bedtime by 9:30 P.M. A practice or game that lasts until 8:00 P.M. leaves little time for schoolwork.

When teens don't get started on homework until late in the evening after other activities, they may be too tired to think clearly or to reason their way through an assignment. If grades slip, parents will need to remind their teens that school is the top priority.

Know Your Kids

"My parents don't understand that I love cars and I don't like playing football at all. Shouldn't I be able to choose my own hobbies?"
—A middle schooler

"Life feels very fast-paced. I feel busy a lot with sports and homework. So I would just want them to know that I'm very busy and always tired. But overall I think my parents love me and understand. They're great parents."
—A middle schooler

It's a good idea to stay tuned in to how your middle schooler is handling the pressure and time demands of school with extracurricular activities. Teens who are pushed too hard—or who push themselves—may get sick or at least be more irritable than usual. In addition to grades, relationships with friends and family may suffer. An observant parent will know when to insist on skipping a practice, or when to encourage dropping out of an activity. This isn't an easy decision for any of the parties involved, so it's important to keep the goal in mind: what's best for the teen's physical and emotional health.

Some warning signs:

- a calendar so full of practice schedules and games that important commitments (a cousin's band concert) or appointments (orthodontist) are forgotten
- frequent family arguments over whose activities are the most important
- teens who have neither the energy nor the desire to spend time on fun activities, like friends' birthday parties

Here's a Thought:

Just for fun, next time you're all together, ask family members what they would do if they had four extra hours a day. Talk about how different (or maybe alike) the answers are.

The Halfway Mark

"Every year it seems like I can get good grades in the beginning but then I don't know what

happens—I just get tired of working so hard.
Then I get in trouble for my bad grades."
—A middle schooler

～～～

"Are we there yet?" If you've ever gone on a long road trip, especially with children, this question is overly familiar. It usually starts about halfway through the trip, and it's often asked because what began as a new and grand adventure has now become a little boring and tedious. There may have even been a few bad experiences along the way, and now there's a longing for the comforts of home.

Middle school can be a lot like that, only this trip doesn't have a return route—and the journey, instead of being a vacation, is the road to a whole new destination.

Halfway through the year, your student may be getting less and less enthusiastic about school. You may be watching grades and motivation slip accordingly. It's getting close to the holidays and the end of the first semester—and everyone seems to be losing steam.

You need an infusion of energy. Fortunately, there are some practical ways to help you *and* your middle schooler keep the momentum going.

When School's Almost Out

～～～

"I'm having a pool party at my house right at the beginning of the summer."

"Cool! I hope you aren't inviting Heather."

"Are you kidding? She doesn't like us anyway."

"I know—she's going to a different school next year."

"Oh, no—she was going to be on the volleyball team next year!"

"I thought you didn't like her."

"Oh, yeah. I don't. But I can't believe she's not coming back."

—Conversation between two middle schoolers

The countdown begins in late spring: "Nine more class days!" "One more Monday!"

As the end of the year quickly approaches, emotions run high—but not just with excitement about summer. Everyone looks forward to a break from school: time to play, lots of hours to sleep in, relief from homework. But for some it causes as much stress as it does joy. The school year has become a comfortable routine, and now everything's about to change again.

Middle school teachers refer to the end of the year as the "Drama Season." As the school year winds down, students realize they won't be seeing each other all summer (or even longer), so they tend to react in one of two ways: (1) They invest more energy in having good times together, even making an effort to show more patience and tolerance for kids they don't like, or (2) they decide that since they won't be returning (they're graduating or moving), they have an attitude of "Doesn't matter what I say, because I won't be seeing you anymore anyway."

They can also become behavior problems in class, even if they weren't any trouble earlier in the year. Regardless of which of these two happens, these middle schoolers usually have no idea why they're acting the way they are.

Why So Sensitive?

"I just feel all mixed up. I can't wait for school to be over, but then I get sad when I think about not being able to see my friends every day."
—A middle schooler

Some middle schoolers get overly sensitive or extremely moody as the end of the school year approaches. It's not unusual for a teen to go from elation and relief to moping and depression a few weeks before school ends. Shrugging, sighing, and a loss of interest in regular activities are all symptoms of a teen who's suddenly realized the whole summer is stretching ahead, and at the end lies another year of changes. It's frustrating for parents, since they're often at a loss over how to deal with their child—who's worried about all kinds of things that haven't even happened yet.

For middle schoolers who have become dependent on friends and social connections, the prospect of being apart all summer can cause some anxiety. They aren't old enough to drive, so getting together with friends can only happen when it's convenient for a parent or another willing chauffeur. Internet and texting are good options, but neither can take the place of a good punch in the arm, or giggling together until you can't breathe. Most middle school social interactions take place at school or revolve around school schedules, and kids know they'll miss that in the summer.

For teens who need order and structure, anticipating a summer full of unscheduled time can cause stress. Not knowing how to fill all those empty days stretching into the future may make them edgy or tearful. Again, watch for chances to listen and be understanding, or to have a chat to see where your child is emotionally. Of course, this won't be accomplished by marching up and asking, point-blank, "How are you feeling about the end of the year?" You have to watch for your opportunity: a mellow moment at the end of the day, a relaxed time while watching TV, a lengthy car ride where nobody falls asleep. Then be low-key and ask offhandedly, "Excited about the year ending?"

Be prepared to listen without too many questions or criticisms. Comments of "Well, don't worry . . ." or "Do you think that's a nice thing to say?" will shut down communication. Instead, use empathy with comments like "Oh, yeah, sounds tricky," or "Ouch, bet that hurts." This will get you much further and will show that you're really listening.

An hour or a day later, you can say (again, offhandedly), "I've been thinking over what you said about the end of the year. Want some advice?" If not, let it go. If so, give your advice nonchalantly, as if you don't care whether it's taken or not. It's entirely possible that your offer may be refused at first, but you may be asked to advise later on.

If you find yourself in the middle of more outbursts than usual, consider the possibility that it's caused by all those end-of-the-year feelings. You can try helping your middle schooler to verbalize his feelings, but it can be a tough task. He's likely to deny it's his fault at all, placing the blame on you or on school or on being too overwhelmed by homework.

You'll need all your best empathy skills. Or maybe you'll just need to create a little space and ride it out. Keep in mind that middle schoolers don't have much control over what happens once school's out, so involve them in any decisions you can. Feeling like they have even a small amount of choice can help lessen the stress.

Here's a Thought:

Since it often helps if your middle schooler feels a sense of control, why not involve her in the process of planning part of the summer vacation or a family outing. If she is going to be spending a lot of time alone while you're at work, include her in the decision about where and how she spends her days.

I'm Bored!

"When school's out it's fun for the first few days, but after a few days it gets old. I feel like I want to do something."
—A middle schooler

"It's boring because I have to do all the chores and then I just sit and watch TV."
—A middle schooler

School's out—and you get to spend a lot more time with your kids. Okay, there may be at least a few reasons parents don't look forward to school breaks as much as their children do. Sometimes spending more time as a family can spark as much conflict and strife as it does togetherness and shared memories. The good news is that we've got some ideas to help you enjoy your family time and *celebrate* time off!

One of the most common complaints, especially from middle schoolers, is boredom. When you tell them that boredom is a *choice*, they may object. "But what if there's nothing to do?" That's when you need to remind them that there's always *something* to do if they really want to overcome their boredom. The problem is, too often kids get bored because they expect entertainment to come from outside sources. So "I'm bored" translates into the unspoken command, "Amuse me." It can also mean, "Since you won't let me spend any more time on the computer or with my video games, I'm going to make your life miserable by bothering you."

When parents decide they don't need to play the role of "cruise director," life can get much easier. Chances are good that your home contains at least a few unused books, games, outdoor toys, and art supplies. Middle schoolers can also choose to cook something, clean something, or build something—or join parents in whatever projects they might be doing. It may take time and patience to convince them that there are other enjoyable things to do besides playing on screens, but when you can tear them away, middle schoolers are often surprised at how much fun they can have *not* playing video or computer games.

Learning something new—thereby keeping their middle school brains in shape—is also a good boredom buster. Reading may seem just a little too educational to your kids, but they may be surprised to find out reading is enjoyable when it's on a subject they find interesting. For example, here are some topics middle schoolers can get excited about:

• how to earn $100
• cheat codes for every video game
• weird and gross facts about the human body

In addition to reading, fun learning options might include Sudoku, crossword or jigsaw puzzles, or Mad Libs with a friend or family member (all can be found online). You might even want to have a family cooking competition, in the spirit of certain television shows. Learning to cook (or trying new recipes) is good for improving reading comprehension, math, and problem solving skills. If your kids resist everything but electronic entertainment, you might try letting them earn video game time by spending an equal amount of time in the non-digital world.

Family Vacation: Wish You Weren't Here?

"My dad likes to take long road trips, and I mean long. I get so sick of sitting in the car that sometimes I poke my sister just to pick a fight. At least it's something to do!"
—A middle schooler

"I used to hate road trips when I was younger, but now they're okay. I can keep in touch with my friends on my phone, so I don't mind so much being in the car all those hours!"
—A middle schooler

When your children were little, it was often easy to keep them happily occupied on a family road trip—and you could usually count on a nap or two along the way. Unfortunately, that changes when they hit middle school. Dealing with unpredictable moods is tricky enough at home, but in the small space of a passenger car it can become a real challenge.

If you're traveling with teens, the two most important things you can buy are a car charger adapter and a power strip. The former is essential for road trips; nothing can make a middle schooler whine faster than dead batteries for his phones or music players. The power strip could be your salvation whether you stay in a motel or at someone else's home. In our society middle schoolers and their parents have so many things that need charging—and not all rooms are equipped with enough outlets for everyone. Plugging in a small, multi-outlet power strip can head off some big arguments.

When you take middle schoolers on a road trip, don't worry too much if all they do is listen to music, text, watch movies, and play video games. To engage their attention once in a while, consider a simple rule: When Mom calls out, "Scenery!" everyone is expected to look up and make appropriate oohing and aahing noises. To prevent overstimulation and sore necks, designate half-hour breaks, giving fair warning that they're coming up: "Ten more minutes . . . five more minutes . . . shutdown time!" Your middle schooler may just go to sleep when forced to turn off a favorite app.

Stops for gas can also be stops for snacks, which will make the trip more bearable for your restless kid. It's a good time to wander into the store, use the restroom, and maybe choose a snack or a drink (with a lid). Nothing keeps teens happy like carbohydrates!

When your middle school travelers get moody, pretend not to notice. If they snap at others in the car, you might impose a "Quiet Zone" for a designated amount of time. Teens will often stake out their favorite spots in the car, but sometimes it's nice to let them sit up front for a while. A change of scenery can do wonders, and the view from the backseat can get pretty monotonous.

Stopping to eat is important, but getting everybody to agree on a fast food place isn't easy. If someone's unhappy about the final choice and decides to sulk, just let her sulk. Everyone knows you can't cheer up a sullen teen (you *do* know that, right?). She can eat or not eat; doesn't matter to you either way (and you save money if she only orders a milkshake).

If you're flying, make sure your children understand the rules for what can and can't go on the plane. Middle schoolers are just as likely to err on the side of caution as they are to break the rules; they've been known to ask if their braces will set off the metal detector. Be sure to warn them about their ears plugging and popping; provide gum if they don't have their own. And don't expect them to understand common courtesy—such as getting out of the center aisle as quickly as possible—without some instruction first.

Missing School

It's the e-mail that makes teachers groan: "We will be taking a family vacation next week, so Henry will miss six days of school. Is there homework he can do early so he won't have to carry any books with him?"

Sometimes in the spring students miss school for a vacation, either because it's cheaper to travel when school's in session, or because it works better for a family's schedule. Before you decide to save money by taking a trip during the off-season, make sure you know all the points to consider.

First, making up written homework will cover only part of what was missed. Copying lecture notes from a classmate can help, but nothing can replace the value of hearing firsthand what the teacher has to say. And if it's a good teacher, the give-and-take of a lively classroom discussion is when the most learning takes place.

Second, the teacher is put in a tough position. Parents may not realize that providing homework early means a teacher may have to take time to run worksheets or create quizzes early. Assignments and tests are then available to be shared with other students, creating the temptation to cheat. In some schools, the policy is that teachers are not required to provide assignments before a student leaves for vacation; it's the responsibility of the student to make up missing work upon returning to school.

Third, there's an emotional aspect to missing several days of middle school. At this age the social scene is far more important than the academic scene, at least from the student's point of view. There could have been a lot of drama among friends when she wasn't there. So when a middle schooler asks, "Did I miss anything important?" she's not asking about homework. Parents may scoff at these "important" incidents, but they play a large part in a middle schooler's world.

—Sue Acuña

There are many advantages to traveling with middle schoolers as opposed to younger children: They can feed and entertain themselves, read signs for you, and do without strollers or booster seats. That doesn't mean the trip will be without challenges of its own, however. Think ahead, be prepared for some speed bumps along the way, and this time vacation may be something to write home about!

Home Alone

"I think it's fun because I can listen to music really loud and run around the house."

"I like being home alone because no one is there to bother me or boss me around. The only time I can actually relax is when I'm home alone."

"If I'm home alone all day, the first couple hours are cool. I watch TV and shoot hoops and play video games. I like it when my sister comes home and we can play cards."

"It's fun except at night—because my house creaks and it's scary, and I live in a bad neighborhood."

"Being home alone is very boring: Wake up, do chores for no pay, sit home alone and wish for someone to argue with me."

"It's nice not having an adult around to yell at you, but being alone for hours and hours is boring and lonely. It's more fun with a friend."

—Eighth graders on staying home alone

Young teens present a unique caretaking challenge for working parents. Too young to get a job but too old to stay with a babysitter, many adolescents wind up staying alone or in charge of younger siblings. At what age are they ready to be left by themselves? And when they are alone, what can you do to prevent them from making bad choices?

Some 12- and 13-year-olds may be ready to stay alone all day, but many will tell you it's scary being home without any adults in the house. They're aware of the danger of opening the door to strangers, and it's easy to imagine those strangers lurking outside in the bushes, just waiting for the parent's car to drive away. Usually they're restricted to the house for their own safety and security, and boredom quickly sets in.

Home Alone Safety Checklist

Before being left home alone, middle schoolers should know:

_____ where to find the first aid kit and how to use it

_____ when to call a parent at work vs. when to call 911

_____ rules for cooking

_____ how to use kitchen utensils such as can openers and paring knives

_____ never to leave the kitchen while the stove is on

_____ how to wipe up spills

_____ to clean up the kitchen when they're finished

_____ where to find emergency numbers, including neighbors' or family members'

_____ to always lock the door when leaving home

_____ what to do if, upon arriving home, they find the front door open

_____ safety rules for lighting candles

_____ expectations for doing chores

_____ time and content limits for electronics

_____ never to open the door unless they've actually met the person on the other side

_____ how to escape in case of fire and where to meet

Others may relish the freedom but be susceptible to temptation, especially when joined by a friend for the day, or when invited to join in questionable activities via text or the Internet.

And there are those who aren't ready for the independence—those who wouldn't know what to do if the power went out or the stove caught fire.

If you have no other option than to leave your middle schooler home, try not to make it for 40 or 50 hours per week. Look for alternatives such as spending one or two days a week with a relative or a friend, or enrolling in daily classes. At this age there are many options for sports, drama, music, or religious camps in various price ranges. There might even be volunteer opportunities at a nearby YMCA or other club.

Be clear about expectations when you're not home, including what chores should be done and what the time limits are on electronics. As we mentioned in Chapter 6, many game systems and computers have parental controls that allow you to set passwords or choose specific times when the devices can be on. Check with your user's manual (in print or online) if you're not sure what options you have.

Here's a Thought:

Create some "what-if" practice scenarios with your kids and role-play what they'd do if something happened. Let them make up some of the scenarios, but don't get frustrated if they don't take it completely seriously. Even the lighthearted practice sessions will get the message across.

A Final Word

The middle school years are a very interesting road trip, and no two days will be exactly the same. You'll be excited, bored, frustrated, thrilled—and there will be days you wish you could put a lot more miles between you and the destination. But this only happens once in a lifetime with your child. Enjoy the ride, work on staying close, stay as positive as possible, and nurture your relationship while you can.

It's important to hold your child accountable—no one should get away with bad behavior. But often the negative effect of punishment, especially when it's harsh and repetitive, is that everything simply grinds to a halt. Now, more than ever, you need momentum, and incentives can keep you moving forward. After all, you can't steer a car that's parked—and if you figure out what will drive your child in the right direction, you're bound to reach the destination sooner!

~~~~~~~~~

Remember when they were three years old and were unhappy? You could usually cheer them up with a hug and a cookie. It's way more complicated now, isn't it? You ask, "What's wrong?"

And you get "Nuthin'" or "Stop bugging me all the time!" Or a defeated shrug. Any further attempts on your part to communicate are either ignored or greeted with an outburst that lets you know your efforts aren't appreciated.

And yet—when I shared this reality with my eighth graders a couple of years ago, there was a thoughtful pause. Finally one student said, "I'd still like that cookie!"

And from the corner of the room a soft voice said, "And I'd kinda like that hug."

—Sue Acuña

Notes

1. "The Growth Spurt," BBC Science: Human Body and Mind, found at http://www.bbc.co.uk/science/humanbody/body /articles/lifecycle/teenagers/growth.shtml.
2. "Late Nights and Laziness," found at BBC Science: Human Body and Mind: http://www.bbc.co.uk/science/humanbody /body/articles/lifecycle/teenagers/sleep.shtml; "Sleep Drive and Your Body Clock," National Sleep Foundation, found at http://www.sleepfoundation.org/article/sleep-topics /sleep-drive-and-your-body-clock.
3. Victor C. Strasburger, M.D., and Marjorie J. Hogan, M.D., "Children, Adolescents, and the Media," *Pediatrics* (November, 2013), found at http://pediatrics.aappublications.org /content/early/2013/10/24/peds.2013-2656.full.pdf+html.
4. Bob Waliszewski, *Plugged-In Parenting* (Focus on the Family /Tyndale House Publishers, 2011), pp. 10-12.
5. "The Teen Brain: Still Under Construction," National Institute of Mental Health, Publication No. 11-4929, 2011, found at http://www.nimh.nih.gov/health/publications /the-teen-brain-still-under-construction/index.shtml.
6. Cynthia Ulrich Tobias, *Every Child Can Succeed: Making the Most of Your Child's Learning Style* (Focus on the Family /Tyndale House Publishers, 1996), pp. 94-98.
7. Cynthia Ulrich Tobias, *The Way They Learn* (Focus on the Family/Tyndale House Publishers, 1994).
8. Ibid., pp. 81-93.
9. Ibid., pp. 94-122.

Meet Sue and Cynthia

The authors of this book are eminently qualified to address the issues of middle schoolers, and passionate about helping parents do everything they can to help children succeed.

Cynthia Tobias uses her experience as a teacher, author, and speaker—as well as her expertise in learning styles—to give parents insight and encouragement as they navigate this difficult phase of their children's lives.

Sue Acuña has been teaching and working with middle schoolers for over 20 years—and enjoys the students more than ever. They love her right back. Because she's so invested in helping them be their best, she consistently goes the extra mile. Sue grasped the importance of learning styles many years ago and immediately had a vision for how she could combine that knowledge with her love of middle school students.

Cynthia received her master's degree in education from Seattle Pacific University. Her background includes 25 years of private practice, eight years of teaching public high school, and six years in law enforcement. She is a best-selling author of nine books, a featured guest on radio and television, and a popular presenter for business, government agencies, and churches and schools throughout the U.S. and the world. She's also the mother of twin sons, who are now young adults. Cynthia and her husband live in the Seattle area.

Sue received her master's degree in education from Concordia University, Portland. She loves teaching middle school so much she also tutors, leads mission trips, directs the middle school choir, and helps with the dance and track teams. Her students claim she's one of the few adults who "gets" them, and they're eager for her to share what she knows with their parents. She is a frequent speaker at parenting workshops, and a popular blogger for parents of teens (http://mrsacuna.wordpress.com). Sue is a wife and the mother of three sons, now young adults, who managed to survive middle school and go on to experience success in high school and college.

Sue and Cynthia have taught together at the Summer Institute for Seattle Pacific University as well as local parent and teacher workshops—where their practical, encouraging approach receives great reviews.

For information on scheduling Cynthia Tobias for speaking engagements, please contact Ambassador Speakers Bureau (Info@AmbassadorSpeakers .com).

The Family project™

A Divine Reflection

FOCUS ON THE FAMILY®

Welcome to the Family

Whether you purchased this book, borrowed it, or received it as a gift, thanks for reading it! This is just one of many insightful, biblically based resources that Focus on the Family produces for people in all stages of life.

Focus is a global Christian ministry dedicated to helping families thrive as they celebrate and cultivate God's design for marriage and experience the adventure of parenthood. Our outreach exists to support individuals and families in the joys and challenges they face, and to equip and empower them to be the best they can be.

Through our many media outlets, we offer help and hope, promote moral values and share the life-changing message of Jesus Christ with people around the world.

Focus on the Family MAGAZINES

These faith-building, character-developing publications address the interests, issues, concerns, and challenges faced by every member of your family from preschool through the senior years.

THRIVING FAMILY®	FOCUS ON	FOCUS ON	FOCUS ON
Marriage & Parenting	THE FAMILY	THE FAMILY	THE FAMILY
	CLUBHOUSE JR.®	CLUBHOUSE®	CITIZEN®
	Ages 4 to 8	Ages 8 to 12	U.S. news issues

For More INFORMATION

ONLINE:
Log on to
FocusOnTheFamily.com
In Canada, log on to
FocusOnTheFamily.ca

 PHONE:
Call toll-free:
**800-A-FAMILY
(232-6459)**
In Canada, call toll-free:
800-661-9800

Rev. 3/11